Cole shook Jennie's hand slowly, measuringly.

She was glad she hadn't removed her kid glove, because the warmth of his grasp was hot enough even with the thin barrier between their palms. Flustered, she released her hat feather, which promptly fell back across her vision.

Cole yanked it off her hat and tossed it in the dirt. "There. That's better."

Openmouthed, she stared at the feather, then at him. "I can't believe you did that."

"It needed doing."

Jennie felt her temper rising, pressed her lips together and turned away from the presumptuous Cole…and the danger that lurked in his beautiful, storm-colored eyes.

of the

Harlequin Historicals is delighted
to introduce Ann Collins
and her terrific debut book

Protecting Jennie
Harlequin Historical #542—December 2000

Protecting Jennie

Ann Collins

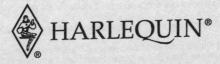

HARLEQUIN®

TORONTO • NEW YORK • LONDON
AMSTERDAM • PARIS • SYDNEY • HAMBURG
STOCKHOLM • ATHENS • TOKYO • MILAN • MADRID
PRAGUE • WARSAW • BUDAPEST • AUCKLAND

ISBN 0-373-29142-6

PROTECTING JENNIE

Copyright © 2000 by Ann Collins

This edition published by arrangement with Harlequin Books S.A.

® and TM are trademarks of the publisher. Trademarks indicated with
® are registered in the United States Patent and Trademark Office, the
Canadian Trade Marks Office and in other countries.

Visit us at www.eHarlequin.com

Printed in U.S.A.

Available from Harlequin Historicals and
ANN COLLINS

Harlequin Historicals

Protecting Jennie #542

Please address questions and book requests to:
Harlequin Reader Service
U.S.: 3010 Walden Ave., P.O. Box 1325, Buffalo, NY 14269
Canadian: P.O. Box 609, Fort Erie, Ont. L2A 5X3

For Grandmother Esther McCarthy Collins,
a Boston beauty who came West, an avid reader
and my biggest supporter.

Acknowledgments

I am grateful to Daniel F. Mulvilhill, M.D., my medical consultant; Andrea Dearing, librarian at the public library of Williams, Arizona; Maxine Edwards, curator of the Arizona Hall of Fame Museum's "Fred Harvey and the Harvey Girls of Arizona" exhibit; John Rotsart, curator of the San Diego Model Railroad Museum; the members of RWA-San Diego; and Tracy Farrell and Melissa Endlich of Harlequin Historicals.

Chapter One

Emporia, Kansas
April 1897

From the edge of the depot's crowded platform, Jennie Andrews peered over her shoulder again and scrutinized the strangers' sunlit faces. Nervously she tapped her silk reticule against the folds of her deep green traveling suit. When her gaze landed on a tall, powerfully built man wearing a black sack suit and leaning lazily against the red station building, she froze. Was he watching her?

Without changing his position, the man stuck a hand-rolled cigarette into his mouth and lit it with a match swiped on the rough, planked wall. Wisps of smoke curled upward past a face shadowed by a faded black Stetson. His hair, as black as the jet beads Jennie had left behind, reached unfashionably to his shoulders. And yet, the length of it looked right on him somehow.

Jennie swallowed against the sudden prairie dry-
in her mouth, wished she could see the man's

eyes clearly, know if they were focused on her. Had he been hired to find her, drag her back to Boston?

Despite the warmth of the spring day's sun, she shivered. The man looked all too capable of carrying out such a task.

Rae Hansen, her friend, fellow waitress and traveling companion, put a warm, ungloved hand on her arm. Concern narrowed the younger girl's bright, innocent blue eyes. "Are you all right, Jennie?"

Jennie glanced at the stranger once more, saw him push away from the wall, lean down to pick up a bag and disappear inside the ticket office. Relief weakened her knees. She covered Rae's hand with her own gloved one.

"I thought someone recognized me." She tried to elicit a smile for her friend. "But I was being foolish."

She briefly shut her eyes, heard the murmur of conversations, the rattle of a carriage and the thumping of horses' hooves. Then she again searched the crowd waiting to board the westbound train sitting on the tracks. Men in suits checked their pocket watches while cowhands chewed tobacco and spat over the sides of the platform, raising little clouds of dust. Most of the women clutched traveling bags and wore simple calico dresses like Rae's.

A dry breeze sent one of Jennie's red curls flying upward to tangle with the tall green feather atop her stylish hat. She absently fingered the curl loose. Ten more minutes remained until the conductor opened the doors and she and Rae could take their seats. Ten long minutes.

She forced herself to look away from the faces concentrate on something else. Near the front train, a young boy crouched under the coal car. His floppy hat skimmed the metal edge while the hem of his shabby, oversize coat brushed the track. Jennie smiled, suspecting that the train and its mechanical workings fascinated him. Trains had always fascinated her father, too. Her smile faded. She didn't want to think about her father now. Nor about the marriage he'd arranged for her.

Suddenly the train lurched, catching the boy unawares. He fell and lay still on the tracks.

Jennie gasped. "Oh, no!" She hitched up her skirts and started running, her shoes thumping down the stairs.

Rae's quick steps followed behind her. "Jennie, what is it? Where are you going?"

"The train hit that boy in the head," she yelled back. "His injury could be serious. A concussion." Or worse, she feared. A skull fracture. What could she possibly do for him if that was the case? Her training was so limited. And Dr. Nicholson wasn't here to instruct her.

She passed the express car and dropped down beside the now-stirring boy. "Stay still," she ordered. "You mustn't move."

He glared at her and sat up.

Jennie reached for his shoulders, but he jerked away from her. "Please, you must keep still."

"What fer?" he demanded, his face smudged with dirt.

"You've injured your head."

He scrunched up his nose at her. "I didn't either."

"But I saw the train knock you down." Could she have been wrong?

"It got the back of my arm." He rubbed the afflicted area.

"Take your coat off and let me look at it." She also wanted to feel for any swelling on his head, just in case. Several years ago, she'd witnessed a young boy run over by a carriage on a cobblestone street back home. Though dressed in near rags, he'd had the warmest, gentlest brown eyes. Jennie had seen those eyes close on the boy's last breath, and she'd never felt so helpless. Never wanted to feel such helplessness again.

The boy's eyes widened in horror. "Hell no! I'm not takin' my clothes off fer you. I'm gettin' outta here." He jumped up.

"Please. I only want to help you," Jennie said, terrified he might leave without getting the care he needed. But he twisted around and ran, coattails flapping. She stared after him, then let Rae help her up. No one else had ventured from the platform to see about the scruffy boy.

"I'm sorry, Jennie." Rae tucked a tendril of blond hair behind her ear. "I guess you can't help someone who doesn't want to be helped."

She dusted off her skirt. "I can try. I can always try."

Back in Boston, at the dispensary where Dr. Nicholson ministered to the poor, the patients had come voluntarily and accepted Jennie's presence. She had served as a nurse, learning all the doctor could teach her. She also read his medical texts. Her oh-so-proper Beacon Hill parents had refused to allow her to apply to medical school, let alone give her the money to pay for it. "A woman doctor?" her mother had scoffed. "Why, Jennifer, it's just not done."

Going against her parents' wishes, Jennie had fought to learn the skills of a doctor. Now she was fighting for her very freedom, the right to choose her own husband, a man she could love and who would love her in return.

The boy vanished around the corner of a nearby saloon. "Men always make the worst patients," Jennie said.

Rae giggled. "Isn't that the truth? Whenever my dad or brothers had to stay in bed, my mother was fit to be tied with their surly demands."

Jennie envied Rae her big Iowa farm family and fond memories. She rarely saw her own two sisters, who had married young, just as their parents had intended. Not like her, who at twenty-five was practically a spinster.

Rae tucked her arm in Jennie's. "Come on. Let's go back to the platform." They exchanged smiles and started forward. Halfway there, two cowhands staggered into their path. Clownlike grins stretched across their unshaven faces. "Jennie?" Rae's voice rose.

Jennie patted her hand. "It's all right. Don't worry. They look harmless enough." She hoped she was right. Until a month ago, when Rae left the farm due to a drought and too many mouths to feed, the girl had never had to fend for herself. "Just keep walking and ignore them."

One of the men removed his hat and bowed, lurching sideways in the process. "Whoa," he said, righting himself and chortling. "Good mornin' to you, ladies. And how are you doin' this fine day?" He squinted up at the cloudless morning sky, winced and replaced his hat.

Jennie steered Rae around him.

The men separated, flanking them. One belched as loud as a pig's snort. The other scratched under his arm. "Hiram, these girls ain't bein' friendly to us."

"No, but they sure is purty." Beside the express car, Hiram stepped in front of them, blocking their way. "Hey, Teddy Boy, take a gander at that big, fancy green feather standing up on Red's hat."

Jennie scowled at him. She liked her feather and hated being called Red. "Let us pass."

"I think they ought to be more friendly-like," Teddy Boy said from beside Rae. He grabbed her, hauled her backward against his chest.

Her mouth opened, but no sound came out.

Jennie thrust her finger at him, her reticule swinging wildly from her wrist. "You release her this instant!"

"Hiram, Red talks real hoity-toity, don't she?" Teddy Boy nuzzled Rae's neck with his stiff whiskers. "Maybe you ought to teach her some Kansas talk."

"You done read my mind, Teddy Boy. You know hows I like to talk with my hands." His arm whipped around Jennie's waist.

"Get away from me!" She slammed the heel of one sturdy French button shoe onto his instep.

He howled like a coyote and shoved her to the ground.

She landed with a thud, felt her bones rattle. Her feather flopped forward and hung in her eyes. Dust billowed upward. In the next instant, Hiram hit the ground beside her. His hat floated down and landed in the dirt between them.

Jennie blinked. Her gaze swung from Hiram to an upright pair of worn beige cowboy boots, most of the decorative stitching hidden beneath black trousers. The black trousers of a familiar sack suit.

Jennie licked her lips, tasting dust. She pulled her feather aside and peered up the length of the stranger's body, from long, trim legs to broad shoulders and a broken-in black Stetson she'd seen not ten minutes ago on the platform. Her heart pumped hard and fast. Had this man come to her rescue only to see that she was returned to her parents and the man she was supposed to marry?

As Hiram sat up and rubbed his jaw, the newcomer's eyes, a stormy blue-gray, fastened on the cowhand. Jennie caught her breath at the beauty, power and danger in those eyes.

Hiram worked his jaw back and forth and touched a grimy hand to his teeth. "Hey, what did ya go and do that fer?"

The man dismissed him, turned to Teddy Boy. "Take your hands off that girl." Each quietly spoken word sounded as powerful as the punch that had toppled Hiram.

"You want 'em both for yourself, huh?" Teddy Boy said, possibly too intoxicated to understand the peril he faced.

"I won't tell you again."

"Mister, I don't care what you say. She's mine."

Behind him, the express car's wooden door slid quietly open several inches. Jennie's eyes widened when the double barrels of a shotgun emerged to press against the cowboy's head.

"I think you'll do what the man told you," said the male voice behind the gun. "Let her go."

Teddy Boy inched his shaking hands upward. Rae bounded away from him.

Jennie picked herself up off the ground and hugged her friend. "You're all right now, Rae."

The girl's body shook. "I was so scared."

"I know, but everything's all right." Jennie hoped she spoke the truth, hoped no one had sent this stranger after her.

The express car door slid farther open and a young man around Rae's age popped his head out. "You okay, Sunshine?"

"Yes." Rae's voice trembled, but she smiled at him. A blush crept into her cheeks. "Thank you for helping me."

"It's always a pleasure to help a pretty girl." Using the gun, he nudged Teddy Boy aside. "Get over with your friend." As the cowhand followed orders, Rae's savior jumped to the ground, the ends of his ribbon tie slapping his clean-shaven chin. Jennie stared at his short black hair and blue-gray eyes, saw his uncanny resemblance to the man who'd come to her aid.

The young man shook the taller one's hand. "Hey, Cole. Good to see you. When I first heard the scuffle out here, I thought someone was trying to trick me into unlocking the door. I've got a full Wells Fargo box in there. But then I heard your voice and decided to lend a hand."

"Your timing was just right, little brother," Cole said.

"I'll say." Hiram gathered up his hat, jammed it on his head and stood, favoring the foot Jennie had stomped on. "But we were just havin' us some fun with these purty gals. Didn't mean no harm."

"You boys've been liquored up long enough," Cole said. "It's time you rode on home. Unless you'd like to be introduced to the local sheriff. He's a personal friend of mine.''

Hiram and Teddy Boy exchanged glances. ''Nah,'' Hiram said, ''we'll git.'' They lumbered away together, Hiram limping.

Through her drooping hat feather, Jennie noticed Cole keeping the men in sight even as he turned toward Rae and her. She didn't know what to think about his acquaintance with the local sheriff.

''Sorry about what happened here, ladies.'' He touched the brim of his hat. ''I'm Cole Bryant. He's Matt.''

Jennie pushed her feather aside and nodded at them. She resisted the impulse to introduce herself. First she had to know more about Cole Bryant. ''Were you watching me earlier, Mr. Bryant, when we were on the platform?''

He pushed his hat further back on his head, glanced at his brother. ''Matt, were you expecting to receive a little gratitude and maybe a polite introduction from these ladies?''

''As a matter of fact, I was,'' Matt said.

Rae bit her lower lip, and Jennie could tell the girl was eager to give both men what they wanted, but she remained silent.

''Please answer my question, sir,'' Jennie said.

''What was it again?'' His expression gave away nothing, but she got the distinct impression he was making fun of her.

While holding the feather out of her face, she lifted her chin a notch. ''Were you watching me up on the platform?''

''I was,'' he answered.

"Why?" She had to know for sure, hated being afraid.

"I watch everything that's going on around me. Everyone, too. Especially a beautiful woman who stands out in a crowd. Why do you ask?"

Jennie knew no more than before he answered, but oddly, she liked knowing this man thought her beautiful. An unbidden heat rose into her cheeks. Embarrassed and ill at ease, needing to distract herself, she extended her free hand. "My name is Jennie Andrews." She decided if her parents had given him her name, there was no reason to hide it now. And if he didn't know it, she wanted him to, even though she knew she shouldn't. "This is Rae Hansen. And, yes, we are grateful for your assistance."

"Very grateful," Rae added, her gaze on Matt.

Cole shook Jennie's hand slowly, measuringly. She was glad she hadn't removed her kid glove, because the warmth of his grasp was hot enough even with the thin barrier between their palms. Flustered, she released her feather, which promptly fell back across her vision.

Cole yanked it off her hat and tossed it in the dirt. "There. That's better."

Openmouthed, she stared at the feather, then at him. "I can't believe you did that."

"It needed doing."

Jennie felt her temper rising. "But it was part of *my* hat."

"And now it's part of the prairie."

Matt cleared his throat loudly. "Where are you girls headed anyway?"

To keep her temper in check, Jennie mashed her lips together and turned away from the presumptuous

Cole. She considered Matt's question, but would not answer it aloud. She was on her way to a new life in the Arizona Territory, far from the reach of James Easton III, her so-called fiancé. At least she hoped it was far enough. Jennie rubbed her wrist. The bruise James had inflicted on her had faded, but not the memory of his threat to hunt her down if she chose to run from a marriage to him.

Jennie shivered, would not divulge her final destination. She couldn't risk word of her whereabouts getting back home.

"We're headed to our first assignment," Rae answered cheerfully, making Jennie cringe. "We're Harvey Girls. We just finished our month of training in Topeka, and we're changing trains here."

Cole's gaze narrowed on Jennie. She saw the questions in his eyes, the first and foremost being why did a fashionably dressed young woman become a Harvey Girl waitress in the West?

Over a month ago, Jennie had been desperate to escape her father's plans when she spotted an ad published in the *Boston Globe:*

Young women, 18 to 30 years of age, of good character, attractive and intelligent, to work in Harvey Eating Houses in the West. Apply, Harvey Company, Chicago, Illinois.

It had seemed the answer to all her problems. Without a word to anyone, she'd traveled to Chicago and was hired and sent to Topeka for training. While suffering through long hours on her feet, heavy breakfast, lunch and dinner plates, and patrons who barely acknowledged her, she'd met Rae. Only the young farm girl knew her secret. Jennie wanted to keep it that way.

"Rae," she said, "we've imposed enough on the gentlemen's time." She took her friend's arm.

"No, you haven't," Matt said. "Stay a little longer. The train won't leave for a while yet."

"You'll have to excuse my brother," Cole said. "Matt doesn't get much companionship locked up in that express car."

Jennie thought she heard a note of disapproval in Cole's voice, but his expression told her nothing.

"I get out once in a while," Matt said. "Even eat at some of the Harvey restaurants along the Santa Fe line. Where will you be working?"

Jennie gave Rae's arm an extra warning squeeze, which the girl ignored. "Williams in the Arizona Territory."

Jennie groaned inwardly.

"Williams?" Matt laughed. "Really?"

Jennie found nothing to laugh about. She noticed Cole wasn't laughing, either. "What is so amusing, Mr. Bryant?"

"You girls are in luck," Matt said. "Cole here has got a cattle ranch a few miles south of Williams. He can give you an escort. Keep you out of trouble. Right, Cole?"

A vein throbbed in Cole's neck, and Jennie realized with relief that he wasn't chasing her after all. In fact, he didn't want to escort them any more than she wanted him to. "That won't be necessary," she said. "We appreciate your earlier assistance, but hereafter, you need not concern yourselves with us. Good day." She nodded curtly and turned away.

Pulling Rae along with her, she started toward the

platform, where the passengers had finally begun filing aboard the train. Her friend glanced back at the men. Jennie stifled her own desire to look back, as well as the twinge of guilt she felt but didn't understand just yet.

"Rae, you'll give them ideas if you keep looking back like that."

"I was only looking at Matt. Oh, Jennie, wasn't he wonderful with that shotgun?" She released a long sigh. "I'll never forget it. Or him."

Jennie would never forget Cole, either. Or the danger that lurked in his beautiful, storm-colored eyes.

Chapter Two

Beside the express car, Cole took a flat packet of rolling papers and a cloth pouch of Bright tobacco from his coat pocket. He watched the two young women march away. The redhead, Jennie, kept the blond's feet moving fast. Their dresses swished against long limbs, both girls taller than average. Jennie still only came up to his chest, but she acted like she towered over him.

Cole busied his fingers rolling a cigarette and recalled thinking Jennie's fair skin would burn quick in the West's relentless sun. She reminded him of a rose, a prickly rose, but one that smelled awful good. The dust clinging to her hadn't masked her fragrant scent.

"Hey, Cole, aren't you ever going to smoke machine-rolled?" Matt asked.

"Nope." He struck a match on the express car and lit the cigarette. "They don't taste as good."

"They're a heckuva lot easier."

"Don't care. I know what I like."

"Yeah, you do at that." He glanced toward the girls now mounting the platform. "I noticed you kinda liked that redhead."

Cole snorted. "That touchy, headstrong woman? She doesn't need an escort, she needs a caretaker. She's beautiful, but she's trouble and I'm steering clear."

Matt raised one dark brow. "You fooled me, then."

Cole shrugged one shoulder. "I'm curious about her is all."

"Oh, yeah? And why's that?"

"On the platform earlier, when I was watching her, she was looking over her shoulder like she expected trouble to come looking for her. And she's definitely not the usual Harvey Girl."

Matt lifted the shotgun, rested it on one wrist. "I noticed that high-priced dress, too. And her Eastern way of talking."

"Boston's my guess." Cole exhaled a stream of smoke. "Upper crust."

"You think she's running from something?"

"Maybe."

An impish smile shifted Matt's lips. "Well, since you're going to be keeping an eye on the girls, you'll have time to find out more about her."

"Now just a doggone minute. I did not agree to escort them."

"I know, but you'll do it anyway."

Matt's smile was starting to annoy Cole. It reminded him of the boy who'd been so full of mischief while knowing exactly what he could get away with. "Miss Jennie Andrews does not want me around. Thankfully."

"You shouldn't have plucked her feather," Matt said. "You riled her plenty with that move."

As he remembered her flashing green eyes, Cole

felt the unfamiliar sensation of a smile tugging at his mouth. "She's got a temper, that one. I'd rather not be around to experience it firsthand. You didn't see how hard she branded that cowpoke's foot." Cole had to admit to some admiration for her quick reflexes.

"She's real different from Ray." Matt peered toward the passengers boarding the train. "That's an odd name for a girl, isn't it? But it fits. She's a ray of sunshine. I could get used to having her around."

"You know where to find her."

"I sure do."

"And when you live on the ranch, you can go to town and see her real regular." Cole stopped breathing, waited for his brother's response.

Matt's forehead creased. "Is that why you're here, Cole? To talk me into quitting my job?"

"I had some banking business to take care of, but yes, it's time you came to live on the C Bar M. Ran it with me." Got out of this dangerous business.

Matt shoved the shotgun back into the car. "You mean you want me to quit guarding express shipments."

Cole threw down his cigarette, ground it out with his toe. "I want you safe, Matt." He'd do anything to protect his brother.

"But you worked as an express messenger yourself. Then you really put yourself in danger by tracking down train robbers. Why should your choices be right and mine wrong?"

Cole said nothing. He *had* taken chances with his life. But he'd been good at his job, and being a Wells Fargo detective paid well. He'd needed that money to send Matt to school. And to buy the ranch he'd dreamed of owning, a real home.

"Cole, the C Bar M is yours. That's not the life I want."

"Do you know what you want?"

"Maybe. Maybe not. I do know it's time I made my own way."

"Matt, I…" Cole thrust a hand in his pocket. Couldn't his little brother understand his worry? How much he loved him? He was the only family he had left, and outlaws killed messengers guarding express shipments.

Matt leaned back against the doorsill. "You can't always protect me, Cole. I may still be your 'little' brother, but I'm not little anymore. I can take care of myself."

Cole knew he could never stop protecting his brother. He'd kept Matt from their father's fists and raised him after their mother's death. He understood Matt's need to break away, but letting him go was another matter. Maybe the blond Harvey Girl would have more luck keeping him close to home. It was worth considering.

Cole decided to drop the subject for now. "I came after you for another reason, too."

"Oh, yeah?" Matt's eyes narrowed, and he cocked his head. "What else?"

"I got myself engaged."

He straightened. "What? Engaged! As in, to be married?"

"Is that so tough to believe?"

"Well, yeah."

"It's no joke."

Matt shook his head, paused. "Okay then, who is she?"

"Katherine Dawson. A reverend's daughter."

"You are joking. You must be. A reverend's daughter?"

Cole ground his teeth. "Matt..."

He held up his hands. "Okay, okay. Sorry. Katherine Dawson. Tell me more about her."

"She's well brought up, quiet and dutiful. She'll be a good wife."

"Quiet? Dutiful? Cole, I can't picture it. She sounds like a mouse. You need a woman who'll stand up to you, stir you up and keep you guessing. Like that Jennie you were watching so closely a few minutes ago."

"Matt, I'm about to lose my patience with you."

"That would be a first." His little brother chuckled. "And you *were* watching her," Matt said.

"I observe everyone. It's a habit that's kept me alive."

"You know what I mean. Admit it, Cole, she's perfect for you."

He nearly choked. Perfect for him? Never. "Matt, I want a quiet life with a woman who respects and accepts my wishes, not someone who fights me at every turn. My children will grow up in a peaceful home."

"I know they will, Cole. And you'll make a good father. I can attest to that."

Warmth stole into Cole's heart. "Thanks. And you'll make a good uncle." If he didn't get hurt, or worse, doing the job he seemed bent on keeping.

"How'd you meet Katherine?"

"Through her father. It's an arranged marriage."

Matt slapped himself on the forehead. "Arranged! Arranged?"

"Love isn't everything," Cole said.

"Of course it is. Without love, there's nothing."

Cole knew his brother barely remembered their mother's suffering, how she'd died of a broken heart. She'd never stopped loving the man who'd stopped loving her.

"There's respect," Cole said. "And that's what Katherine and I have for each other." He had no intention of ever falling in love, let alone marrying for it.

"Cole, I think you're making a mistake, but when's the big day?"

"May thirty-first. Six weeks away. And you'd better be there. I want you to stand up with me."

"I'll wear my best suit, and I'll even be happy for you."

Cole knew better than to believe that, but he looked forward to having his brother by his side. And hopefully out of the express business.

The whistle shrilled from the locomotive.

Matt climbed into the express car. With a hand on the sliding door, he said, "Cole, promise me you'll keep an eye on Sunshine and her friend for me, okay?"

A third of the way back in the nearly filled passenger coach, Jennie arranged her skirt over the cushioned seat. Rae sat to her left, next to the window. Her temper cooled now, Jennie realized why she felt so guilty. Cole had punched a man to help them, and she'd never determined if his hand needed medical attention. She wouldn't feel easy until she'd examined it.

"Jennie, do you think Matt will be stopping in Williams, too?" Rae asked.

"I have no idea, but if he does, I'm sure he'll take the time to come and see you."

Her blue eyes sparkled. "You think so?"

"Isn't he the one who asked where we were going?"

Pink stole into Rae's cheeks. "I was so glad he asked. I know I shouldn't have told them, but I couldn't help myself. I'm sorry, Jennie. Can you forgive me?"

"Of course. Since they were protecting us, I suppose I don't have to worry about their knowing." She hoped they would keep the information to themselves.

Rae beamed her a smile. "Cole seemed rather taken with you."

"Don't be ridiculous. Besides, how would you know? You noticed no one but Matt."

"I saw Cole rip off your feather."

"He had no right to do that."

"It needed to be removed. Admit it."

"I was planning to pull it off as soon as you and I were alone." She stuffed her reticule deeper into her lap, careful not to poke herself with one of the needles in her sewing kit. "And don't you dare get any matchmaking ideas, Rae Hansen."

Jennie faced forward, just in time to see Cole enter from the vestibule. He dipped his head under the doorjamb, stopped and surveyed the coach. Her pulse climbed.

She planted her eyes on the bald spot of the man sitting in front of her. It didn't help. Cole sauntered down the aisle, stopping close enough to touch. When he lifted his bag onto the overhead rack, his coat stretched across his back, revealing muscles that could never have been acquired in an office. Jennie swallowed hard.

He sat down across the aisle from her, next to a prune-mouthed old woman dressed in widow's weeds. Cole tipped his hat back, looked at Jennie, then lowered the hat over his eyes.

"Mr. Bryant?" She refused to let him fall asleep before she checked his hand.

"The name's Cole," he said from under the hat.

The whistle blew again, followed by a clanging bell. The coach lurched forward.

"Could you do me the courtesy of looking at me...*Cole?*"

He sighed and tipped his hat back. "Yes, ma'am."

"The name's *Jennie,*" she retorted.

"Yes, *Jennie.* What do you want?"

"Your right hand." She reached across the aisle.

He jerked back, squeezed the widow lady between himself and the window. She squealed in surprise, and Jennie stifled a laugh at both her and the man who was acting so like the scruffy boy she'd tried to help earlier.

"Uh, sorry, ma'am." He turned back to Jennie, scowled at her outstretched arm. "What do you think you're doing?"

"I am concerned about your hand. You hit that man's jaw very hard. You could have done yourself an injury."

"It's fine." He held it up, opened and closed it several times. "See. Still works."

Men! Would she have to hold him down to get a good look? "Let me see it up close. Please."

"There's no need." He muttered something under

his breath. Jennie thought she heard the word "trouble."

"Then prove to me it's fine."

"By letting you see it, right?"

"You have a quick mind," she said. "I'm impressed."

"I think your flattery is less than sincere, Jennie."

"Possibly, but my concern is very real. Cole, I feel responsible. If you take an infection and die, I'll never forgive myself."

He peered over at her, his expression inscrutable. Then he groaned and thrust out his hand. "I don't want anyone feeling responsible for me. Make it quick."

Mr. Gracious. "Thank you."

She took his hand—big, warm and rough from hard work. It was also scrubbed clean. No dirt burrowed under his nails, and no grime was embedded in the creases of his palm. She liked the way his hand felt and looked, didn't want to let go. Only a few slight abrasions reddened his knuckles.

"Will I live?" His voice was rich and deep and sincere when she'd expected sarcasm from him.

"Yes," she managed to say, not looking up. She turned his hand over, slowly trailed the tip of her finger over the thick callus covering much of his palm.

He yanked his hand away from her and shifted in his seat. "That side didn't connect with anyone's jaw."

"Oh, of course not. I was, uh, checking for… swelling. It looks all right. And the abrasions on your knuckles are minimal." Jennie rearranged her skirts. What had come over her? "However, I suggest you visit the lavatory to wash them with some soap and water.''

He readjusted his hat. ''I'll do that. Later.''

Jennie turned to Rae, trying to get away from her unprofessional behavior and the man who'd incited it. But Rae chose that moment to lean forward and address him.

''Will your brother be joining you on your ranch, Mr. Bryant?''

He removed his hat, raked his fingers through his hair. ''I'm hoping so.''

''I'm from Iowa,'' Rae said, ''and I already miss my family.''

''I want Matt to help me run the ranch,'' he said. ''I've got a good-size spread and plenty of stock now. The C Bar M will be a good place to raise a family.''

With the talk of family, Jennie twisted the drawstring of her reticule over and over. Despite her parents' lack of understanding and her father's betrayal when he put his signature on a marriage contract, she missed them. She was also worried about her mother's delicate health. Jennie had already risked sending two letters so her mother wouldn't worry about her safety. To keep her location secret, rail passengers she'd served in the Harvey House had posted the letters from places other than Topeka.

Rae leaned around Jennie again. ''What does C Bar M mean?''

''That's the name I gave the ranch. *C* for Cole and *M* for Matt.'' He shrugged. ''Not very original. And so far, Matt doesn't want any part of it.'' He dropped his hat into his lap, fiddled with the brim.

''I'm sorry,'' Rae said. ''Maybe he'll change his mind.''

"We'll see. What about you, Jennie?"

Her fingers tangled in the drawstring. "What? What about me?"

"Where's your family?" As he eyed her fingers, his own stilled on the hat.

She didn't move. "I'm on my own," she answered. "Have you always been a rancher, Cole?"

He angled his head. "You're changing the subject."

She responded with a shrug.

Under his long regard, Jennie felt like a blood sample under a microscope. She tried to guess his thoughts, and didn't like what she concluded—that he was a man who didn't like secrets.

Eventually he answered her. "I've only been a rancher for a year and a half. Before that, I worked for the Company."

"The Company? I don't understand."

"Wells, Fargo and Company. I started as an express messenger, like Matt. Then I moved into detective work. Tracked down train robbers."

Jennie's heart skipped a beat. A detective? Was that how he'd become a personal friend of the sheriff in Emporia? The urge to flee slammed into her. But changing seats now would really raise his suspicions.

"You're not working as a detective anymore though, right?" she asked too quickly.

"What's your interest?"

She curled her fingers around her reticule. Couldn't the man answer a simple question? She tried for nonchalance. "Just curious."

"I see. Or maybe you're just passing the time of day?"

"Yes, it's a long trip."

"You got that right." The hours ahead of them didn't seem to please him, either.

"So," she said, "are you still doing some detective work?"

He paused, and Jennie held her breath.

"Not anymore. Now all I want is a quiet life on my ranch."

She let herself breathe again. Tight muscles eased until she slid down in her seat.

Rae leaned forward again. "Your former profession must've been dangerous, Cole. Do you still carry a gun?"

"I use one when I need to."

Jennie pulled herself back up, anxious to keep the conversation about him rather than her. "Have you ever been shot?"

Cole rubbed a spot on his upper arm. "Yeah, but you don't want to hear about that."

"Yes, I do." Jennie wondered if the bullet had gone straight through or lodged in muscle or bone.

"I do, too," Rae added.

"All right then," he said grudgingly. "About three years ago, a posse and me were tracking a gang of train robbers. They'd gotten away with gold bullion. We captured all except one man. While the posse took the others into Prescott, the Yavapai County seat, I went after him."

His story was interesting, but not quite what Jennie had wanted to know.

"What happened?" Rae asked breathlessly.

He stared straight ahead, as if he were seeing himself in another place. "The man, a boy really, name of Fred Hardin, refused to surrender. He fired on me. I fired back. Hit him in the heart. He still didn't go down easy. Got off two more shots, and I took one of them in the arm.''

Jennie stopped thinking about her medical interest in his experience with a bullet wound. Cole had killed a man, had protected himself by taking another's life. She didn't know what to think, except that she was glad Cole seemed to regret what he'd had to do. "Did you leave your job after that?"

"No. Not till I'd saved enough to buy the ranch." His gaze swept over her traveling suit. "I can see you come from money, Jennie. Now it's your turn to answer a question. Why is a well-bred Eastern miss working as a Harvey Girl?"

Chapter Three

Jennie stared at Cole. His unrelenting gaze didn't flinch. Once again he was asking a question she didn't want to answer. Did she dare tell him anything?

She hesitated. The train swayed on a curve. Metal wheels clattered and screeched over the rails. The whistle blew, signaling a crossroads.

"You ask a lot of questions for a man who claims he's no longer a detective."

"I like to know about the people I'm traveling with."

"You are *not* traveling with us," Jennie said. "You took the seat beside us is all."

"Matt asked me to keep an eye on the two of you."

Jennie heard Rae draw an excited breath. "And you always do what your brother asks?"

"No."

"Then why now?"

He glanced at Rae. "I've got my reasons."

"And I've got mine for becoming a Harvey Girl. None of them concern you."

He shrugged and put his hat back on. "Maybe." Before he pulled the hat over his eyes, she saw the

light of anticipation there, the anticipation of a challenge to be met. *She* was that challenge. Jennie willed
the train to go faster.

Stark fear enveloped her. Relentless footsteps
pounded behind her, closer and closer.

Jennie ran. Her lungs burned, fought for air. She
twisted her head and saw her pursuer's dark, cavern-
ous eyes. They swallowed the moon's light. She
stumbled. Almost fell. *No! Keep going. Faster.*

"Jen-ni-fer," he coaxed. "I told you I'd hunt you
down. You will be mine."

No! She had to get away. Run harder. Never stop.

She forced her feet ahead. Struggled over the un-
seen path. The ground moved. Rocked and swayed.
Tried to throw her down. She wanted to shout for
help, but didn't. She wouldn't risk someone else's life
to save her own.

She kept running. When her skirt threatened to trip
her, she gripped it in her fists. But the ground shifted.
A creaking noise screamed through her brain, matching her own silent scream.

She was falling.

Jennie jerked awake, heart racing. Her stiff fingers
clutched the fabric of her skirt. Beads of perspiration
trickled down her body.

To get her bearings, she glanced around. Rae slept
beside her, a dark coat wedged between her head and
the window.

I'm on a train. Jennie panted, her breathing loud.
*The ground isn't moving. No one is chasing me. I'm
safe.*

Just in case, she looked behind her. A few snores
rumbled through the coach, but no one moved or

spoke. She released a shaky sigh. Until she saw Cole Bryant. His long legs were angled into the aisle, and his forearms rested across his trim waist. His gaze pinned her to her seat. She gulped. What had he seen?

"Bad dream?" His voice was low and matter-of-fact, reassuring and solid. Jennie held the sound of it inside her and drew strength from it.

She nodded in answer, and for the first time since her living nightmare had begun, she felt…safe.

"You okay?" he asked.

"Yes, th-thank you."

"You don't sound okay. And you've still got a death grip on your dress."

She glanced down at the white knuckles forming mountains across the back of her hand. Loosening her rigid fingers took some moments. "I'm quite all right now."

"Jennie, you're not fooling me." He leaned across the aisle and took her stiff hands in his. "Damn, these are ice-cold. That must've been some dream."

Jennie wanted to pull back, but she didn't have the will to fight him. And when the warmth of his hands seeped into hers, it spread through her body until she felt no desire to move at all. He massaged her fingers, slowly bringing the blood and life back into them. Jennie moaned, couldn't imagine letting anyone else touch her like this.

He put his long thumb across her knuckles and gently pulled her fingers back, stretching them. "Feels good, doesn't it?"

"Yes." Languid, she let him continue, but she imagined her mother's shocked expression. "But you shouldn't be doing it. It's not proper."

"I'm not concerned with proper."

She didn't know whether to be pleased or wary about that. She only knew she didn't want him to stop. When his calluses scraped over her flesh, a heated shiver moved through her body. "Do you make a habit of massaging women's hands?"

"Nope," he answered. "Usually it's a man's. Outlaws often hole up in canyons or mountains, where it's cold a lot of the year. Sometimes the men out tracking with me suffered frostbite on their hands." He released her hand. "If I didn't do for them what I just did for you, they could've lost their fingers."

"Oh," she said, already missing his warm touch. Jennie liked that Cole shared her desire to help others, to heal their injuries. Peering over at him, she realized it would be dangerously easy to let herself depend on him.

But she couldn't do it. She was on her own now and could take care of herself.

He leaned back in his seat. "Jennie, does your nightmare have something to do with why you've become a Harvey Girl?"

"You're digging into my life again. And I don't want you to."

"A good detective digs until he finds the answers he needs."

"But you don't *need* to know anything about me."

The corners of his mouth lifted the tiniest bit. "I'll be the judge of that."

Slim Carter stepped out of the saloon and into the cold, late-morning air of Flagstaff, Arizona Territory. On the peaks to the north, deep snow still covered several thousand feet of altitude. He shivered, then snarled. He wanted to get back to south Texas and warmth, but first he had a job to do and money to collect.

He surveyed the street and rows of buildings, hunched deeper into his sheepskin coat and crossed to the telegraph office.

"What can I do for you?" the ruddy-faced clerk asked.

"The name's Marsh." Slim gave him the name he'd been told to use. "I'm waitin' on a wire."

"Oh, yes, Mr. Marsh. It came in just a little bit ago. Unsigned, though." The clerk handed him the telegram, looked him over then lowered his eyes. "I expect you know who it's from."

Slim ambled over to the cast-iron stove. With his back to the clerk, he slowly walked his index finger under each word.

NO 1 WESTBOUND CARRYING CARGO STOP TAKE DELIVERY AT PREARRANGED DESTINATION STOP

Slim smiled, opened the stove door with his gloved hand and dropped the paper inside. The fire flared and crackled before he clanged the door shut.

He left the office and returned to the saloon, stopping at a round table where his gang sat. Jack spread out a full house, then scooped up his cash winnings. The other four men tossed down their cards and grabbed their whiskey glasses.

"Drink up, boys," Slim said. "We got us a train to catch."

The locomotive chugged and groaned as it dragged its load onto the Colorado Plateau of the Arizona Territory. Cole checked his pocket watch for the third time in the past twenty minutes. Two hours till their evening arrival in Williams. He drummed his fingers on the armrest and glanced at Jennie and Rae. He'd made no progress with the troublesome redhead whose mouth could close as tight as a canning jar.

He still knew nothing about her, except that she had the softest hands he'd ever touched. Her fingers were long and elegant, soothing and stirring at the same time.

He shifted in his seat. His body's continued response to Jennie was getting to be a dang nuisance. Especially when he should've been thinking about Katherine instead.

He checked the time again, watched the pine forest along the tracks crawl past. The train was moving like a snake in winter.

Cole tensed, and the back of his neck prickled, reminding him of his former tracking days. Once, he had ignored the raised hairs on the back of his neck, and Billy Baker, a new Wells Fargo man, had been gunned down as a result. His needless death still weighed on Cole.

Wrenching his head from left to right, Cole saw no sign of anything untoward. He reached for his bag anyway and pulled it down to his lap. Inside, he gripped his Colt .45 caliber single-action army revolver.

Within seconds, metal screeched on metal. Brakes shrieked. Passengers braced themselves with hands shoved against the backs of seats.

Cole's bag flew to the floor. When the train shuddered to a halt, his gun remained in hand. The widow woman saw it, screamed and fainted. Probably thought he was holding up the train.

Cole jumped into the aisle. He lowered the woman's head onto his seat, where she'd be safer if someone really was holding them up. Leaving his hat on the rack above, he scanned the coach and what he could see outside. A tree could've fallen and blocked the tracks, but his instinct told him otherwise.

A jumble of confused, indignant and fearful voices spread through the car. Beside him, Jennie was reassuring her friend. Gunshots erupted outside, and an ominous silence followed.

His fingers tightened on the gun, and his stomach roiled. Matt! Cole's heart and soul shouted at him to run forward, protect his brother. But his mind commanded patience and restraint. If he didn't evaluate the situation first, he might never make it to Matt's side.

Another gunshot split the quiet. Cole saw Rae duck her head below the window. Jennie craned for a better view.

"Get down, you fool!"

She turned to him, green eyes flashing.

He pushed her face into her lap. Despite the outraged gasp and muffled words filtering from the folds of her skirt, Cole kept his hand on the back of her head and felt a mulish sense of satisfaction.

He leaned over the two women and peered out the window. A short, wide-chested man wearing woolly chaps strode toward the front steps of the passenger coach. A navy-blue neckerchief masked his face. Two six-shooters led the way.

Cole spun toward the rear of the car. He raced through the aisle, his steps light and quiet. Softly he shut the door behind him just as the coach moved under the other man's considerable weight. Cole crept to the vestibule's outer door, itching to make a move. But what move?

The robbers would go after the express car. If Matt refused to open up, they would most likely threaten one of the crew members until he did. Another possibility came to mind. The outlaws could have a charge of dynamite to blow the door open.

Cole's heart hammered, and his breathing shortened. He poked his bare head beyond the edge of the passenger car door for another look. A wide clearing opened along one side. Jittery saddle horses tied to the trees pulled at their tethers, stamped their hooves and blew out clouds of breath. Two men on foot, hats worn low over their eyes and wool scarves wrapped around their noses and mouths, approached Matt's car. Another had his shotgun pointed toward the back of the train. A fourth man sat atop a large bay mare. He wore a sheepskin coat and held a Winchester repeating rifle aimed toward the locomotive. A red kerchief hid his face, but Cole got the impression of youth.

When a fifth man headed toward the second coach, Cole slipped out the other door, crept several feet forward and sprinted for the express car.

With the weight of Cole's hand gone from her head, Jennie sat bolt upright. *How dare he!* She whirled toward his seat.

But the widow woman was draped across it.

Before Jennie could look for him, the front vestibule door crashed open. A short, stout man wearing a big, dust-covered handkerchief around his head stormed into the coach. "Don't nobody move!"

"I don't believe this," she whispered to Rae.

"First we're assaulted by drunken cowhands and now the train is being robbed."

Rae dug a quivering finger into her thigh and shushed her.

When a woman at the front whimpered, the man aimed one of his guns at her. "Shut up!" The woman bit the white hanky clutched in her hand.

Jennie slumped down, but after a few moments she couldn't bear not knowing what was happening. She'd also begun to worry about Cole. Where was he?

She lifted her head and peered through the lowest part of the window. Tints of orange and pink clawed their way across the sky as dusk began to fall. Pines jutting high surrounded a wide clearing of bare earth and patches of snow. Armed men held the train at bay. One of them sat atop a large horse and burrowed into a sheepskin coat. His breath puffed white, and Jennie realized how cold the Arizona mountains could be. Staying inside suited her fine. She hoped the robbers didn't expect them to leave the coach's warmth.

Suddenly the mounted robber jerked his head from side to side, as if trying to avoid a pesky insect. He swatted at his face, catching his mask. It fell around his neck. He quickly yanked it back into place, but not fast enough. Jennie would know him if she saw him again.

Cole raced silently along the right side of the train, the cold unfelt. The clearing didn't extend to this side, so his dark suit, the forest and the darkening sky camouflaged him.

Between the first passenger coach and the express

car, he peered over the couplings. The outlaws didn't look his way, and he slipped forward.

The sliding door loomed above him. Cole's heart pounded against his ribs. He waited, listened, but heard nothing from the inside. Matt, despite sweating palms and a churning stomach, would have his shotgun and a revolver ready to protect the shipment. Cole would protect Matt.

Footsteps crunched through snow on the other side. Cole wiped his own sweating palms on his pants. He barely breathed.

"Hurry up and do it, would ya?" a deep, gravelly voice said. "What are ya, yellow?"

"Shut up, Jack! Unless you want to be blowed to hell," answered the other. "I needs my concentration."

Cole's stomach cramped, but he kept still, listening, waiting for his chance.

"Just hurry it up," said the one called Jack.

"I'm doin' it. Keep your pants on."

"I wouldn't have to if the boss'd let us help ourselves to whatever's ridin' in them treasure boxes inside. Then we'd be outta here, and I'd be enjoyin' me some nice little see-noritas on our way south."

"We'll be paid soon enough."

"Not enough compared to what's inside this car, I'd wager. Once it's kindling, why shouldn't we help ourselves?"

"That's not the plan. Here, hold this for me."

"It's a damn fool plan if you ask me. We should just shoot the messenger. Why bother wastin' good dynamite on him?"

"Quit your jawin'! I'm finished."

Cole's breath came fast now. These men wanted

his little brother dead. What kind of train robbers went after the expressman instead of the treasure he guarded?

Cole fought to keep himself hidden, fought for control. An instant later, he heard boots running over snow and dirt. And the hiss of a wick burning toward an explosive charge.

Oh, God! Matt!

He dropped his gun, threw himself under the coach. His body rolled across the wood ties. The momentum carried him over the steel rail and he vaulted to his feet, no time to worry about the robbers spotting him.

He focused on the doorsill. Wedged in the grating, two sticks of dynamite lay bound together. The few seconds' worth of remaining fuse sparked yellow dots of light.

No! he screamed silently.

Cole reached for the dynamite, grappled with it, then finally yanked the sticks free. He spun away from the car, his right arm outstretched.

The sputtering stopped.

Chapter Four

In the silent passenger coach, Jennie kept her head low and eyes open. The gunman trained his revolvers on the faces staring back at him. Running footsteps thudded outside. The man on the horse wheeled his mount away from the train.

"What are they doing?" she whispered, more to herself than to Rae.

A thunderous explosion shook the air.

Jennie jerked. "Oh, my goodness!"

The blast echoed around the clearing. Passengers gasped. Some screamed. Jennie thrust her face toward the window.

Smoke filtered through the pines. Frantic horses strained against their rawhide tethers. The man whose mask had fallen fought to control his rearing horse and stay in the saddle. Jennie wished the horse would bolt and take his rider with him.

Rae clutched at her hand. "Jennie! Jennie, what's happened?"

She squeezed the younger girl's hand. "I don't know, Rae. I can't see anything from here."

"What about Matt?" Rae's hand shook. "He could be hurt."

"We'll go find out as soon as—"

The vestibule door banged shut, and the stout gunman ran toward the horses.

"—the coast is clear," Jennie finished, already scooting out of her seat.

Rae grabbed her skirt, held her back. "Are you going now?" Her voice was pitched high.

"Aren't you coming?"

Rae didn't release her skirt. "Y-yes, but—"

"Good, keep your head down and let go of my skirt."

They crept out of their seats and along the aisle. As they entered the vestibule, a barrage of gunfire erupted outside. Jennie dropped to the floor with Rae, hands over their heads. The loud reports bounced between the train and forest, shattering nerves.

A man's shout followed. "Let's get outta here." Hoofbeats faded into the trees.

Jennie jumped up, pulled open the door and cautiously surveyed the now quiet landscape. "They're gone, Rae. Let's go." With her reticule hanging from her wrist, she leaped down from the coach and started forward, Rae close behind her. She dreaded what she might find after such an explosion and all the gunfire, but she kept on.

The sight of a man lying motionless beside the express car stopped her short. He was wearing a black sack suit and beige cowboy boots. Jennie's stomach twisted into knots, then she broke into a run. "Cole!"

Before she could get to him, the express car's bullet-ridden door slid open and Matt stared at his brother. Jennie's heart clenched at the naked pain on his young face.

He jumped down, stumbled to his knees amid the wood splinters littering the ground. Tears streamed over his cheeks as he scrambled to his brother.

Jennie's steps slowed. She was too late. Her eyes blurred and burned. Cole had protected her yesterday, comforted her in the night. Made her feel safe. And now she could never offer him her gratitude again, do nothing in return.

Matt sat at the top of Cole's head, gently stroked the shoulder-length hair away from his brother's smoke-blackened face. His other hand covered Cole's right arm.

"Cole. Wake up. You gotta wake up. I know I shouldn't have taken this job, but I wanted to be like you. I'm sorry. Cole!" He sobbed out his brother's name. "Wake up. You can't die now. Don't you dare die!"

He wasn't dead? Jennie scrubbed her eyes, rushed forward and dropped to her knees beside him. She bent her head to Cole's chest. The beat of his heart thumped in her ears. Relief as powerful as a locomotive rushed through her. But he was unconscious. Did he have a head wound?

"Matt," she said. When he didn't answer, she pinched his arm hard. "Matt!"

He lifted his vacant gaze to her, then raised his right hand. Blood dripped from his fingers. Cole's blood.

Her breath caught deep in her lungs. Rae gasped, the sound sending Jennie into action. She crawled to Cole's right side and blanched. His hand and wrist had vanished.

She gritted her teeth and took charge. She knew what to do and would not allow Cole Bryant to die. He was her patient now, and she owed him.

Blood soaked his torn sleeve, but the bone and tendons were cleanly severed. She yanked what remained of his sleeve out of the way.

"What are you doing?" Matt cried.

"Please, Matt," Rae said in a softly pleading voice. "Jennie can help. Trust her."

He studied Rae's face. "All right."

"Matt," Jennie said, "give me your necktie. Quick."

The tie appeared in her palm. She silently thanked Rae for getting through to him. Jennie placed the narrow strip of fabric in position, looped the ends under each other. She continued giving orders until she had a tourniquet tightened in place with a narrow piece of wood. Thankfully, Cole remained unconscious.

Jennie wished she had anesthetic, wished Dr. Nicholson were here to do what she must. Could she remember everything he'd done when she'd helped him with a similar injury? Would it matter in these primitive conditions?

Two men dressed in grease-spattered overalls ran to them. "Is he okay?" one asked.

"I never seen such a thing," the other said. "He come from right under the car, grabbed that dynamite and tried to toss it away."

Jennie glanced at Matt's white face while Rae placed a comforting hand on his shoulder. Cole had risked his life to protect his brother, loved him enough to die for him.

Moisture stung Jennie's eyes. She blinked it away,

needed to see clearly if she was going to do him any good at all.

"Gentlemen, I need your help," she commanded.

"Our help? But, ma'am, we got to clear the logs from the track and get this train moving. I'm the engineer and he's the brakeman."

"This man's life may depend upon you. Please, I need water, soap, blankets, alcohol and a hot fire."

"Well, okay, I guess," the engineer said. "But does the fire have to be right here?"

"No, but I'll need a lamp to sterilize my needle and scissors and give me light to see by." The daylight was almost gone.

"All right, ma'am. The fireman can build up the fire in the locomotive, and we'll get you the other items."

"Fine. Rae, can you help them?"

The girl gave Matt an encouraging smile, then joined the men.

"Ma'am, we'll be back directly with everything you need," the brakeman said. "Don't worry."

"Thank you." She returned to her unconscious patient and his brother, who held the tourniquet in place. A tear slid down Matt's cheek as he stared at his brother's grayish face.

Jennie looked away, then stood up and reached under her skirt. She unfastened her white petticoat and stepped out of it, trying her best to keep it from touching the ground.

A faint, masculine voice asked, "Wh-what are…you d-doing?"

Jennie jerked her head toward Cole. "You're awake," she stated, then scowled. He *would* awaken at the precise moment she was removing her undergarment for his benefit.

"Sh-shouldn't I be?"

Jennie's annoyance dissolved at the weakness in his voice.

Tears brimmed over Matt's dark lashes. "Cole, my God! I thought you were nearly dead."

Cole frowned as if trying to remember something. Suddenly he searched his brother's face. Fear and love mingled in the pewter eyes that only yesterday had glittered with danger. Jennie had never seen such love, and her breath caught.

"M-Matt, you o-okay?"

Jennie stood alone, felt like an interloper as she witnessed a love so raw it hurt her to see it. But she couldn't tear her gaze away.

A huge grin spread across Matt's face. Merely seeing Cole awake gave the younger man strength. "I'm just fine, big brother. You always knew how to keep me—" his voice cracked "—out of trouble."

"Yeah, I've gotten you…out of a few…scrapes over…the years."

Cole rested for a moment. When he looked at Jennie again, frown lines grooved his forehead. "Why…your petticoat?"

She knelt beside him, the garment in her hands. "Your arm has been wounded." She forced herself to speak matter-of-factly, concentrate on him instead of what she'd seen in his eyes, or what would happen to him if she couldn't help him. "We need bandages. As clean as we can get."

"Oh." He tried to lift his head, but it fell back. "I don't…feel…pain." His eyelids drifted closed.

"Matt, back to work," Jennie ordered.

She gave him her petticoat and tied down the piece of wood keeping the tourniquet tight. He tore the petticoat into strips, laying them over his shoulder.

"I'll need something metal to heat and cauterize the smaller arteries. Do you have anything?"

He lifted Cole's pant leg and pulled a lethal-looking knife from the boot. "Will this do?"

Jennie looked from the knife in his hand to the man he'd taken it from. She swallowed. "Yes. That will do nicely. Now go find that fire and heat the knife till it glows."

Matt ran forward.

Alone with her silent patient, Jennie decided to do something she hadn't even done after leaving Boston. She bowed her head in prayer. "Dear God, please help me to do everything correctly. And protect Cole from infection. Amen." When she lifted her head, the engineer, brakeman and Rae arrived, their arms laden with blankets, a variety of clinking bottles and all the other items she'd asked for.

Rae spread one of the blankets over Cole's body, careful to avoid his injury. The engineer lined up the bottles and flasks near Jennie, and the brakeman placed the lamp and more blankets close at hand.

Jennie disinfected her hands and the wound as best she could, then wielded her scissors, needle and thread. Matt returned with the knife and bandages.

Fifteen minutes later, night had fallen. Jennie strapped what remained of Cole's arm to his body. His pulse was weak but constant. His color had already improved. Now, if they could just get him warm. A group of male passengers, having cleared the tracks, carried Cole inside the passenger coach.

Jennie stumbled after them, shivering from the cold

and aftermath of what she'd done. Inside, she fell into her seat, rubbed her gritty eyes and worried. Had she done everything possible for Cole? Would he live?

For the rest of the night, after the train arrived in Williams and while Jennie tried to sleep in the Harvey House dormitory room she and Rae had been assigned, Jennie worried about Cole.

She'd finally fallen asleep near dawn, but when she awakened late in the morning, an overpowering need to see him hurried her dressing. Was he in pain? Were her stitches holding? She could think of a hundred reasons to see the man who had risked his life for his brother. Most of all, she had to know if Cole had lived through the night.

Crossing the dirt street to the two-story brick Grand Canyon Hotel, Jennie noticed the sun glittering in a sharp blue sky. The scent of pine drifted on the breeze. Crisp mountain air seeped through her clothing, and she pulled her wool coat tighter.

Inside the hotel, she passed an open door to the attached mercantile and approached the reception clerk, a sallow-complected young man. "Cole Bryant's room, please."

"That'd be number two, ma'am. Up the stairs and down the hall. It's on the front side of the building."

Jennie thanked him and started up. At the door marked 2, she lifted her fist and hesitated. Was Cole all right? She sucked in a deep breath and knocked lightly.

Matt opened the door. Dark crescents underlined his eyes. She gave him a tentative smile. "I came to see my patient. How is he faring?"

He motioned her into a large room decorated in

gaudy reds and golds. Velvet drapes were pulled back from the windows by golden ropes hung with tassels.

"According to Dr. Goodman, he's as well as can be expected."

Jennie felt her shoulder muscles ease slightly. She hadn't realized just how heavy a burden she carried. "Thank God."

She took several steps toward the bed and observed her patient. He lay quiet under two quilts spread over a high double bed. His color had improved, and his respiration appeared even and regular. Jennie's throat tightened, and she had to look away.

Matt followed her into the room. "Dr. Goodman said I shouldn't worry, but I do, Jennie. Cole hasn't been awake since that one time yesterday."

"He lost a lot of blood. I'm sure it's just his body's way of resting up," she said, though she worried, too. Anything could happen. Especially if she'd done something wrong. "The doctor would know best."

"You're probably right. Maybe Cole will wake up now that you're here. You're much better looking than Dr. Goodman." Matt smiled.

"Tell me about the doctor," Jennie said, unable to enjoy the compliment.

"He's the town physician. He and Cole are friends. I think he'd like to meet you."

"Why is that?" Had she forgotten to do something important?

"Because he said your work was exceptional. There was nothing he could do that you hadn't already done."

"Really?"

At Matt's nod, the fears and uncertainties plaguing her dissipated. Her concerns now turned to the threat of infection and Cole's psychological response to losing his hand and wrist.

"Did the doctor say anything else about Cole's treatment? What needs to be done? I want to help you, Matt."

"Just about changing the bandage regularly, and if his pain gets too bad, giving him some laudanum. The bottle is on the nightstand."

Jennie bit her lip. Dr. Nicholson had explained that some people became dependent on the liquid drug. She didn't want that for Cole. "Why don't you keep the bottle aside, Matt. When Cole needs the drug, give him a little bit at a time. It's better he not take too much of it."

"That's what Dr. Goodman said, too." Matt removed the bottle to a table across the room. Returning, he dropped his voice to a whisper. "Jennie, I don't want Cole to know about his injury yet. He's always been stronger than me, but something like this..." He drew a ragged breath. "I'm afraid he won't take it so well."

"He'll see it soon enough. Wouldn't it be better to tell him before that happens?"

"I don't know."

"Matt, listen to me," Jennie implored. "You said yourself Cole is a strong man. He'll get over this and get on with his life."

His gaze bounced around the room. "I guess. I don't know why I'm worrying so much. He'll be fine. He has to be."

"Of course he will," Jennie said, but she carried her own doubts. She had no idea how he'd react.

A rustling of the bedclothes drew Jennie from her thoughts. When the bedsprings squeaked, both she and Matt rushed to opposite sides of the bed. Matt leaned over his brother.

Cole woke and looked straight at him. "Matt," he croaked, "are we in Williams?"

"We sure are, big brother. In the Grand Canyon Hotel."

Cole licked his dry lips and swallowed several times. "Hotel? But I got to get to the ranch. Carpenters are building me a barn. I can't leave it all to the foreman."

"Relax, Cole. There's nothing to worry about. When you're feeling stronger, we'll head out to the ranch."

A frown creased Cole's brow. "We?"

"Yeah, we, as in us."

"I thought you were staying with the Company."

"I changed my mind." Matt tucked his thumbs into his waistband.

"Why?"

"That's not important."

Cole didn't move. "Yeah, it is important."

"Okay, fine. All my life you've been helping me, now it's my turn to help you. It's as simple as that."

Jennie knew there was more to it. She'd heard Matt's confession to an unconscious Cole. He blamed himself for what had happened.

Cole's eyes brightened. "Really? You're going to help me with the ranch? Make your home there?"

Jennie watched Matt's mouth open, then close again. Cole had misunderstood.

"Uh, that's right, Cole. It's time I learned the ranching business."

"I'm glad," he said, the rugged lines of his face relaxing. "It'll be good having you home, little brother, but right now, I'm thirsty.'' When he tried to sit up, he grimaced. And he spotted her. ''What are *you* doing here?''

''It's so good to see you, too,'' Jennie said.

His lips thinned. ''Why can't you just answer the question?''

''I came by to see how you were feeling. Does that satisfy you?''

''No.'' Again he tried to hoist himself up in the bed. When she came closer to help him, he flinched from her. ''I can do it.''

Matt worked two pillows in behind his back, but didn't get any thanks for it. Jennie schooled her expression into a calm facade, but it hurt that Cole didn't want her help. Unwilling to give up yet, she poured a glass of water and put it to his lips.

He glared at her. ''I'm not an invalid. I can do it myself, or didn't you understand me the first time?''

''Humor me. You seem to have forgotten you were injured.''

He paused. ''I have a vague recollection of lying on the ground for some reason. But what I really remember is you.'' Cole's disturbingly direct gaze dipped below her waist. ''Are you missing a petticoat by chance?'' Amusement lightened his tone.

''That's not funny.'' Jennie forced the glass against his teeth and started pouring.

Cole sputtered through the first mouthful, then drank down the entire glass. She hadn't exactly given him a choice.

''Thanks for nothing. Your nursing is about as gentle as a mustang being ridden for the first time.''

''You're welcome.'' She dropped the glass onto the

nightstand with a thunk. "And I forgive you for stuffing my face into my lap during the robbery."

"You ought to be grateful. You could've gotten your fool head shot off. Or didn't you think about that?"

Heat rose into her cheeks. He'd been protecting her again, but with her quick temper and everything else that had happened, she hadn't considered he was being anything but insufferable. "Your methods leave much to be desired," she said, though she spoke less abruptly than before.

"But they're effective."

"Uncomfortably so." She started straightening the bedclothes. "Are you hungry?"

"No. And stop fussing."

Matt grinned. "Jennie, you'll have to excuse his surliness. He's not one to accept help easily. In the past, if there was any nursing to be done, he did it. Cole practically raised me."

"Shut up, Matt." Cole's grayish-blue eyes darkened to the color of winter storm clouds.

His irritation piqued her curiosity. Was he being modest? Or just plain difficult? "Go on, Matt," Jennie invited.

He smiled defiantly at his severe older brother. "We grew up in Omaha, see. Pa skipped town when I was about five. Ma worked two or more jobs to take care of us and make sure we got some education. She died when I was eight, but Cole had already been looking after me."

Matt spoke as though his father's desertion and his mother's death meant little to him. Had he been too young to understand? Or had he needed only Cole?

Jennie heard Cole's teeth grinding behind his rigid

face. Matt was obviously the good-natured one in the family, but then, he'd been protected from the hardships his brother had had to face. Jennie couldn't imagine their life. How had Cole supported them? Another piece of her heart went out to him, to the man whose love for his brother went as deep as what she hoped to have one day from the man she married.

"Matt!" Cole said with absolute authority. "That's enough! Jennie doesn't need to hear our life story."

A mischievous smile curved Matt's mouth. Was this his way of reassuring himself Cole would live? "Ah, come on, Cole. Jennie's practically family now."

"What have you been drinking, Matt?" Cole's eyelids began to droop. His body sagged against the pillows.

"I haven't been drinking anything. I'm trying to tell you Jennie saved your life. What do you think of that?"

Chapter Five

Cole tried to open his eyes again. Jennie had saved his life?

No. That was crazy. He'd been protecting her, not the other way around. She was the one who continued to get into trouble. Her absence was what he wanted. Then he'd finally have some peace.

Cole knew he ought to be out getting supplies for the ranch, but a bone-deep tiredness pulled at him. He felt like a flower in a hot spell. What had happened to him? He couldn't be laid up when he had so much to do: run the C Bar M, teach Matt the cattle business, marry Katherine, and...

There was something else he needed to handle. Something to do with what happened on the train. What was it? He couldn't think now. Later. He would remember later.

Matt stood at the foot of the bed and stared at the even rise and fall of Cole's chest beneath the quilts. Jennie had left an hour ago, after Cole had fallen back to sleep. Matt wanted to sleep, too, but he couldn't. Not last night when he'd watched every reassuring movement of Cole's chest, and not now. Each time his big brother twitched, Matt froze, holding his breath until he knew Cole still breathed, still lived. Only then could Matt breathe again, too.

A light knock drew his attention.

He crossed the room and opened the door a crack. Bright blue eyes met his. His mouth moved into an automatic smile, and his fears and anguish dropped away. He hadn't realized how much he needed to see his ray of sunshine.

"Hello, Matt," she said shyly.

"Hi, Sunshine."

Rae's smile wiped out all remnants of his gloom. Matt slipped into the hallway, leaving the door ajar so he could watch and listen to his brother.

"My name isn't Sunshine," she admonished him.

"No, it's Ray, for a ray of sunshine."

She laughed softly. "Not *r-a-y,* silly, *r-a-e.* It's Scandinavian for female deer."

"Maybe so, but I'll always think of a bright summer day when I say it. Or see you."

Shyly she dropped her gaze. "I suppose I won't mind if you think that."

He lifted his hand and caressed her smooth face. She leaned her cheek into his hand, closed her eyes for a moment. Too soon, she straightened and stepped back. His hand fell.

"I saw Jennie," she said. "She told me your brother is doing better. I'm glad."

"Yeah, she stopped by earlier. I think he's going to be okay, but I can't stop worrying about him. I don't know what to do." He hauled in a harsh breath. "I feel so damn helpless."

She took his hand, and Matt held on to hers like a man hanging from a cliff.

"You're doing everything you can, Matt. Cole just needs to heal now. And he will with both you and Jennie keeping an eye on him."

A chuckle escaped his throat, the sound surprising him. But he couldn't help laughing. Every time his brother and Jennie got together, sparks flew.

"Why are you laughing?" she asked.

"Because Jennie has a very odd effect on Cole."

"What's that?"

"She drives him crazy. She talks back to him, and he's not used to that. Especially from a female."

Rae giggled. "Jennie doesn't take any guff if she doesn't have to." Her smile disappeared, and her eyes clouded with concern. "She's a strong woman."

Matt cocked his head. "If she's so strong, why do you suddenly look worried about her?"

"It's nothing. Really."

"Okay, if you say so," he said, knowing it wasn't nothing. "During the train trip, did Jennie tell Cole anything about herself?"

Rae's gaze became wary, shifted to the partially open door. "Why do you ask that?"

He shrugged as if it really didn't matter to him. "Just something Cole said back in Kansas. He thought she was running from something."

Rae clasped her hands, wrung them together. "He did?"

"Yeah. He wanted to know what." Matt leaned against the flocked wallpaper. "So, is she on the run?"

"I have to go now." Rae started to turn away.

He snagged her arm. "Rae, talk to me. Is Jennie in trouble? She's not wanted by the law, is she?"

She gasped. "No, of course not."

"Then what?"

"Let go of me, Matt. Please."

Reluctantly he let her go. "Tell me what's going on. Are you safe with her?"

"I'm perfectly safe. There's no cause to worry about me."

"Good, but what about Jennie?"

"I'm sorry, but I can't say anything. I made her a promise, and I'm not going to break it. I'm also not going to tell Jennie of Cole's suspicions. She has enough on her plate."

"She's an intelligent woman, Rae. She most likely knows already. Cole isn't real subtle when he decides he wants information."

"I doubt he'll be thinking about her problems for a while."

"I wouldn't bet on that. She's a distraction to him. And a pretty one at that. He's going to need distractions when he realizes his hand's gone."

Rae's brow furrowed with her worry. Matt wanted to calm her, but when he reached for her hands, she stepped back.

"Matt, please promise me you'll say nothing to Cole."

"You haven't given me anything to tell. Nothing that he hasn't already figured out."

"Promise me."

"All right," he said, unable to resist pleasing her. "I promise. Now will you let me hold your hands?"

She tucked them behind her. "I really do have to go. Jennie and I are meeting with our supervisor at the Harvey House. We have to learn where everything is before we start work tomorrow morning. I'll see you again, though. I do promise that.''

He nodded slowly. It wouldn't be soon enough.

Evening fell, fast and dark. Thousands of stars, which Jennie had never seen above the lights of Boston, glittered in the Arizona sky. She hoped they symbolized good things to come. Good things for Cole.

She entered the hotel, climbed the stairs and knocked on his door for the second time that day. Matt greeted her with a glowing smile. ''Cole woke up a few minutes ago and ate some supper.''

''That's wonderful, but…how did he manage?'' She peered around Matt's shoulder. Did Cole know the extent of his injury?

''I told him his right arm was wounded and shouldn't be moved, so he let me cut his meat for him. But he fed himself. Cole's always been good with both hands. In school, he purposely switched his pencil from hand to hand just to make the teacher mad, 'cause she tried to force all the kids to use their right hands.''

''He's a talented man.'' Jennie wished she'd known Cole as a youth. ''So he doesn't know about—?''

Matt shook his head slightly. ''Come on in.''

She laid her coat, scarf and gloves over the chair near the door, then approached the bed. ''Good evening, Cole.''

''Back so soon?'' he asked from his semi-sitting position. ''Don't you have customers to serve over in that Harvey House?''

Jennie showed him a sweetly medicinal smile.

"Rae and I start work at breakfast tomorrow. You'll be overjoyed to know I've gotten special permission from the Harvey House manager to come and check on you around midmorning."

"Lucky me. Why do I rate such devotion?"

Matt strolled to the other side of the bed. "Cole, be nice to your doctor."

His eyes narrowed. "My what?"

"You heard me. Your doctor. I told you before that Jennie saved your life, but I don't think you believed me. Or maybe you didn't hear good. Jennie stopped the bleeding and sewed you up. Right there next to the train."

Cole's jawline tensed. "Is that true, Jennie?"

"I knew what to do, how to help. Any life is threatened by the continued loss of blood. Even yours."

"Then…I'm indebted to you." The words came from between gritted teeth.

"No, we are square now. If you'll remember, you saved Rae and me from those unpleasant cowhands back in Kansas."

"I remember." Some of the tension eased from his voice, but she could tell he didn't like owing anyone anything.

"Good. Then you know there is no debt to be repaid. Unless it's on my side. You gave me the chance to practice my medical skills."

The gray of his eyes darkened. "Why am I suddenly worried?" he asked the room. "It must be because my teeth still hurt from their earlier encounter with a drinking glass. I hope your doctoring is better than your nursing."

She leaned toward him, one finger pointed at the patch of black hair peeking out above the quilts covering his chest. "My doctoring is the reason you're in this bed instead of a box, Mr. Bryant. If you wish to complain, do it silently."

Matt quickly intervened. "Jennie, that's just Cole's way of making fun. He's joshing you."

"I'm not joshing," Cole said tightly. "Matt doesn't know what he's talking about." He shifted his weight, and the bed creaked. "Are you really a doctor, Jennie?"

She hesitated. Already the questions were beginning again. But this time he had the right to ask. A patient deserved to know the credentials of the person who treated him.

"No, I'm not a doctor. Or a nurse."

Two creases dented the area between his dark brows. "Then how come I'm…still alive."

She wandered to the foot of the bed. "Back home, I used to work as a volunteer in a medical dispensary."

"In Boston?"

She stared at him. "How did you know?"

"Your accent is kind of hard to miss. Go on."

"I, uh, well, the dispensary is in a poor section of town and pays little to nothing, so very few qualified nurses work there. I ended up helping the doctor with just about everything. We had a case similar to yours not too long ago, so…" She shrugged, didn't want to explain the similarities any further.

"I see." He glanced down at the quilts covering his arm. "So what did you have to do to save my life?"

Cole watched her mouth open and close twice. She tucked a stray red curl behind her ear, then repeated the motion for no good reason. For a woman who usually had some comment or retort, she was awful quiet now. "Jennie?"

When she exchanged an anxious look with Matt and still said nothing, Cole's heart started to pound. Why wouldn't she answer? A trickle of sweat slid down his temple.

"Matt," Jennie said, "I think you—"

"No!" Matt took a step back. "You're the one with the medical experience."

Cole swallowed hard. His mouth tasted like the harsh desert south of the mountains. From another room, men's laughter reverberated into the corridor. The scent of cigar smoke snaked in under the door.

Few things in life frightened Cole. Not knowing the truth of a situation was one. Being less than the man his brother looked up to was another. What had happened to him?

"Tell me, Jennie."

She shifted her weight from one foot to the other, shot Matt another glance before moving closer to the bedside. Her expressive eyes glistened in the lamplight. Was it sorrow he was seeing in them? Or pity?

"Just tell me, damn it! Everything."

Matt dashed to the window and stared out.

A door slammed, and louder laughter came tumbling down the hall. Cole heard men slapping each other on the back.

Jennie cleared her throat. "Cole, the train we were on was held up. Apparently—"

"Tell me something I don't know," he blurted, hearing his own impatience when he'd always considered himself a patient man.

"Then let me finish." She glared at him, but her

eyes were moist, the dark red lashes clumped together.

"Go on."

"Apparently, you went to help Matt during the robbery. To protect him. The outlaws had placed some dynamite in—"

"Dynamite? I don't remember that."

"Do you want to hear this or not?" Her green eyes flashed, and Cole took comfort from her temper. This was the woman he'd met at the depot, not the one with pity in her gaze.

"Go ahead."

"The engineer said you grabbed the dynamite from the doorsill and threw it away. However, the charge exploded very close to you. Too close, Cole." Her voice shook, and she inhaled deeply. "It took your right hand and wrist with it."

The men in the hallway guffawed as they thumped down the stairs. Cole didn't move. This had to be a cruel joke. He could feel his fingers. His hand was still there. It had to be.

"You're lying."

Jennie twisted the bedclothes in her fingers. "Matt, Rae and the train's crew helped me treat you. They were all wonderful. I think you'll be just fine."

Just fine? How could he be "just fine" if his hand was gone?

"I said you're lying." His pulse hammered in his ears, grew louder with each passing second. "I can feel my fingers."

"Cole, I truly wish I were lying. I'm so sorry." A single tear trailed down her cheek. "Phantom pains are common in cases like yours."

Cole's stomach knotted. "No," he whispered. He'd

asked for the truth, but now he didn't want it. Desperate for someone to reassure him he was still the same man, Cole looked to his little brother. "Matt?"

Matt kept his back turned. His shoulders heaved, and Cole heard him haul in a ragged, pain-filled breath. His last hope vanished. It was true.

Jennie leaned over him and started to pull down the quilts.

"Don't!" he shouted, making both her and Matt jump.

Her hands stilled. "But you should see—"

"Later. I'll look later." He shut his eyes. "Leave me alone."

She didn't move. He heard her soft breathing, smelled the scent of roses. In his mind, he saw again that one tear caressing her cheek after she'd told him he would never be the same.

Finally, with a rustling of her skirt, she stepped away. "All right. I'll go. But I'll be back tomorrow morning." He heard her pick up her things from the chair and ease open the door. "Good night, Cole."

He didn't respond, because inside he was screaming.

Chapter Six

"Come on up, gentlemen." Dr. Earnest Goodman adjusted his gold-rimmed spectacles. "My office is at your disposal."

Beneath the glowing gas lamp hanging on the two-story building, Walter Gray, Benjamin Porter and Jefferson Stark clomped up the side staircase after him. Inside, they pulled up chairs around his desk.

"So what did you ask us here for, Doc?" Gray asked. He was the most successful merchant and hotelier in town. His gaze strayed to the deck of cards next to the inkwell.

"After the attack on the Number 1, I should have thought that would be obvious, Walter." The doctor withdrew a bottle of whiskey and four glasses from his bottom desk drawer. "Drink, gentlemen?"

They all nodded as he splashed the amber liquid into the glasses. They were the town fathers, their fortunes tied up in the Arizona Territory. They grabbed for their drinks.

Earnest sipped his. "I wish to discuss how to stop the criminal element from plaguing our part of the territory."

Jefferson Stark, owner of the Saginaw Lumber Company, fingered his bushy brown beard and stretched out legs as powerful as the trees his company felled and milled. "You think that train holdup was too close to home?"

"I do, indeed. Don't you?"

He gulped down half his drink and shrugged, disappointing the doctor with his apathy.

Gray stroked his goatee. "The doc has a point, Jefferson. An assault like that could frighten off potential citizens. If we want Williams to continue growing, we can't have outlaws causing problems for us."

"We might even lose some of the folk we've got," said Benjamin Porter, owner and chief operating officer of the Northern Arizona Savings Bank in Williams. "Either way, we all lose valuable business."

"Yeah," Gray said, his gaze aimed at Stark. "Your lumber built most of this town. Where will your company be if everyone leaves?"

He frowned. "The same place you'd be. Broke."

"Exactly."

"So," the doctor said, "what can we do to protect our homes and citizens?"

Porter folded his arms over his broad middle. "We've already got a sheriff. Does he need to hire more men?"

"That would cost us more money," Gray said. "The town coffers are low as it is."

"I think it's up to the Santa Fe Railway and Wells Fargo." Stark helped himself to more whiskey. "They need to take charge, show they mean business. Don't they put up a reward after a robbery?"

"What robbery?" Porter asked. "I heard nothing

was taken. Wells Fargo would be foolish to send somebody out here for nothing.''

''There was damage to the express car,'' Gray said. ''That gang must've unloaded every last bullet they had into it. Some of the cargo had to have been destroyed. Wouldn't Wells Fargo send someone because of that?''

''I doubt it,'' Porter said. ''They've got cases keeping them busy all over the country.'' He spread his arms expansively. ''The world even. I heard from one of my banking colleagues in San Francisco that Wells Fargo went after a fellow who skipped to the South Pacific with a bundle. One of their own trusted employees.''

Gray reached for the cards, fanned them with his nimble fingers. ''There's no money involved here.''

''No,'' the doctor said, ''but there's an injured man. A past Wells Fargo man and one of our own.''

''Yeah, Cole Bryant.'' Porter clucked his tongue. ''I heard about it when I got back from Prescott. Terrible thing.''

''Bryant's going to make it, though, isn't he?'' Stark asked, his wiry brows drawn together. ''I already sent out the last shipment of lumber for his new barn. It'll be a beauty when it's finished, but I haven't received payment for that load yet.''

Gray dropped the deck on the desk. ''He owes me as well. It's been nearly a month since his last payment at the mercantile. And he's staying at my hotel right now.''

''My bank's got the mortgage on his land,'' Porter said. ''And I believe his savings account is currently rather low. Tell us the truth, Doc. Did he really lose his arm? Is he going to be laid up for long?''

Earnest sighed. He'd made no progress with these men at all. "Gentlemen, I'm sure that you will all get the money you are owed. And no, Cole did not lose his arm. He lost his right hand and wrist."

Stark and Porter tossed more whiskey down their throats. Gray picked up the cards and laid several down.

"How did he live through such an ordeal?" Stark asked.

Earnest took another sip from his glass. "A new Harvey Girl treated him, a redhead by the name of Jennie Andrews. She did a remarkable job. Bryant should recover fully. Except, of course, that part of his arm is gone."

"A shame about that," Gray said. "I hope he gets back in the saddle quick."

Earnest heard what Gray didn't say outright, that he wanted his money sooner than later.

"It will take some getting used to," the doctor said, "but I think Cole is the kind of man who adapts easily. I wouldn't be surprised if he went after those outlaws himself."

The three men stared across the desk at him.

"I thought his detective days were over," Porter said.

"Well, sure, but this is personal. It was his brother in that express car. Wouldn't you do the same once you were feeling fit?"

The other men hesitated, exchanged uncertain glances.

Earnest corked the bottle and stood. This meeting had gone on long enough. Playing poker with his so-called friends would make the evening interminable.

He hoped he would never have to count on them for anything.

"Gentlemen, I fear I must say good night now. I hope you will consider what we've discussed here and think about how we might better protect our town."

They hemmed and hawed as they rose to their feet. Gray eyed the cards longingly before turning for the door.

Earnest locked his office and followed the men's loud steps down the staircase and into the street. One of them veered from the usual route. Earnest thought nothing of it. The fellow was probably going to the saloon for a nightcap.

One man stood alone in the shadow of the Williams depot. Clouds had crept in overhead to hide the moon and stars.

He stared at the darkened, sleeping Harvey House just a few steps away and didn't know whether to curse or thank the redhead named Jennie Andrews.

He turned his attention to the east, in the direction of the robbery site.

"Damn! Those idiots can't even blow up an expressman," he grated. "Well, I've waited three years, Cole Bryant. I can wait a little longer."

Cole stared up at the austere white ceiling. One tiny brown spot had captured his attention after Jennie's evening departure hours ago. Or had it been only minutes? He had no idea, had lost all concept of time and of what was real. He could've sworn his fingers still existed. His entire arm.

Now he had to see for himself.

"Matt," he blurted, "get out."

His brother kicked at the Oriental rug next to the bed. "I don't think so, Cole."

"Don't argue with me. Not now."

"What are you planning to do?" His gaze was uneasy.

"Don't question me, Matt. Just get out!"

"But—"

"Now!" Cole slammed his fist on the mattress, and instantly regretted it. Pain surged through his body.

"All right. I'm going." Matt shuffled away. "But I'll be right outside the door."

"Fine."

When the door closed behind his brother, Cole whispered, "I have to know for sure."

Beads of sweat trickled down his forehead, stung his eyes. He wished he were out tracking the most dangerous of outlaws instead of lying in this bed about to do what he must.

He lifted his gaze to the spot on the ceiling, then dragged the soft cotton quilt away from his injured arm. But he couldn't look yet. His breath came in rapid pants. Cole forced himself to take a steadying breath, but he couldn't draw enough air to fill his starving lungs. Was this how it felt to drown?

Just do it. Look at it.

Finally he peered down at his right side. And stopped breathing. Denting a pillow was a stump swathed in white muslin. Everything was gone. Fingers, hand and wrist.

"No," he choked out in a whisper. His head fell back. What little breath he still had shuddered out.

A moment later he inhaled, instinct overriding his horror. Desperate to wipe out the sight of nothing where there should've been bone, muscle and flesh,

Cole refocused on that little spot on the ceiling. But it was useless. The image of his missing hand haunted him.

"She should've let me die."

Jennie slid a plate of poached eggs in front of a gentleman traveler, then hurried toward the woman beckoning from the U-shaped curve of the lunchroom counter. The clink of china and silver vied with the constant buzz of conversation.

Jennie glanced toward Rae, who rushed back and forth along the other half of the wood-topped counter. She was serving her share of Harvey House breakfasts during the train's allotted thirty-minute stop. More Harvey Girls, all dressed in their nun's habit of a uniform, waited on the customers in the adjoining dining room. Miss Olive Thompson, the supervisor, kept a vigilant, policing eye on all the girls.

As Jennie hastened toward the female customer awaiting her assistance, a large man in a frock coat called out, "Miss?"

Jennie sighed inwardly. What could he want now? She'd already brought him his coffee.

"Miss!" He leaned his barrel-sized chest over the counter.

She stopped in front of him. "Yes, sir?"

"I ordered coffee." With a manicured fingernail, he tapped the blue chain pattern rimming the white cup.

"I did bring you coffee, sir."

"No, you did not bring me coffee." He shoved the cup across the counter at her. "It's tea."

Jennie peered into it, then gnashed her teeth at another mistake. She hadn't displeased this many customers since her first week of training. But her mind kept drifting across the tracks to the Grand Canyon Hotel and Cole. Had he looked at his arm yet?

"I'm sorry, sir. I'll bring you a new cup right away. It'll just—"

The train emitted a long whistle.

"Don't bother," he grumbled. "I don't have time now."

He shoved his bulk out of the high-backed wood swivel chair and followed the other customers streaming out of the restaurant in an orderly rush. Jennie dismissed him and started toward the woman who'd been trying to get her attention. But she was gone.

As the door swung shut behind the last patron, Jennie blew out a breath that stirred the damp hair falling over her forehead. Welcoming the blessed quiet, she leaned against the counter's edge and closed her eyes. How had Olive Thompson managed to work as a Harvey Girl for so long? Fifteen years, Jennie had heard.

Was Miss Thompson's pinched face the result of serving food to too many hungry people in a hurry? The woman, her figure as thin as a broom handle, wore her graying hair severely pulled back in the least flattering style possible.

"Are you all right, Jennie?" Rae touched her shoulder.

She wiped her forehead with the back of her hand. "I'm already exhausted, and we still have lunch and dinner to serve."

"You need more rest. I know you haven't slept well since we got here. You have to stop worrying about Cole."

"I can't help it. He's my patient. I can't stop caring for him."

"Or *about* him," Rae said.

Jennie shrugged, didn't really understand why she felt this gnawing need to be with him, help him, comfort him.

"Do you think he'll be any more accepting of his injury today?"

"I don't know." Jennie picked up a cleaning rag from beneath the counter and wiped up a nearby spill. "I guess I'll find out as soon as I get my station cleaned up and go see him."

"Ladies," Olive Thompson announced as she hustled up in front of them. "You are to refrain from chitchat during working hours. Is that understood?"

Jennie and Rae came to attention. "Yes, ma'am," they answered crisply.

"Good. Now, Rae, return to your station please. I wish to speak to Jennie."

The pulse beating in Jennie's ears sounded as loud as the train chugging out of the station.

Rae stepped away, glancing back over her shoulder. At the end of the counter, one of the busboys cleared up the dirty forks, spoons and knives, dropping them with a clatter onto a round silver tray.

"Is there something wrong, Miss Thompson?" Jennie asked, struggling to keep her apprehension out of her voice. She couldn't afford to lose this job.

The woman rolled her dark eyes. "Do you really have to ask that?"

Jennie said nothing for fear she might incriminate herself unnecessarily.

Miss Thompson pulled a small notebook from the black uniform beneath her spotless white apron. She snapped a finger against the top sheet of paper. "In the past hour I have seen you commit four infractions against what is considered to be competent Harvey House service. Did you learn nothing during your training in Topeka?"

Below the countertop, out of Miss Thompson's sight, Jennie curled her hands into tight fists. She wanted to tell the woman to go jump in the Grand Canyon. But she bit her tongue. If she lost this job, she had no place else to go.

"I'm sorry, Miss Thompson. I've been preoccupied."

"By that *man* from the train." Her nose wrinkled with distaste.

"Yes, ma'am. He's badly hurt."

"He is no longer your concern. Dr. Goodman is perfectly capable of looking after him."

"I know, but—"

"But nothing. If you don't pay more attention to your job, you'll lose it. There will always be another girl in training ready to replace you."

At the implied threat, Jennie's heart skipped a beat.

Miss Thompson went on. "Harvey House establishments do not tolerate mistakes. Our customers have only a short time to enjoy their meal. We want them to leave highly satisfied with the food, coffee and service."

"Yes, Miss Thompson," she said as contritely as she knew how.

The woman stuffed the notebook back in her skirt pocket. "Against my better judgment, the manager has given you permission to look in on that man at the hotel this morning." She lifted the brooch watch pinned to her apron and peered down at it. "Before I let you leave, I expect your station to shine." She let go of the watch. "Or you won't go at all."

Jennie's fingernails dug into her palms. Oh how she hated being subservient to this unfeeling woman. To anyone, for that matter. "It will shine, Miss Thompson."

"I hope so. Consider yourself warned." She replaced her notebook and squared her bony shoulders. "I'll be watching you."

Chapter Seven

Cole lay in bed, the heavy velvet drapes drawn against the midmorning light. He didn't want to see the sun, the day that dawned even when he felt his life had ended.

A hearty knock echoed in the dark room. Cole recognized Jennie's bold touch and groaned. Would the woman never leave him alone?

"Cole, Jennie's here," Matt announced from the door.

"Tell her to go away."

"Too late. I'm already in," she said, removing her coat and handing it to Matt as if he were a servant. "Goodness, this place is as gloomy as a tomb. I can't see a thing."

"I like it this way," Cole said.

She strode to the window and flung open the drapes. "There. Much better."

He grunted, squinting against the light. "Close those damn drapes now!"

She stood beside the window, her hands braced on her hips and a too-cheery smile on her face. "Good morning to you, too."

"I said shut those drapes."

"I heard you the first time, but they will stay open unless you get out of bed and close them yourself."

With every intention of doing just that, Cole lifted his legs toward the edge of the bed. But the movement sent a shaft of pain through what remained of his arm and into his shoulder. He still considered getting up, just to show Jennie who the trail boss was in this outfit. But then he remembered if he left the bed, he'd face seeing his injury again. He lay back down.

Matt hurried over to him. "Can I do something, Cole?"

"Just let me be."

Jennie stepped away from the window, her hands still on her hips. Cole eyed the high-collared white bib that covered a long-sleeved black shirtwaist. From beneath a white apron and black skirt, black button-hook shoes peeked out. She would fit right in with the penguins he'd seen drawings of in one of his books.

"That drab uniform is about as unfashionable as one of my old flannel shirts," Cole said, although Jennie had enough color in her eyes, hair and skin to look good in anything. "Not the fancy Eastern clothes you're used to, I'd wager."

"It's a different look, but Rae and I have decided our virtue is safe because of it."

"No doubt," he said, though it wouldn't have stopped him before he'd gotten engaged, and before he became a cripple.

She gave him a thin smile. "I'm so glad to see you're feeling better, Cole."

"I am not feeling better."

"Ah. You're wallowing, then."

He winced at the term he'd never expected would apply to him, but he couldn't deny it. "I'm entitled. I've lost my arm."

Matt fingered the belt loops on his canvas pants. "Jennie, he's been talking foolishness ever since last night, after he looked at his injury. He thinks he's useless now."

She crossed her arms over her chest. "Well, that's ridiculous. He's just feeling sorry for himself."

"I know, and I can't blame him but—"

"Do you two mind?" Cole said. "I'm in the room here."

"And I hate it," Matt continued. "The brother I've looked up to all my life has given up."

A different kind of pain speared through Cole. One that had nothing to do with his physical ache. He was letting his little brother down.

Jennie's gaze dropped to the floor. "I'm so sorry, Matt. That's awful."

"He'd rather be dead," Matt added.

"What?" Her eyes flashed with disbelief and anger.

"That's enough!" Cole shouted.

"Is that true, Cole? You'd rather be dead?"

He didn't answer.

"Cole Bryant, I did not go to the trouble of saving your life just to have you wish you were dead."

"I'm a cripple now, Miss Sew-it-up-and-you'll-be-fine. Half a man. How do you think that feels?"

"I imagine it feels terrible, but, losing a *part* of your arm does not divide out to half a man. Yes, you'll have to do some things a little differently, but you are strong and intelligent. You'll figure it out."

"Your confidence in me is astounding." Cole realized that right now she had more confidence in him than he had in himself.

"I've seen you in action," she said. "You *face* danger, you don't run from it." She turned to the window, stared out.

Cole dismissed her sudden melancholy, had enough of his own burdening him. But he admitted she was right: he was running scared.

She turned back. "Cole, I don't mean to be unkind, but you're not the first man to lose part of a limb."

No, it only felt like he was. "Don't you think I know that? I've worked around trains all my life. Railroad men often lose arms and legs. It's just hard for me to remember that right now."

"I know." She moved closer, smoothed a wrinkle in the quilt. "It takes time, but you'll be working your ranch again sooner than you think. Especially with Matt helping you."

Cole observed his brother, who smiled. "That's right, Cole. As soon as you're feeling up to the trip, we'll head out to the C Bar M."

Cole stared at him as realization struck like a hammer to his head. "You didn't quit Wells Fargo to work the ranch, did you, Matt? You quit because of my arm. Because I wouldn't be able to manage."

Matt and Jennie exchanged glances, and Cole saw the truth all too clearly. Until now they'd let him think what he wanted. He shook his head, wanted a cigarette, but with one hand, he couldn't even roll his own anymore.

He laughed, the sound rough, harsh, nothing like a laugh. "I thought you'd finally figured out how dangerous guarding express shipments can be. I thought you wanted to try ranching. I'm such a fool."

Matt stuffed his hands into his pockets. "Cole, I always knew being a messenger was dangerous. How do you think I felt when you were doing it? I never knew if I'd see you again, if something terrible might happen to you. Just because I was a kid didn't mean I worried less."

A knot of regret clogged Cole's throat. He'd never thought about how Matt felt. "I'm sorry. I didn't know."

"Well, now you do. After you're your old self again, I might go back to the Company, or I might not. I don't know what I want to do with my life yet. But I will help you with the ranch for a while."

"I—" Cole cleared his throat noisily, wanted to say so many important things to his little brother. "I appreciate that."

"I should be doing a whole lot more." Matt's eyes shimmered wetly. "You're hurt because of me."

"Don't even think that way. You're not responsible for what those outlaws did."

"I'm responsible for what happened to you. If I hadn't been in that express car, you wouldn't have grabbed the dynamite."

"Maybe. Maybe not. But I'll tell you this, I'd do it again if I had to." And Cole realized he would, without any hesitation and knowing he could lose more than just his hand.

Matt blinked rapidly, breathed through his mouth and turned toward the door. "I need some air."

Cole understood his brother's need, wished he could go out himself. The emotions in here were piling up higher than hay bales. He needed a distraction, too. "On your way back up," he said gruffly, "stop in the mercantile and get that item we talked about. Put it on my account.''

"Sure, Cole," he said without looking back. "I'll get it."

After the door clicked shut, Cole turned his attention to Jennie. She was dabbing the corner of one eye with her finger.

"What item is that?" she asked, dropping her hand.

Cole readjusted his position. "Has anyone ever told you you're too curious for your own good?"

"A few people."

"I thought so."

"So what's he getting?"

"Nothing."

"It must be something."

Cole ground his teeth, feeling better already. "Are you going to pester me as long as I stay in town?"

She leaned toward him, eyes narrowed. "I do not pester."

"Of course you do, but let's not argue about it. You'll just make me madder and your medical handiwork hurt more."

"I intend to check on you, your wound, that is, as often as I wish. Provided I can get away from the Harvey House. My supervisor does not approve of my coming here."

"I already like your supervisor."

Her lips thinned. "You and Olive Thompson could be best friends. You're both bossier than I am."

Cole nearly laughed out loud, which took him by surprise. He rarely, if ever, laughed, even when he was feeling good. But no one could be bossier than

Jennie. "I think I've discovered the incentive I need for getting better quick."

"And what's that?" She tapped a foot on the Oriental rug.

"Once I'm on the ranch, I won't have to reckon with you anymore."

"You would miss me."

"I doubt it." As Cole responded to her outrageous statement, he got the strangest feeling he might be lying.

Moments later, the door of Cole's room banged open. Jennie watched Matt enter, carrying a package tied up in butcher paper and string.

"I got it, Cole."

She was just as glad for the interruption. Jennie didn't want to think about Cole's leaving town. Even if he wouldn't miss her, as he claimed, she knew she would miss him. He gave her something to think about besides herself, kept her from remembering that she had run from her own problems rather than face them down. Also, Cole made her feel safe, despite his current limitations.

"Show it to me," Cole ordered Matt.

"Cole, it's a lady's petticoat. You want me to open it in front of Jennie? With us in the room?"

"Since I was wearing her other one for a time, it would hardly be a crime to see this one. I have to make sure it's good enough."

Jennie glanced at Cole. "You bought me a petticoat?"

"I owed you."

She started to shake her head.

"Don't argue with me, Jennie. I told you before I always pay my debts."

She did want to argue with him, but his generosity touched her. He'd had so much else to think about, and yet he'd thought about her.

Cole hitched himself higher against the headboard. "Unwrap it, Matt."

"There is no need to open it," she said quickly.

Cole's jaw clenched. "Beside the train, and me, you took the petticoat off without a second's hesitation. Now it's not even on you and you're balking."

"The situation was entirely different then." She reached for the package. "I'm sure this will be perfectly all right."

"Open it, Matt."

Matt shrugged at Jennie, then pulled the taut string through the knot. Stiff paper crackled and dropped to the rug. "Here, Cole." He thrust it toward him.

"Hold it up."

Matt pursed his mouth. "The only reason I'm doing this is 'cause you're sick in bed."

"I'm not sick. I'm injured."

He held up the white muslin garment. A flounce of lace circled the hem.

"It'll do," Cole declared.

Jennie fingered the lace. "It's beautiful. Nicer than the one I had."

"Package it back up and give it to her."

"I'll do it." She snatched the undergarment and picked up the string and paper.

"It's all yours." Matt approached the bed. "Hey, Cole, that merchant downstairs gave me a hard time about putting the petticoat on your account. It took some discussion before he finally let me do it."

"Walter Gray?"

"I don't know his name. Short, middle-aged fellow with a funny little beard."

"Yeah, that's Gray."

"Well, he doesn't trust you to pay your account. Said he'd prefer cash in all your future transactions."

"I don't understand. The Grand Canyon Mercantile has supplied me with goods ever since I bought the ranch. I've always paid my bills on time."

"Big brother, while you're trying to solve that mystery, I've got another one for you."

"And what's that?"

"Figure out why those train robbers drilled my express car full of holes and then took off without forcing the door open. There was plenty of silver, gold and paper money in there for the taking."

As she finished packaging her new petticoat, Jennie watched Cole tip his head. Deep creases formed in his brow. "Is something wrong, Cole?"

"There's something I need to remember, but it keeps disappearing when I think I'm close to pulling it out."

"Something about the robbery?" Matt asked.

"I think so, but I just can't remember."

"I'm sure it will come back to you eventually. Thank you for this, Cole." Jennie indicated the package tucked under her arm. "I appreciate your thoughtfulness."

"I wasn't being thoughtful."

She smiled. "I know. You were paying a debt. I thank you just the same. Now I have to go. I've already stayed too long. I will be roasted alive if I miss the lunch service. I'll come by tonight before the Harvey House curfew."

"Don't trouble yourself," Cole said.

"It's no trouble."

"Can't you take a hint, Jennie?"

She chuckled. "I can take one, but heeding it is another matter. See you this evening."

He groaned as she opened the door. Once again, Jennie thought she heard him say something about "trouble." Then he said, "Matt, go with her. See that she gets back all right."

She turned around, warmed by Cole's concern but also annoyed by it. "I do not need an escort. Why, it's the middle of the morning."

"I don't care. And Matt will bring you here and take you back at night, too, if you insist on coming."

"I do. But I really don't—"

"Williams can be safe, but you never know when some cowhands visiting town with their wages might get ideas. Remember Kansas?"

She frowned. "I remember, but I wasn't afraid then and I'm not afraid now."

"Then you ought to know the hills southwest of here are a haven for outlaws. If a few of them get a hankering for flour, jerky, whiskey or women, they'll come on in to town."

Matt nodded in confirmation.

She swallowed hard. "I will keep your warning in mind." But escort or not, Jennie intended to see her patient whenever time, and Olive Thompson, would permit.

Night closed in early, the moon obscured by clouds scuttling across it. Just south of the Williams livery, near a forest of tall ponderosa pines, Slim Carter slipped into the shadowed doorway of a run-down shack.

An older man already occupied most of the space. He wore an expensive frock suit and stood twirling his gold pocket watch. "You're late, Carter. Don't do it again."

Slim frowned at the man whose name he didn't know, the face he hadn't seen till now. They'd commenced their association through a mutual acquaintance, and then via telegraph.

"Just give me my money and you'll never have to wait again." Slim pulled his sheepskin coat closer to ward off the chill breeze sawing the pine needles against each other. He scanned the area. "Doesn't this place ever get warm?"

"Shut up and listen to me."

With a gloved hand, Slim tapped the butt of the gun in his holster. He'd come here for his money, not insults. "Don't—"

"You botched the job," the man interrupted.

"What are you talking about, old man?"

"Exactly what I said. You bungled the job. The express messenger is still alive."

"But how?" Damn. Nothing had gone right with this job. "You gotta be wrong. We shot the hell out of that car. Nobody coulda lived through that."

"Well, he did, you moron. Not a scratch. And you didn't do any better with the dynamite. Idiots."

Slim's trigger finger started itching bad, but he didn't have his money yet. "We didn't expect some tomfool to grab a live charge of dynamite. I expect *he's* good and dead. Serves him right."

"He's as alive as you and I. Got fixed up minus one hand. And you'd better be glad of it. If you'd

killed him, I would've had your hide. I want Cole
Bryant to suffer for a long time to come.'' He leaned
closer, his breath smelling of cigar and whiskey.
''You owe me, Carter.'' His unwavering gaze penetrated the shadows.

Slim felt his first sense of foreboding. ''I don't owe
you nothin'. You owe me two thousand dollars.''

''You'll get it when you earn it.''

Slim flexed the fingers of his gun hand. His men
had been grumbling ever since the holdup, their loyalty only going as far as the next dollar. If he'd let
them loot the express car, they could've skipped out
on this guy. They'd now be livin' the high life in
every saloon between here and Texas.

''Mister, we coulda robbed that train, but we didn't
'cause of your instructions.''

He straightened, rubbed a thumb over his shiny
watch. ''That's the only thing you did do right. I don't
want Wells Fargo sending in their detectives.''

''We don't give a mule's hind leg about no detectives. 'Cause we'll be long gone from here. With our
money.'' Metal rasped against leather as Slim pulled
his gun. He pressed the barrel into the man's gut.

The older man's jaw tightened. His breathing
slowed when Slim expected to hear it coming in
gulps. A horse whinnied at the nearby livery stable.

''Don't threaten me, Carter. I have no money with
me. As I said, you'll get paid when the job is done
to my satisfaction.''

Slim clamped down on his temper, lowered his revolver. ''Okay, Mr. Big Man, so where's the expressman now? I'll unload my gun into him and be done
with it.''

''Not yet, Carter.'' The moon burst out of the
clouds, and the gold in the man's smile glimmered.
''I have another plan.''

Chapter Eight

"It's about time," Cole said as Jennie entered the hotel room with Matt. "What took you so long?"

She smiled through her fatigue. "You see, you did miss me."

"I was talking to Matt. I thought he might've tripped over the tracks in the dark."

"Uh-huh," Jennie said, recognizing his loneliness.

Matt dropped into the chair by the door. "I waited in the Harvey House while Jennie cleaned up. It took longer than I thought."

"He must've drunk five cups of coffee, all of them served by Rae," she teased.

"Why doesn't that surprise me?" Cole stated.

Matt blushed, and Jennie had to admit he and Rae made a cute couple. He wriggled in the chair. "Their supervisor tried to throw me out for consorting with one of *her* girls. I swear, Cole, the woman looks like a pinyon pine fence post."

Jennie strode to the bed and began pulling down the quilts.

Cole hauled them back up. "What are you doing?"

"Checking on your wound. If the bandage needs changing, I'll do that, too."

"There's no need. Doc Goodman did it this afternoon."

"Oh." Feeling strangely bereft, she smoothed her hands over her apron. "That's good then. How did it look?"

"I didn't watch."

Matt came to stand at the foot of the bed. "The doc said it was healing nicely."

"I'm glad. That's very good." And she was glad, except that in a matter of days, when Cole grew stronger, he would leave.

"Tell her what else he said, Cole."

"You're so good at saying everything, why don't you tell her?"

Jennie stifled a smile at the petulant tone underlying Cole's deeply masculine voice. He was still miffed by Matt's long absence.

Matt laughed, an impish sparkle in his eye. "Dr. Goodman said he'd be obliged, Jennie, if you'd change Cole's dressing in a couple days. The doc'll be making rounds to some of the outlying ranches and won't be back in time."

Her spirits lifted. "I'd be happy to."

"Good, now I'm going to go have a smoke out front. Cole, if you need me, give a holler."

"I won't need you."

"Since your wound has already been tended, you apparently don't need me, either," Jennie said. "I'll be going."

"No. You stay," Cole ordered.

"But—"

"We have things to discuss."

She heard the determination in his voice and started to worry. She'd heard that tone before, on the train when he tried to goad her into discussing her past. Jennie considered following Matt out the door anyway, but it shut tight before she could take a step. To avoid talking about herself, she asked, "Did you wish to know something about your treatment?"

"No."

"The phantom pains? What you can expect in the next few weeks?"

"No, I don't want to know any of that." He hoisted himself higher in the bed. "Why did you come west, Jennie?"

Her mouth went dry. This man would follow his quarry along steel tracks until he reached the end of the line. "Now who's pestering who?"

"I think you're running from something," he said.

Her mouth dropped open. She'd underestimated him. Had she given herself away after waking from her nightmare?

"I can see I guessed right on that. Now why would a well-educated, fancy-dressed Boston woman be on the run? Could she have stolen something?"

She lifted her chin to a haughty angle. How dare he suggest such a thing! "I stole nothing."

He rubbed the dark stubble on his jaw. "Or maybe you killed a man."

Jennie gasped, couldn't even respond to that outrageous hypothesis.

"Nah," he said, "you're more likely to save a man than kill him. My guess is your running has something to do with your marital status."

She stared at his too-intelligent gaze, the pewter eyes that already seemed to know the truth. Had he heard something in Kansas? Cole had said he knew the sheriff. Had her parents sent her picture around, put it on a poster like the wanted criminals? Or had Cole seen a newspaper story about a missing Boston society girl? A girl on the run from an arranged marriage?

Cole went on. "You're looking more and more worried, Jennie, so I'm on the right track. I'd say you're close to twenty-five, too old for some men. But you are a beauty. On the other hand, you can be as stubborn and willful as a contrary mule. Is that why you're not married yet, 'cause you're too contrary?"

Disregarding his comment about her beauty, Jennie flexed and fisted her hands. No one had ever compared her to a mule. Not even her father, who complained at length about her willfulness, independent nature and advanced age. Her two older sisters had married at the age of twenty. Not Jennie. She was the one who didn't fit the Beacon Hill Andrews mold.

"I am not married for a very good reason. I choose to wed for love. If you must know, I've given up everything for my conviction—my family, my home, my money and my volunteer work. Everything. Wouldn't you?"

"No. I wouldn't and I'm not."

A sick feeling she didn't understand lodged in her stomach. "What do you mean, you're not?"

"I'm engaged to be married. At least, as far as I know I am. My fiancée hasn't come to see me yet."

Engaged? "Is she…here in Williams?" Jennie found it difficult to talk.

"She's the reverend's daughter up at the First Methodist Episcopal Church. Katherine Dawson is her name. It's an arranged marriage."

A wave of disappointment rolled through her. "That's what you want? A marriage without love?"

He hesitated a fraction of a second. "It's exactly what I want."

Jennie didn't understand. How could a man with so much love in his heart want to be part of a loveless marriage?

His gaze dropped to the quilt covering his injured arm. "If she'll have me now, that is."

"Oh, I'm sure she will." Jennie hoped so for Cole's sake. He needed Katherine Dawson to believe in him, needed to know that the loss of part of his limb would not affect his future. "You're strong and smart. A rancher. Surely she won't see you any differently. I know I wouldn't."

"You wouldn't?" His eyes darkened.

Her gaze locked on his and her breathing turned shallow. "I *don't* see you any differently." Without thinking, she reached toward the beard shadowing his cheeks. He'd begun to look like a desperado, but buried somewhere inside him was the love she'd seen in the aftermath of the explosion. She wished she could see it again. Her fingers touched the stiff whiskers of his chin.

He jerked his head away. "Don't."

As if she'd stabbed herself with a sewing needle, she yanked her hand back. His rejection struck deep, much more deeply than she ever expected, or imagined, or wanted. She stiffened her spine. "Is my touch so repulsive?"

"Repulsive? Oh, no. A temptation would be closer to the truth."

"Really?" A smile bloomed inside her.

"But I'm an engaged man, Jennie. Even if I wasn't,

your touch wouldn't get you what you claim you want. I'll have nothing to do with love."

"I don't expect you to feel anything for me, but I do feel sorry for you and your fiancée. Love is what binds two people together, not a marriage contract or ceremony."

"You're a fool if you believe that. The truth is love blinds you, and in the end it makes your life a misery."

"How can you say that?"

"I saw it happen to my own parents. They loved each other once, but my father's love for my mother vanished like a puff of smoke. He started beating her when I was too little to do anything. Eventually he took off, which was a good thing because I might've killed him after I grew a bit older."

"Oh, Cole, I'm so sorry." Jennie's heart ached for him, for the dreadful childhood he had endured.

"I don't want your sorrow. I want you to realize love is not the answer. My mother would've been better off never loving at all. Then her heart wouldn't have been torn apart when she lost it. She worked herself to death keeping Matt and me in school and putting food on the table. An arranged marriage to a kind, hardworking man would have spared her."

"You can't know that. She might have been betrothed to a man every bit as vicious as the one she married for love." Jennie rubbed her wrist, felt the pain of James Easton's grip all over again. "I think you're the fool, Cole. You won't even open your heart to give love a chance."

She turned away from him, felt a desolation inside her soul. But as she walked toward the door, she decided she couldn't give up on him. He needed a woman's love, be it from Katherine Dawson or another woman. Jennie intended to help Cole learn what he was missing. But how was she going to do it?

Silver polishing cloth in hand, Jennie stood beside Rae at the vacant lunch counter. The afternoon dragged on, but she had to keep working, keep Olive Thompson happy and her little notebook empty. Fortunately, the woman had disappeared into the upstairs dormitory. But how long would she be gone?

"Jennie, do you believe in love at first sight?" Rae asked.

"At first sight?" She remembered the variety of men she'd met and danced with at society parties back in Boston. They'd been nice enough, and some quite handsome, but she hadn't fallen in love with any of them. Not at first or any other sight.

One man came unbidden to her mind. Cole Bryant.

Jennie stifled a short laugh. She definitely hadn't fallen in love with him at first sight, though he'd certainly made an attractive protector. But that man would fight love till his last breath, or until she convinced him otherwise.

"I'd like to believe in love at first sight, Rae. Perhaps once I meet the right man, I will. Why do you ask?"

Rae's shoulders lifted and dropped with her deep sigh. "My folks fell in love the first time they saw each other. It was at a picnic at the end of corn harvest. They were young, but they knew right away. I often wondered if it would be the same for me." She hesitated, her innocent blue eyes serious. "It is."

"Matt," Jennie stated.

Rae looked out the window toward the Grand

Canyon Hotel. "Yes, from the moment he asked if I was all right back in Kansas. Oh, Jennie, I can't believe it. It's so wonderful. I've never felt like this. I wish I didn't have to work. I want to be with him." Rae bit down on her thumbnail, her enthusiasm ebbing.

"What's wrong? Doesn't he feel the same way?"

"That's not it. I know he cares for me. It's just, well, I have a confession to make."

"You? A confession?"

"Maybe not a confession. More like an apology. I wasn't very good company for you on the train ride. My mind was so full of Matt. I kept thinking about him all alone up in that express car. When the explosion went off…oh, Jennie, I was so scared for him. And now I feel so guilty."

"Guilty? Whatever for?"

Her eyes glistened with tears. "Because I'm so relieved what happened to Cole didn't happen to Matt. I don't know if I could've stood it."

Jennie peered toward the hotel, imagined Cole lying in bed, suffering both physical and emotional pain. "I think if you really love a man, it doesn't matter what he looks like," she said softly. "Whether he has one hand or two."

"Yes, of course. In my heart I know that, but I still feel guilty. I'm so sorry for Cole, for what he must be going through."

"I am, too." Jennie set the polishing cloth on the counter. "But nothing can change what happened. We have to go on from here. Just as he does."

"You're right, of course. You're so much more practical than I am, Jennie."

"I don't know. With all that's occurred recently,

I've had my ups and downs. When I've been low, you've known the right things to say and do."

Rae offered her a smile. "And vice versa."

"We're good together." She rearranged the salt and pepper shakers. "Rae, I'd like to make a confession, too. I don't know what I would've done without you over the past five weeks." The girl had been, and still was, an anchor in turbulent seas. "I want you to know that you're the best friend I've ever had." Jennie's eyes threatened to leak tears. She'd never been one to cry easily, but the last few days had taken their toll.

Rae touched her cheek. "What's this? Don't tell me you're getting as emotional as me? You know, if you start crying, then I'll start, and pretty soon our uniforms will be soaking wet. Then we'll have to change them, because no spots are allowed."

Jennie laughed and sniffled. "Well, I just wanted you to know. After what happened to Cole, I guess I've realized you never know what's around the corner."

James Easton III stroked his fingers over the desk chair's smooth, red leather arms. He sat behind his uncle Richard's immense carved-wood desk in the Beacon Hill mansion.

This will belong to me one day, he told himself for the thousandth time. Unfortunately, Jennifer Andrews was the key. Marrying her would bring him the money and power he needed to destroy his uncle, the man who abandoned his own brother, James's father. After his brother's death, Richard Easton had even refused to save James's mother from being committed to the asylum in New York City.

Thomas Fuller, a young man with limp brown hair, approached the desk. His hands filled the pockets of his oversize brown coat. Fuller glanced at the nearby chair, but James hadn't invited the private detective to sit down, nor did he intend to do so.

"Take your hands out of your pockets when I'm talking to you," James ordered. The man clumsily complied. "Now tell me what you've discovered."

"Mr. Easton, I've run into more dead ends than a man in one of those garden mazes. Your future bride doesn't seem to want to be found. She could be anywhere."

James's stomach churned. "That's not what I want to hear, Fuller. It's been over five weeks. Don't give me excuses."

"I'm sorry, sir, but very little has changed since we last met." Fuller's fingers rubbed up and down against his coat. "She hasn't withdrawn any money from her bank account."

James pulled out a drawer and slammed it shut. "She's got to be living on something. Jennifer is a well-bred young woman who is used to the finer things in life. Have you checked Newport, Marblehead and the other society watering holes?"

"Yes, sir. Not a sign." Fuller reached for his pockets again, then met James's gaze and dropped them by his sides.

James relaxed a fraction. Behind this desk, he felt all-powerful. He loved it when a man thought twice before doing something that might displease him.

His pleasure vanished when he remembered how Jennifer Andrews had run from him. Her disappearance after the publication of their engagement announcement had caused tongues to wag. But only for a short time. Edmund Andrews, her gullible father, was so intent on gaining himself a son-in-law he believed capable of succeeding him at the bank that he told people she'd gone to Europe to purchase her trousseau. But how much longer until her friends and the rest of Boston society suspected the truth?

"Tell me something I want to hear, Fuller."

"I have a theory, sir." One side of his mouth lifted in what appeared to be a hesitant but self-satisfied smile. "Miss Andrews's parents received another letter."

James sat up. "From where?"

"According to my source, the postmark was San Francisco."

"California!" James pounded his fist on the desk. A pen jumped on the leather blotter.

"Yes, sir, but here's my theory," Fuller rushed to say. "I don't believe she's there. Each of the letters has been posted in a random pattern. I believe Miss Andrews is sending her correspondence with railroad passengers or personnel who post them for her. She's quite clever, Mr. Easton."

"Don't compliment her, find her." James picked up the pen. "If you don't, I'll see that you never work in this city again. Is that understood?"

The man's Adam's apple bobbed. "Yes, sir."

Fuller retreated from the room. James's gaze followed him until he turned a corner forty feet along the marble hall.

James stabbed the pen into his palm, drawing blood. "You can't escape me, Jennifer," he whispered. "I'll find you, and marry you. Then, you'll pay."

On Cole's fourth day in the hotel, afternoon sunlight illuminated the pages of a book Matt had borrowed for him from the clerk. But the exploits of Wild Bill Hickok held no interest for him. Cole preferred his own books, ones on law, police work, geography, nature and ranching that he'd read during his years spent riding the rails.

Even those books, however, couldn't have kept his mind from the mysteries around him and the pain that only a swallow of laudanum numbed. He kept the medicine bottle handy, even though Matt and Jennie had both given him grief about it.

Cole's mind strayed to the troublesome redhead, who refused to stop coming to see him, even though she looked ready to drop from too much work and not enough sleep. Guilt that he was partly to blame for her state pricked at his conscience, but he honestly looked forward to her visits, her expressive eyes, unruly red hair and staunch refusal to treat him any differently than the first time they met.

He wished she would confide the rest of her story to him, the specifics behind her departure from Boston, but so far, she'd told him nothing more. He also wanted to know who might come after her. Cole wanted her trust, even though he should've been grateful that she refused to involve him in her troubles.

When a knock sounded at the door, he sat up straighter. He'd sent Matt to the depot in search of the Wells Fargo agent, Bill Jacobs. Cole wanted answers about the robbery, and he wanted to know exactly what was being done to catch the men who could've killed his brother.

"Come on in," he called out.

A thin, middle-aged man with a small, narrow face stuck his upper body past the door. "Hey, Cole, good to see you." He slipped inside.

Though Cole had known Bill for several years, his gaze settled briefly on the man's abnormally large ears. For the first time since they'd met, Cole wondered how Bill felt when men, women and children stared at his ears. Did he feel awkward? Or did they feel awkward around him, avoid his gaze entirely?

Carrying one of the new-style clipboards with the spring clip at the top, Bill ambled over to the bed. "I'd been wondering when I'd hear from you."

"I've been a little preoccupied."

"Yeah. I was real sorry to hear about your injury." His gaze dipped to the flattened area under the quilts where Cole's hand and wrist should've been. "A real shame, but it was for a good cause."

Cole nodded, but he preferred to avoid conversing on the subject.

"Your brother seems real taken with that new blonde over at the Harvey House," the agent said.

"And how do you happen to know that?" Cole said, though he didn't really need to ask.

"I eat at the Harvey House as often as anybody, and my eyes see as good as my ears hear."

"And you hear better than anyone I know." The compliment was no lie. "Which is why I wanted to talk to you, Bill. I'm looking for some answers."

Chapter Nine

Bill sauntered up to the bedside. "If I have any answers, I'll be glad to give 'em to you, Cole. You know that."

"Yeah, I do. Thanks. I'd like to see the waybill for Matt's last shipment on the Number 1."

"Sure thing. Got it right here." He held up the clipboard, a sheet of paper clamped to it.

"Anything unusual on it?"

Bill scratched his chin. "Not that struck me any. You lookin' for something in particular?"

"I don't know. From what I've heard about that charge of dynamite, I'm thinking it would've done a lot more than just open the door. Maybe someone wanted to destroy something being shipped."

The agent handed him the clipboard. "Take a look."

He scanned the list. "Gold coin, bullion, silver certificates, money orders, clothing, hardware, canned foods, bicycle, tobacco, stuffed duck, etcetera." Wanting to tap a finger on the list, Cole unthinkingly started to pull his right arm from beneath the quilts.

Pain shot through his shoulder. He locked his jaw and slowly lowered the limb back to the pillow.

"You okay, Cole?" Bill's face was taut with concern.

"Yeah, fine. I had an itch." He wanted to kick himself. How did he expect to figure out why the robbers left empty-handed when he couldn't manage to remember part of his arm was gone?

"Anything interesting on the list?" Bill asked.

"Nothing." Cole handed back the clipboard. "Matt said the coach was shot up pretty bad."

"Real bad. Amazing your brother came through it okay."

Cole had to swallow several times before he could speak. "Where's the car now?"

"Sitting on a siding over at the depot." He gestured toward the window. "After the Number 1 come in, some of the men from the warehouse guarded the shipment till we could send everything on with the next westbound train."

"How did the shipment come through it all?"

"The coach was smellin' nice and sweet from canned peach juice." Bill laughed. "The bicycle had a flat tire and was dinged up a mite. And the stuffed bird got another hole shot through it. But all in all, most of the express escaped harm."

"That's lucky." Cole rubbed his smooth chin, which he'd shaved earlier while Matt held the mirror. Though Cole still tired easily, he felt himself growing stronger by the day. Soon he would be walking around, facing the people on the dusty street below. He started to sweat. "Uh, has anyone been making noise against the Company? You know, grudges and such?"

Bill scratched the top of his head. "Not that I've heard."

"How about any unhappy Santa Fe men?"

"Nope, but I can ask around."

"It was just a thought," Cole said. "From what I do remember, the robbers didn't look much like railroaders, more like hired guns, but keep an ear out anyway."

"To the rails." Bill leaned his head over in mock imitation and smiled.

Cole rolled his eyes at the man's humor, but inside he felt a chuckle trying to work its way out.

Bill straightened and snapped the board's spring-loaded clip. "So any other ideas about the attack?"

"Not that I can think of, but I know I'm missing something. Some little piece of information that could clear up this whole case. I wish I could remember everything that happened."

"Maybe it'll come back to you."

"Yeah." Frustrated, Cole pulled at the quilts. "Has Sheriff Conklin found the robbers yet? Matt said he went after them."

Bill snapped the clamp again. "Well, now, the sheriff and his deputy rode out to the site, sure enough, but they lost the trail in the woods. By now the gang will be long gone and the trail cold."

Cole ground his teeth. "What about Wells Fargo? Who are they sending in?"

"I hate to tell you this, but the Company's got bigger problems. On the Southern Pacific, an expressman and brakeman were killed. Two chests of gold and silver were stolen. All available men are headed there." Bill shrugged. "I wish I had better news for you."

"I wish you did, too."

Bill rubbed his ear. "I guess it's up to you then, Cole."

Two days later, Cole still ruminated over Bill's ludicrous comment, that it was up to him to solve the mystery of the holdup. But what could he do? How could a weakened, one-handed man track a gang of outlaws, let alone bring them in?

He'd regained some of his strength, sure, but not nearly enough. When he'd forced himself to get up yesterday and walk around the room for an hour, he'd needed Matt's help to lower his exhausted body back into bed. He would have let himself fall into it except that any jarring movement sent pain ripping through him. Cole peered over at his brother, who sat in his usual chair keeping vigil.

"Do you need something, Cole?"

He pushed himself higher, leaning against the pillow and tall wood headboard. The quilts dropped to his waist, but he didn't pull them back up. He'd done enough of that. "No. I'm just thinking."

"About what?"

"About the two hours I'm going to spend walking the floor of this room later."

Matt leaned forward, worry lines etched into his face. "Two hours? No, Cole. It's too much too fast."

"I want to get out of here. I need to get my strength up so I can go home. I can recuperate there as well as I can here."

"But at the ranch you won't have Dr. Goodman or Jennie."

"I don't need either one of them," Cole said,

though something jabbed his conscience at Jennie's name.

When someone rapped at the door, Matt bounded up and yanked it open.

Miss Katherine Dawson stood in the hall with her father, the Reverend Robert Dawson.

Cole stared at them. The woman he planned to marry was finally here. His muscles tightened. How would she react to his injury? To him? He grabbed the quilts and pulled them above his bare chest.

She reached for her father's arm, a look of uncertainty, possibly even fear, in her brown eyes.

Cole tried not to worry, refused to give up on his plans. He needed to go forward with his life. He wanted a family. "Matt, I'd like you to meet Reverend Dawson and his daughter Katherine, my fiancée."

Matt ushered them in. "Good to know you both. I'm Matt Bryant."

They acknowledged him as they entered, then stopped halfway into the room and faced Cole. "Good morning, Mr. Bryant," Katherine said in a voice to match her diminutive size.

"Mr. Bryant?" Cole said carefully. "What happened to calling me Cole?"

Her father put a bony hand on his only child's shoulder and guided her closer to the bed. Cole found himself comparing her small, hesitant steps to Jennie's graceful, long-limbed strides.

Katherine looked at the floor. "I'm sorry. I, uh, just haven't seen you for a while, Cole."

His name didn't roll off her tongue as easily as it once had. And never as smoothly as it did off Jennie's.

"It's good to see you, Cole," the reverend said, a half smile pasted below his silver-rimmed spectacles. A stiff black suit hung on his spare frame. Soft-spoken, he was no Bible-thumper, just a solid, honest-minded man living in the parsonage of the First Methodist Episcopal Church and serving the needs of two denominations in a small town.

"Good to see you, too, Reverend."

"Father and I were so aggrieved to hear of your accident," Katherine said, now looking at the headboard. "Are you in great pain?"

"It comes and goes." Cole noted her pale face and the smattering of freckles across her nose. Thin brown hair sat in a tidy knot on her head. After seeing Jennie's coloring so often, Katherine appeared terribly plain. And oddly enough, her clothing struck him as unbecoming when only two weeks ago he'd seen this same dress and thought it pretty on her.

"Father and I have said a great many prayers for you, haven't we, Father?"

"Yes, indeed. A great many."

"I appreciate that," Cole said, though he'd never thought much of prayer. A man made his own luck.

"The ladies in the quilting bee met yesterday, and they all said what a hero you are." Her soft voice was starting to annoy him.

Again Cole found himself comparing Katherine to Jennie when there was no comparison. The two women were complete opposites. Katherine spoke softly, frequently deferring to her father. Jennie didn't defer to anyone, just spoke her mind.

Reluctantly Cole had to respect Jennie for the way she stood up to him, as well as the way she'd taken care of him beside the train. However, she was *not* the kind of woman he wanted for a wife. Cole wanted a woman who would make his life comfortable and quiet, not fight him at every turn. "The ladies in your sewing group are too generous, Katherine. I'm no hero."

"But of course you are." Her gaze centered on another fascinating part of the headboard. "You risked yourself to save your brother from harm. That's very commendable."

"I did what I had to. That's all."

"Well," the reverend said, reaching toward Cole's right shoulder, "we're very proud of you."

Cole drew back, grimaced from the pain the small movement produced.

Reverend Dawson jerked his hand back as realization struck. "Oh, dear me. I'm sorry. I didn't think."

"It's all right, Reverend." At least Katherine's father was willing to touch him. Katherine hadn't even looked at him. Cole felt his future slipping away and decided he wanted to settle matters now. "Katherine, I realize things have changed since we last spoke. I won't hold you to our agreement."

Her gaze finally met his, her eyes wide with surprise. "You don't want to marry me anymore?"

"I didn't say that. I'm giving you an out, because of this." He nodded at his arm.

She followed his gesture, and an unrestrained shudder rippled over her body. Her father put his arm around her. She focused on the headboard again and licked her lips. "Nothing's changed, Cole. The wedding arrangements are progressing well. The ladies from the quilting bee are helping me. Besides, I couldn't leave the man who sacrificed a part of himself for another, just as God gave up his son for us."

"I'm nothing like God, Katherine. I rarely go to church."

"That can be remedied easily enough."

Cole wasn't so sure he wanted to remedy that.

She fidgeted with her reticule. "If you haven't changed your mind about me, then in five weeks I will marry you, Cole."

He noticed she was already deferring to him, letting him make the final decision no matter how she really felt. Her deference didn't please him as much as he once thought it would.

"I gave you my word and I stand by it." He expected to feel relief that their marriage would take place after all, but he didn't. How could he be happy about hitching himself to a woman who shuddered at the sight of him? How would she bear his touch long enough to give him the children he wanted? Would any woman want to make love to a man with a mutilated body?

Cole remembered the excitement he'd felt when he first told Matt about his engagement. Now dread filled him.

"Katherine my dear," her father said, "I think we should allow Cole his rest and take our leave."

"Yes. We want you to mend quickly, Cole. Will you and your brother stay in town until the spring dance at the Opera House?"

Cole, having completely forgotten Matt was in the room, saw his brother standing by the door. Matt had already mentioned the dance twice. He would be going with Rae Hansen. Cole decided to make it his coming-out party. With Katherine on his good arm, he would face the townsfolk. But the dance was three weeks from now, and he had no intention of staying away from the ranch that long.

"I'll be heading to the C Bar M in a few days, but I'll be back for the dance. Shall I come for you at the parsonage?"

She glanced at her father, who nodded at her. Katherine brought her gaze back to the headboard. "Uh, that would be fine. Until then, I'll keep you in my prayers."

Cole watched the door close behind them, then he sagged into the mattress.

Matt strode over to the bed. "Cole, I know you gave your word, but you don't really want to marry her, do you? That woman will spend more time on her knees in prayer than on her back in your bed."

If she would share his bed at all. "Shut up, Matt. I'm marrying her and that's that."

"But she can't even look at you."

"She did before, and she will again. It'll just take a little time."

"Ah, Cole, I sure wish you were marrying for love."

"You know how I feel about that."

"I know, but just because the feelings between our folks turned sour doesn't mean it will for you or me."

Cole wasn't willing to take that chance. "You put too much stock in feelings, Matt. You always have."

"But with the right woman, you could be really happy."

"I am happy," he said, but deep down Cole wondered if he was lying to his brother, and to himself.

Jennie approached the bed as Matt drew the drapes against the night. To see better, she repositioned the lamp on the nightstand.

''Put the lamp back,'' Cole said so tonelessly that Jennie wondered where the man she usually locked horns with had gone.

''I need it to see by. Or have you forgotten Dr. Goodman's request that I change your bandage?''

He stared at the ceiling, saying nothing, so Jennie started to pull the quilt down. He batted her hands away.

She took a step back and braced her hands on her hips. ''Cole, what's wrong with you tonight?''

''Nothing. I just don't feel like visitors.''

''I'm not a visitor. I'm here in a medical capacity.'' She reached for the quilt again.

He blocked her efforts. ''I don't care who or what you are as long as you leave me be.''

''So help me, Cole,'' she said, ''if you don't let me look at this arm, I'll get out my sewing kit and put some stitches in the other one.''

He glared at her. When she tried once more, he turned onto his side, offering her his back end in blatant dismissal.

''All right, Mr. Bryant, you asked for it.'' Jennie crossed to the chair where she'd laid her things. After rummaging through her bag, she returned to the bedside. ''This is your last chance.''

He paid her no attention.

She extracted her needle from the sewing kit, tested its sharpness against the pad of her thumb. ''I think you're going to regret this.'' She wouldn't cause him too much pain, but he needed something to snap him out of this melancholy.

Matt watched from the foot of the bed. "Jennie, I don't think this is such a good—"

She silenced him with a look, took aim and poked the needle through the bedclothes.

"Ow!" Cole cried, his body springing to the far side of the bed. He flopped onto his back, his face a study in pain. He shoved his hand under his bottom. "You—"

"Are you going to be still?" She held the needle high. "Or do I have to make good on my original threat?"

"Get that dagger away from me!"

"Will you let me do what I came here for?"

"Not if you've come to torture me."

She pointed the needle toward him, snaking it through the air as if she were sewing. "Is that a yes?"

"Yes. All right," he said through a clenched jaw. "Do it and get out. Fast."

"I'll take as much time as I need." She returned the needle to her reticule and pulled the quilt halfway down his bare chest. The sight of the soft mat of black, curling hair sent her pulse tripping over itself.

Jennie reminded herself that she'd seen Cole's chest before, that it should have no effect on her. But when she'd treated him days ago, his injury and recovery had drawn all her attention. Tonight, for some reason she didn't recognize, she noticed much more about him: the pronounced delineation of his muscles, the broad expanse of his shoulders and the tanned flesh that proved he must sometimes work without his shirt, perhaps putting in fence posts, or whatever it was ranchers did outside.

Jennie swallowed with difficulty, told herself she should be viewing him as her patient, not as a man who would attract a woman's attention. She tore her eyes from his chest and began unwrapping the bandage. "So why are you so cranky tonight?"

He didn't answer.

Matt rested his forearms on the thick wood footboard. "I can tell you. Cole's intended finally came by. She was kind of…uneasy about all that's happened. In fact, she barely looked at him and, in my view, couldn't wait to get out the door."

Jennie's hands faltered in their work. The oddest sense of relief tugged at her mind, but her heart ached for Cole. How could Katherine Dawson have been so cruel? Jennie wanted to throttle the woman.

Cole scowled at his brother. "Matt, you're worse than the gossips in Katherine's quilting bee. Do you think you could keep your mouth shut for longer than two minutes?"

"Nah," Matt answered. "Jennie, this woman was so meek I could hardly hear her. I keep telling Cole she's not right for him, but he's as stubborn as an old piece of jerky." Matt kicked the bed. "Cole, she's a mouse."

"That's your future sister-in-law you're talking about. She's a good woman," he said, defending her.

Jennie expected nothing less of him, and a twinge of envy made her fingers tighten on the bandage she held.

"She's a good *religious* woman," Matt said. "Jennie, you should have heard her talk. She actually compared Cole to God."

"Now that is a stretch," Jennie said. "Whatever made her think that?"

"'Cause he gave up his hand like God gave up his son."

"I see." Jennie unwrapped the bandage further. "But I don't think the sacrifice was quite the same. What do you think, Cole?"

"I think I'd like to have my hand back," he answered dryly.

She smiled, knowing he would lose it all over again if that would keep Matt safe.

Matt straightened. "Even though Katherine shudders at the sight of Cole, she's saying lots of prayers for him. And she still plans to marry him." He thumped the footboard with his fist. "And it's a big mistake."

"Matt," Cole growled, "if you don't stop hitting and kicking my bed, I'm going to need more laudanum. Being stabbed in my backside didn't help none either."

Jennie didn't react to Cole's remark, barely even heard it. Over and over her mind repeated, "She still plans to marry him." After Matt's description of Katherine's reaction, Jennie expected the woman to cry off the engagement. Apparently not.

A hollow feeling opened inside her. She convinced herself it was due to the probability that Cole might never experience a woman's love and total acceptance of himself as a man.

"What do you think of this marriage, Jennie?" Matt asked.

She removed the last of the bandage. "Cole already knows how I feel about arranged marriages." Jennie felt his gaze on her, making her body heat.

"Well, tell me," Matt said.

"I'm opposed to them. A couple should marry for love."

"Exactly. And he'll never love that mouse. It's obvious she doesn't love him, with or without his right hand.''

Jennie forced herself to concentrate on Cole's healing wound, lifted the remaining limb as if it were delicate porcelain. Thankfully, no infection streaked his warm flesh. ''You're healing very well, Cole. And quite quickly. It looks good.''

''To you maybe.'' Cole was looking at his arm almost as intently as she had been. A sheen of moisture covered his forehead.

Jennie's heart expanded at his growing acceptance of the injury. Maybe he would be all right after all. Using a fresh dressing, she began rewrapping his wound.

''I'll be going home soon,'' he stated.

Her fingers paused in their work. ''You will? I mean, of course you will. I was just...'' Jennie didn't know what to say, only knew that her body felt a sudden heaviness very much like what she'd felt stepping onto the train leaving Boston. She didn't want Cole to go.

Chapter Ten

On Monday morning, two days after Katherine's visit, Cole stood inside the entrance to the hotel. He wore Levi's and a long-sleeved white cotton shirt from his traveling bag. The cuff of one sleeve hung empty. He stared out at the gray sky. It matched his mood. Getting fully dressed for the first time in a week had been a humiliating experience.

Though he'd always been good with both hands, he wasn't used to buttoning his shirt or the stiff denim of his fly with his left hand. Matt had done both for him, and Cole had felt like a helpless child, remembered himself doing the same for Matt over twenty years ago. He swore to train his fingers to do everything he needed them to do.

Outside, on Bill Williams Avenue, Cole saw Benjamin Porter, the local banker, escorting his ill-looking wife across the dusty street. She wore a vacant look, as if she were only half alive.

Cole knew the feeling. Every day he suffered ups and downs, acceptance and anger and despondency. He hated it. Had never thought himself capable of such mood swings. But then, he'd never had reason before.

He shook off his gloomy thoughts and noticed Jefferson Stark, owner of the Saginaw Lumber Company, standing opposite the hotel, deep in conversation with Harry Cummings, his office manager. Stark waved an agitated hand toward the hotel.

Cole knew both men but had dealt mostly with Harry, an easy-mannered man of middle age who had more hair on his upper lip than what grew under his black felt derby.

Cole hooked his thumb into his pants pocket. What could the two men be discussing so fervently away from the mill office? He watched Harry shake his head, then look at the ground and nod.

Stark, appearing satisfied about something, turned and headed in the direction of the lumber mill. When Harry started toward the hotel, Cole moved away from the door. He leaned against the wall near the window, where two overstuffed chairs took up space.

Harry entered the reception area and shuffled up to the clerk. "Cole Bryant's room, please."

The clerk peered at Cole.

"I'm over here, Harry." He stepped away from the wall. "What can I do for you?"

"Oh, uh, morning, Cole. It's good to see you up and about." Harry removed his hat, swallowed visibly. "I'm really sorry to bother you. I hope this isn't an inconvenient time."

"No. As I said, what can I do for you?"

Harry fingered the narrow brim of his derby. "I didn't want to come here, Cole, but I wasn't given a choice. I'm really sorry."

"Sorry about what, exactly?" Cole heard the hard-as-steel edge to his voice.

"Well, first of all, I'm sorry about your injury. I know it won't hold you down for long, though. Your ranch will be one of the most successful in the county. The men delivered that last load of lumber while you were away, and I'm happy to say your new barn is nearing completion. It'll look right fine with that handsome white clapboard house of yours. You know you're one of Mr. Stark's best private customers."

"Cut the speech-making, Harry. I saw you and Stark talking. Why did he send you over here?"

He pulled at his sandy-colored mustache. "To be blunt, Mr. Stark wants you to pay up your account. I have the papers right here." He pulled a sheaf from his inside coat pocket.

"My final payment isn't due till the end of the month. That's two more days. What's going on, Harry?"

The papers rustled in his hand. He glanced back at the clerk who was watching them and lowered his voice. "Cole, I'm not supposed to say anything, but you deserve the truth. Word has it your finances aren't in the best of health."

"I lost part of my arm, Harry, not my bank balance." Cole pushed his remaining hand into his pocket. He'd invested wisely over the years, earning enough to keep those investments and pay cash for his land. His loan with the Northern Arizona Savings Bank in town was for the cattle he'd bought. Yes, his account with Porter's bank was a little low right now, but he had two others, one in Kansas and one in Chicago. "Your boss told you that?"

"Yes."

"Do you know where he might've picked up the information?"

"He told me it was a rumor, but he seemed pretty sure of himself."

"Uh-huh." Cole kept his voice even. "Okay, Harry. Leave the papers. I'll take care of it today. Tell Stark he'll have his money." Harry apologized profusely as Cole ushered him out.

Settling his account was no problem. He'd gone to Kansas to check on his investments and buy a Wells Fargo money order. Cole watched Harry walk away and started making sense of the so-called rumor. First Walter Gray from the hotel and mercantile hadn't wanted to extend him any more credit, and now Stark wanted payment. As if Cole didn't have enough trouble, someone seemed bent on undermining his financial standing in Williams. But who and why were the questions.

By the end of today, Cole vowed that everyone he owed money to would be paid. Then he and Matt would leave. Something strange was going on in this town, and Cole didn't like it. The back of his neck started itching again, but he didn't know which way to look. It was time to go to the ranch. His refuge. Home.

To lessen his pain, Cole shuffled slowly down Second Street toward the railroad tracks and the Harvey House. As the midday sun broke through the clouds, the fresh scent of spring teased his senses and warmth hit the dark wool of his coat. Out here, he felt alive again, awake to the red earth beneath his feet, the smell of the pine forest and the anticipation of returning home.

He'd left Matt in front of the Grand Canyon Hotel and Mercantile, filling the wagon with supplies. Walter Gray had oozed apologies and goodwill when Cole paid up his account. Cole considered taking his business elsewhere.

At the Saginaw Lumber Company, an embarrassed Harry Cummings took Cole's money and marked his order "Paid." Jefferson Stark had not put in an appearance though Harry had glanced repeatedly at the man's closed office door. Ben Porter, owner of the bank, had jovially accepted Cole's loan payment.

Now Cole had one last stop to make. Jennie. He owed her, for his life and his will to live. Not being good with words, he didn't know how to express his gratitude, but he was going to try. He was also going to try to find out the rest of her story. Cole wanted her trust, and he wanted to know she would be safe from whatever or whomever she was running from.

He entered the Harvey House lunchroom. Several local men lingered over coffee, their elbows on the countertop. Jennie stood alone behind the counter, polishing a serving spoon. Her black-and-white uniform was crisply starched. "Jennie."

She looked up, surprise and pleasure in her face. He approached the counter, felt himself drawn by her green eyes. They were the last impression she always left with him. Beautiful. Shining. Expressive. Right now, though, they were narrowing on him.

"Cole, should you be out of bed?"

"I'm fine," he said, enjoying her concern for him. "I'm on my way home. Matt's loading the wagon now. We'll head out as soon as I finish here."

"Oh." She blinked several times, and the color of

her eyes dulled. "I hope you have a pleasant journey."

This woman's mood changed faster than a pony express rider had ever changed horses. What had changed her this time? He struggled for something to say. "The ride will be painful, but I have the laudanum." He patted his coat pocket.

"Cole, please don't depend on the drug. It's dangerous. Dr. Nicholson—"

"I know. You've told me before." Cole didn't need Jennie's warning. He knew laudanum was a form of opium. Williams had no shortage of hop joints. Behind each Chinese laundry one could find an opium den. In his detective days, Cole had entered the hazy, smoke-filled rooms in search of thieves spending what they'd stolen from Wells Fargo. He'd never understood the kind of man who lost himself in a drug. At least, he hadn't before his injury. "I promise I'll be careful."

He glanced around the restaurant, saw two other Harvey Girls setting the tables in the dining room. One of them peered over at him, at the end of his coat sleeve. When she saw him watching her, red flooded her face and she spun away. Cole stiffened. "Come outside with me. I want to talk to you privately."

"I can't. I have customers," she answered. "Rae is working in the storeroom, so I'm alone here."

"These boys don't look like they'll need you anytime soon. Come with me."

Her gaze darted between him and the dining room. "I have to remain at my station, Cole. I could lose my job if I don't. I'm not even supposed to be talking to you here. If Miss Thompson sees us—"

"Where is she now?"

"In the back of the dining room, but—"

Cole strode into the other room and spotted the woman Matt had described as a pinyon pine fence post. He wasn't far off, except that Miss Olive Thompson didn't have any bend to her.

"Miss Thompson?" he asked, approaching her.

Her gaze flicked toward his arm, then to his face. Frown lines creased the thin skin of her forehead. "Yes? Is there something I can do for you?"

"I'm Cole Bryant, the man Jennie Andrews helped. I think you know about that."

Her bony chin lifted a notch higher. "I do. You look to be in good health now, Mr. Bryant. I hope this means Jennie's ministrations will no longer be needed."

"It does. I'm leaving town, but first, I wish to speak with her. Outside, where we can have some privacy. I'm sure you can understand."

"She cannot leave her station."

Cole eyed the aging spinster, felt her dislike flying at him like a bullet. Did she resent him for taking so much of Jennie's time? Or was there another reason? "Miss Thompson, I am grateful to Jennie for what she's done for me. I just want a few minutes alone with her to say so."

"That would be highly irregular."

"But not impossible."

"Mr. Bryant, I suggest you be on your way."

He leaned in close, his patience beginning to fray. "And I suggest you do as I ask, or I will send a wire to Fred Harvey himself about your lack of compassion for my situation. You ought to know that I've been in the railroad business as long as Harvey has been running his restaurants, and we've met no less than three times. Shall I contact him, Miss Thompson?''

Her pale skin had gone as white as her spotless apron. ''No, that won't be necessary.'' She started toward the lunchroom.

Cole followed. He didn't enjoy pressuring a woman, but Miss Thompson needed to know who she was dealing with.

''Jennie,'' she said, striding up to the counter, ''Mr. Bryant wishes a few minutes of your time outside. You have my permission. I will man your station.''

Jennie's astonished gaze flitted from the spinster to Cole and back. She put down the spoon and polishing rag. ''Yes, Miss Thompson. Thank you. I won't be long.'' She accompanied Cole to the door. As he held it open for her, she leaned over and whispered, ''How did you manage that?''

''I can be very persuasive when the need arises.'' He let the door close behind them.

''I guess you can. I'm impressed.'' At the edge of the boardwalk, she lifted her face to meet the sun. ''And I'm glad you did. It's beautiful out here. Look how blue the sky is against those puffy clouds.''

Cole peered upward. Clouds like cotton batting drifted leisurely across the crisp blue sky. He never thought much about the sky, unless it was to gauge the weather. ''It's nice,'' he said, bringing his gaze back down to an even prettier sight. With her eyes closed and face tipped up like that, he imagined Jennie waiting for a man's kiss. His kiss.

''It's wonderful.'' She breathed deeply. ''Spring is here. Can you feel it?''

More than you know. He felt much warmer than

the outside temperature warranted. When she arched her back, stretching, her breasts pushed against the bib of her apron. Cole's heartbeat accelerated. Remembering his upcoming marriage, he forced himself to look away. "I didn't come here to talk about spring."

She brought her gaze down. "All right, a simple goodbye will suffice, then you may leave."

A simple goodbye would not suffice. He searched his mind and heart for the right words. "I, uh, came to...thank you for everything you've done. The medical care. You know." His throat was suddenly parched. "I, uh—" He swallowed. "Your doctor friend in the East would be pleased, I think."

She smiled wistfully. "I like to think he would, too. And you're welcome."

He toed his boot in a crack in the boardwalk. "I'm sorry I took up so much of your time."

"I'm not. I don't regret a minute of it," she said. "I'm just glad you're all right."

When his gaze locked with hers, her smile faded into something that pulled him closer. He reached out, couldn't seem to stop himself, and touched the dark smudges still visible beneath her eyes. "I think you lost a lot of sleep over me."

She licked her lips, her tongue making them shimmer temptingly. "I was worried."

He trailed his thumb over her cheek, coming close to her lips. "I'm the one who's worried now."

"Wh-why is that?"

"Because I don't know if you'll be safe here."

She frowned. "I don't understand."

"Jennie, will whatever or whoever you're running from follow you here?"

She stepped back, her body taut. His arm dropped to his side. The short distance between them widened into a chasm that seemed as broad as the Grand Canyon. Why couldn't Jennie trust him enough to confide in him?

"I'm safe here," she answered. "I have Rae and everyone at the Harvey House. There's no reason for you to worry."

"Don't lie to me, Jennie. On the train, I saw how you were during that nightmare. Tell me what you're running from." He held his breath.

She looked away. "I appreciate your concern, Cole, but nightmares are often worse than reality. I'll be quite safe."

He let out his breath in a long sigh. "You don't trust me."

She faced him squarely. "Maybe I'm trying to protect you."

"Me? I've lost one hand, Jennie. I can still shoot a pistol with the other. I don't need *your* protection, but someday, you might need mine."

She started to shake her head, but he caught her chin with his fingers, felt the heat and smoothness of her skin. "The C Bar M is seven miles south of town. There's only the one road south, so the place is easy to find. If you need me, you send for me."

She didn't answer, but her eyes revealed her fear. The indomitable Jennie Andrews appeared as vulnerable as when she'd awakened from her nightmare. Cole's protective instincts flooded him like a river during spring thaw. "Promise me, Jennie."

She dropped her gaze. "I can't promise anything."

A new wound opened inside Cole, the pain deep and piercing. He let go of her chin. "All right then."

He moved back. "I can't force you to accept my help. Take care of yourself, Jennie."

As Cole walked away, Jennie almost ran after him. She desperately wanted to tell him everything, share her fears and the reasons for them, but with his injury, he had so much more to worry about. He needed to mend, learn how to do things one-handed, and help his fiancée get used to the change in him. Jennie wouldn't burden him with her own problems.

She watched him go and her heart bled. Tears burned her eyes. She knew she'd hurt him with her silence. He deserved better, but she really did want to protect him. Even with his limitations, Cole would not hesitate to face danger on another person's behalf, especially when he felt he owed that person.

Jennie wouldn't risk putting Cole in harm's way. And she had no doubt that James Easton III, if he found her, would hurt or kill whoever tried to stop him from marrying her.

Chapter Eleven

In front of the hotel, Cole leaned against the wagon while he waited for Matt, who had run over to the Harvey House to say goodbye to Rae. Cole considered his own goodbye to Jennie, then tried to push all thought of her away. He didn't want to think about her or her problems, problems she refused to share with him.

When Matt returned, his shoulders were slumped. "That was a lot harder than I thought it would be."

"Because you like her."

"I think I love her, Cole."

He straightened away from the wagon. "This sounds serious."

"She cried when I said goodbye." He stared at the ground. "Lord help me, I wanted to cry, too. And I know a man should never admit to that, but..." He didn't finish.

"I guess a man can cry if he's got a good enough reason," Cole said. "But you'll see Rae again soon. The dance will be here before you know it."

Matt dredged up a smile. "Yeah, you're right. And the sooner we get going, the sooner it will be here, right?'' He strode to the back of the wagon and lowered the tailgate. ''Did you see the comfortable riding spot I fixed up for you?''

Cole peered over the planked side, past the crates of supplies to the blankets and pillows lining a space big enough for a man to lie down in. ''I am *not* riding out of town laid out like a corpse.''

''But, Cole, if you ride on the seat, it'll jostle your arm something fierce.''

''I'll manage.''

Reluctantly Matt helped Cole up onto the planked seat. As they drove through town, Cole felt the curious gazes of too many people. Despite the pain from bumping over ruts left from winter snowmelt, he squared his shoulders and looked straight ahead.

Ten minutes outside of town, ponderosa pines lined the uneven road. Bill Williams Mountain, named for a long-ago trapper, stood to the right like a sentinel. On the deserted road, Cole downed a swallow of laudanum. The bitter brown liquid eased the pain reverberating through his body.

''I'm sorry, Cole.'' Matt gripped the reins with white knuckles. ''I'm trying to avoid the ruts, but there're too many.''

''I know.'' He held what remained of his arm to his body. ''I never noticed before how bad this road is.'' He forced back his moans, wanting to spare Matt.

After five more minutes of unmerciful jolts and his little brother's apologies, the blankets and pillows called to Cole. ''Matt, stop.''

''What?''

''Stop the wagon. I've decided to take advantage of that comfort you arranged for me.''

Matt pulled up the horses and smiled.

"Don't expect me to lie down, though."

"Of course not, Cole."

Cole lifted a leg into the back of the wagon and dropped carefully onto the blankets. He propped his back against one pillow and his injured arm against another. When Matt set the horses in motion, Cole flinched and gritted his teeth. He brought out the laudanum again, tipped the bottle to his mouth. The taste wasn't as bad as before.

An hour out of Williams, halfway to the C Bar M, Cole's pain had lessened considerably. His mind felt pleasantly fuzzy, and he even enjoyed watching a pair of squirrels scamper up a tree. When he leaned his head back, an eagle soared across the late afternoon sky. It was some minutes before Cole noticed the itch at the back of his neck.

"Hmm," he muttered. "What could be causing that?" With the half-empty laudanum bottle in his hand, he tried to sit up and look around. But his muscles disobeyed his orders. He struggled harder, his drugged mind finally grasping the danger that might lurk within the trees.

By the time he got a good look around, the itch had disappeared. Cole glanced down at the small bottle he held, realized that he'd let himself and Jennie down. He opened the bottle and tossed it into the road. As the liquid drained into the dirt, he slumped back into the pillows, hoping to clear his mind by the time they got home. He wanted his wits about him when he saw his men.

Near sundown, they arrived at the ranch. Cole felt marginally better, but exhaustion dragged at him. He couldn't even get excited about the sight of his new barn. He just wanted his bed.

As the wagon rolled to a stop in front of the house, Lucas, the foreman and five others hoofed it out of the bunkhouse, hats in hand. Afraid of falling over if he stood up in the wagon, Cole scooted himself to the tailgate Matt lowered and dropped his legs over. Matt helped him stand; Cole had no energy to resist.

He greeted his foreman and acknowledged the men, at least half of whom avoided his gaze. "Most of you have met my brother Matt before. He'll be staying on awhile."

"Good," Lucas said, fingering his hat. "Matt, what would you like us to do first?" All the men looked to Cole's brother.

A band tightened around Cole's chest, making it difficult to breathe. "Lucas," he said, his voice deceptively quiet, "I'm still boss here. Is that understood?"

The foreman glanced at the other men. "Uh, sorry, Cole. I didn't think you—" He licked his lips. "I, uh, just didn't think. You bet you're the boss. Ain't that right, boys?"

They all nodded rapidly and offered their verbal assent.

Cole didn't feel any better. He'd lost part of his arm; with it went the respect and loyalty of his men. He sucked in a harsh breath, vowed to fight his fatigue long enough to give orders.

"Unload the supplies and put up the horses." Cole stepped away from the wagon. "Lucas, tomorrow I want a full report on everything that's gone on while I was away."

"Sure thing, Cole. I'll be there." He replaced his hat. The other men followed suit and scrambled to unload the wagon.

Cole approved of their quick response, but he'd never forget the way they'd dismissed him and his authority as if he no longer existed. As if he weren't capable of running his ranch.

Jennie watched the last of the dinner service passengers file out the door. She wished they weren't leaving. She needed distractions to keep her from thinking about Cole, from remembering the way she'd hurt him and how much she already missed him. She wanted to feel his touch again.

When he'd brushed his finger over the tender skin under her eyes, stroked his thumb along her cheek, she'd nearly melted with longing. A type of longing she'd never experienced before. He wasn't the kind of man she'd envisioned for herself, but she couldn't deny her body's reaction to him. Cole Bryant was a strong, attractive and deeply emotional man. He was also engaged, Jennie reminded herself.

Outside, the locomotive's brass bell clanged and the whistle blasted over the landscape. Steam escaped with a loud hiss as the engine chugged out of the station, headed east toward Boston. Jennie wondered if she would ever go back there. Tonight, she felt stranded between two worlds, unsure where she belonged.

A nudge on her shoulder made Jennie turn. Rae stood beside her. "Evan's been trying to get your attention."

"Oh." She found the busboy shifting from one foot to the other a few feet away. His round silver tray, already heaped with cups, saucers and plates, rested on the counter. She smiled at him. "I'm sorry, Evan. I was wool-gathering."

A blush blossomed in his teenaged face, and he hunched his gangly frame. "I didn't mean to bother you, Miss Jennie. I just wanted to take those dirty dishes for you."

"You didn't bother me a bit." She stepped back from the counter and let him get to the soiled dishes placed beneath it. "Thank you."

The china clinked as he loaded the tray still higher. "Chef said to tell you and Miss Rae that he's tryin' out a new dessert in the kitchen." The powerfully built German cook was a wizard of wonderful dishes. He also wielded a sharp set of knives. His kitchen staff had claimed he could fell a tree with his butcher knife. "The Harvey Girls from the dining room are comin'," Evan said. "Will you come, too?"

"Oh, I wish I could, but—" Jennie stopped the refusal that had automatically flowed from her lips. She'd become accustomed to seeing Cole after her shift, but he was gone now. Despite the emptiness spreading inside her, she forced herself to smile. "Rae, shall we join the other girls and taste one of Chef's new concoctions?"

"My stomach is rumbling already," Rae answered. Jennie was glad to hear her friend's appetite had improved. After Matt's brief but heartfelt goodbye, tears had poured down Rae's cheeks, and she'd eaten nothing at dinner.

"Evan, you tell Chef that Rae and I will be there as soon as we finish up out here."

He beamed. "Yes, ma'am! I'll tell him." Evan lifted the heavy tray to his shoulder and made his way toward the kitchen.

"That boy has a crush on you, Jennie. You do realize that, don't—"

A tremendous crash echoed around the room. Jennie and Rae spun toward the kitchen door. Shattered china showered the floor. Evan stood in the middle of it all, gaping at the porcelain carnage around him.

Jennie started toward him, then stopped as the storm herself marched in from the dining room. Miss Olive Thompson.

Rae's fingers grabbed Jennie's arm. "Oh, no. We have to do something."

Jennie didn't want to see the boy dismissed from his job, either. He was a part of their Harvey House family. "Come on."

Evan crouched in front of the kitchen door, looking as if he might burst into tears. Before Jennie and Rae could get to him, Miss Thompson dropped to her haunches beside him. The fuming anger Jennie expected to see never ignited. Instead, she wore an expression of resigned acceptance. Jennie stopped short.

"It's not the end of the world, Evan," Miss Thompson said. "I've seen this happen plenty of times before. Just don't let it happen to you again."

He nodded sharply. "Yes, ma'am. I mean, no, ma'am. I mean, I'll be more careful, ma'am."

"Make two trips next time."

"I will, ma'am. I won't ever carry so much at once."

"That's fine. Now why don't you get this cleaned up."

Miss Thompson stood, straightened her uniform and eyed Jennie and Rae. Her mouth thinned. "Back to work, girls. No dawdling."

"Yes, Miss Thompson," they answered together.

When Jennie smiled at her, the older woman scowled back. "Don't think what you just saw changes anything between us, Miss Andrews. Good busboys are a lot harder to find than Harvey Girls.'' She turned her back and returned to the dining room.

Jennie's smile shifted into a frown. ''I guess I still have to be on my guard.''

''And I was just feeling kinder toward her,'' Rae said with a sigh. She strolled to her station.

Jennie's thoughts unwittingly drifted back to Cole when she only wished to put him from her mind. Home now, he didn't need her anymore. He was re-starting the life he'd worked so many years to attain. A life in which Katherine Dawson would soon join him.

Jennie didn't think she could manage to eat any of Chef's dessert after all.

Cole awakened to a pounding headache and bright sunlight. As he sat up and lifted his legs over the side of his bed, every muscle screamed in protest. He'd thought yesterday's pain would have departed after a good sleep.

He automatically reached toward the nightstand for the laudanum. His hand stalled midway when he remembered the bottle was lying in the road. ''I need a smoke.''

Naked, Cole pushed himself to his feet and padded over to the chair where he'd dropped his traveling bag. He reached in and pulled out the rolling papers, tobacco pouch and a loose match. The smell of Bright tobacco spurred him on. He could practically taste it. He laid everything on the bureau's high surface.

''I can do this,'' he said, succeeding in laying out one sheet of the flimsy paper. He lifted the pouch and tipped out tobacco.

It fell onto the paper, more mountain than mound. "Damn!" He scowled down at it. With his left index finger, he leveled the mountain by pushing some of the dried leaves onto the dresser. "I am going to do this."

He commenced to rolling, but without a stabilizing second hand, the paper moved. Half the tobacco spilled out.

"Hell!" Every sore muscle in his body tensed. Sweat trickled down his spine. His headache worsened, and his hand shook.

He pinched tobacco back onto the paper. Millimeter by millimeter, his fingers cramping, the paper began to roll. Ten minutes later, Cole stared at a mangled facsimile of a cigarette. It looked like he'd kept it in his pocket for a decade. "Who cares?" he muttered. "I rolled it and I'm going to smoke it."

He jammed it between his teeth, lit it and inhaled with satisfaction. Then he sank onto the bed to rest up for his next challenge—washing and dressing. Shaving could wait for tomorrow. Or the next day.

When his smoke was nothing more than a memory and his body had cooled, he washed at the basin and took a pair of faded, brown Levi's from a drawer. After pulling them on, he only managed the bottom two buttons of his fly. His black flannel shirt came next, the buttons on it easier to manipulate. Then Cole noticed his loose cuffs. "Damn!"

He braced the cuff of his floppy sleeve against his belly and slipped the button through the hole. Impressed with himself, he nearly smiled. Once he got the other cuff buttoned, he would tuck his shirt in, finish fastening his pants and pull on his boots.

Cole reached for his left cuff. He groaned when

there was no hand to do the job. "Why can't I remember such a simple thing?"

He lifted his left wrist to his mouth. His teeth grated against the bone button, and he left a wet spot on the black flannel. "The morning is half-gone and I can't even dress myself properly. How the hell can I show the men that I can run the C Bar M? For that matter, how *will* I run it?" Cole glared at the colorless face in the mirror. "I need a drink."

In bare feet, with his shirttail hanging outside his Levi's, he stalked downstairs and into the parlor. He banged open a cupboard, pulled out a glass and set it on the pine table. A bottle followed. He pulled out the cork with his teeth. Glass clinked against glass as he poured a generous amount of whiskey.

Cole watched his fingers grip the clear glass of amber liquid, and his mind filled with the image of his father doing the same, over and over. Cole pulled his hand back, leaving the glass on the table.

The front door opened and closed. Boots tapped against the wood floor, then were muffled as Matt entered the parlor, one glove tugged halfway off his hand. His gaze landed on the whiskey. "Kind of early for a drink, isn't it, Cole?"

"I know."

Matt dropped both gloves and his heavy leather coat onto the sofa. He lowered himself into a wide, padded armchair. "What brought on your thirst?"

Cole leaned up against the cold stone fireplace. "Frustration."

"With what?"

"My clothes."

Matt's gaze skimmed over his unkempt appearance. "They give you some trouble, did they?"

"Some," Cole admitted.

"What can I do to help?"

Cole lifted his wrist. "My cuff. I can't get the damn cuff buttoned."

"Oh." Matt contorted his left hand, trying to reach his own cuff with his fingers. "That is a tough one. Did you try your teeth?"

"Didn't work."

"Hmm. This is interesting, Cole. Like an engineering problem. We're both reasonably well educated. Those books in your study aren't for show. I'm sure we can come up with a solution. What about skipping the button entirely? You could roll up your sleeve before you ever put the shirt on."

"I'll give that some consideration during the summer," Cole said dryly. "By that time, though, Katherine will be living here. She could move the button over for me."

"That's a great idea! The sewing part, I mean. Then there'd be enough room to push your big paw right through. But, Cole, why wait for a wife when we know a very nice girl who always carries a sewing kit with her?"

Cole rolled his eyes, knew Matt was purposely shifting the topic of conversation from Katherine to Jennie. "Oh, no."

"What's wrong with Jennie's sewing needle?"

"She prefers to use it on my flesh." He rubbed his hand over his backside. "I don't need Jennie Andrews to take care of any more sewing for me. I'm sure that between the ranch hands and ourselves we can get the job done."

"I bet it won't look as nice," Matt said.

"It'll look fine, and when Katherine and I are married she can move the buttons on all my shirts."

"Okay, whatever you say." Matt tapped the padded armrests. "I took a look around this morning. That barn you designed is one of the nicest I've seen. Your white-and-black Appaloosa, a sorrel mare and a very handsome, deep brown stallion named Dancer are already occupying three of the stalls. Lucas was under the impression that Dancer belonged to me."

"He told you that, huh?"

He shrugged. "Not in so many words. But I can read between the lines."

"I didn't know if you'd come here or not, stay or not, but he is yours, whatever you decide to do," Cole said, unwilling to get his hopes up. Even if Matt married Rae, it didn't mean they'd settle on the ranch. "When I'm back to full strength, you can take him with you. Or board him here."

"What's the occasion? It's not my birthday."

Cole avoided Matt's unrelenting gaze. "Call him a welcome-home gift."

"It was awful nice of you, Cole. He's a real beauty. Looks fast, too. I bet he can beat your Appaloosa."

"Not a chance."

Matt laughed. "You want to bet on that? Loser buys the beer at the Cabinet Saloon."

"You're on, but give me a few weeks to get back in the saddle."

"When we go to town for the dance, we'll race part of the way. How's that?"

"I'll be ready," Cole said, promising himself at the same time. "And I fully intend to beat the pants off of you."

* * *

Jennie heard Evan pound the large brass gong on the depot's platform, announcing the dinner hour and directing the next onslaught of passengers to the Harvey House for roast sirloin of beef au jus, pork with applesauce, baked veal pie, or stuffed turkey with all the trimmings. Cole had been gone only a few days, but it seemed like weeks. Jennie hoped he was doing well at home.

The passengers filed in, their faces a blur. Her station filled up quickly with demanding customers, whom she handled quickly and efficiently, taking their orders and pouring Harvey's special blend. The last man at the end, a gentleman, pulled his cup and saucer toward him. "Thank you, miss. On the train, several people raved about Fred Harvey's coffee."

At his pronounced Boston accent, Jennie looked up. The man seemed familiar. Too familiar. "It's well-known," she said, trying to disguise her accent.

He cocked his head as he observed her. "Miss, do I know you?"

"I don't think so."

"I could swear I've seen you before. Where are you from?"

"Excuse me, sir, but I need to pick up the orders." Her heart thumped hard as she hurried to the kitchen, tried to place him. He probably had seen her. He dressed and spoke like many of the men who frequented the society gatherings back home.

Jennie considered running out of the restaurant, feigning illness, but if she did, Rae would have to cover her station, which wouldn't be fair. Returning with a tray of steaming dishes, Jennie allocated them to the correct diners.

The gentleman slid his coffee aside when she held his plate out. "You know, I'm sure I've seen you. Have you ever been to Boston? That's where I'm from."

"I'm sorry, sir. I'm not allowed to converse with the patrons." Which was true. Smiles were encouraged, not conversation. She walked away, asking the other diners if they needed anything. Finally she had to go past him again.

"Just tell me your name then," he said. "That's all."

"I could lose my job talking to you like this."

"Please. My name is George Lampton. Now tell me yours."

Jennie could hardly speak. She knew that name well. Her parents knew the Lampton family. If she remembered correctly, George, the eldest son, had been away at school for years, then had gone to work in the family shipping company's New York office. He came to Boston only occasionally, but it was one time too many for Jennie.

"I'm sorry. I can't," she said, desperate to hear the train engineer ring the bell.

"Never mind. I'll think of it. I have a long trip ahead of me. Plenty of time to remember."

Chapter Twelve

$\mathbf{F}$our nights after his return, Cole struggled through his fatigue to mount the stairs of the home he had built. As a child, living in a hovel in Omaha, he'd dreamed of a white clapboard house like this.

He'd pushed himself hard today, working long hours at putting the final touches on his barn, doing the accounts and so many other things he was too tired to list. But he felt good. The men treated him as they had before, and he was regaining more of his strength and former self. Now, though, his bed beckoned.

Matt followed him up, waving the lamp around. "Cole, you got to stop doing so much so fast. Take it easy."

"I'll take it easy when I'm asleep." He reached the top of the stairs and turned into his darkened room.

Matt stopped at the threshold. "You can't—"

"Matt, I'm too tired to argue with you. Go to bed."

"Fine. Kill yourself working." He turned and stomped down the hall. "I'll see you in the morning," he shouted back.

Cole sighed and went back to the doorway. "Matt?"

"What?" he snapped, glancing over his shoulder.

"Tomorrow I'll take some time out to rest. I promise."

A slow smile crept across his brother's face. "Thank you. Good night, Cole," he said sweetly.

Cole almost chuckled. "Good night yourself."

Inside the bedroom, Cole didn't bother to light the lamp. He stretched out fully dressed across the double bed. Too tired to even use the bootjack, he left his boots on. He'd slept in them often enough out on the trail, and once already this week.

He settled into the soft mattress, anxious for sleep to come. But it refused to take him away from the constant ache of his injured arm. Cole groped for a subject to divert his mind. His wedding night.

He tried to envision Katherine lying naked beside him, touching him, his missing hand of no consequence to her. The image never formed. Cole rearranged the feather pillow beneath his head, tried again to see his future wife beside him.

This time, an image did form. A red-haired, green-eyed beauty, her skin a soft rose hue.

"No," Cole uttered aloud. "I will not think about Jennie." The pine bed frame creaked as he turned onto his side and faced the window. He thought about how many calves would soon drop, how many more horses could go into the barn tomorrow and how Jennie's personality would fill his room with her warmth. The room glowed already.

Cole bolted upright. He stared at the window in growing horror. The glow was coming from the direction of his new barn.

His fatigue forgotten, he jumped to the window, threw up the double-hung panel of glass, leaned out and stared in disbelief. Flames licked at the far end of the barn.

"Fire!" he shouted, trying to rouse the men from the bunkhouse. The flames hissed and crackled. The three terrified horses trapped in their stalls screamed. Cole leaned farther out the window. "Fire! Fire!"

Men in various forms of dress streamed out of the bunkhouse doorway. After drawing a relieved breath, Cole tore across the room. At the door, he collided with a barefoot Matt.

"Cole! The barn!"

"I know. Come on."

A surge of energy sent Cole flying down the stairs and out onto the porch. Matt's footsteps thudded behind him. The flames leaped higher, brightening the sky as they devoured the new lumber. With Lucas manning the pump, four of the men lined up to lug and throw buckets of water onto the blaze. Reynolds ran to the barn doors and banged them open against the building. Cole and Matt peered inside with him.

The horses reared and fought against their confinement. They stamped and screamed, their eyes rolling back.

"Reynolds, you get the mare!" Cole shouted. "Matt, take Dancer! I'll get Storm."

They sprinted inside. Thick smoke billowed toward them from the other end of the barn where the flames burned brightest.

Cole grabbed a saddle blanket, went to his Appaloosa's stall and swung open the gate. With only one hand, he wouldn't attempt to use a halter and lead rope. Storm's wild eyes reflected the yellow flames eating through fresh straw.

"It's okay, boy," Cole said soothingly. "We're gonna get out of here just as soon as I get your eyes covered. Take it easy." He held up the blanket. "I'm gonna put this over your head real gentle-like. Then we're leaving." He dropped the blanket over the horse's head and grasped the corners beneath Storm's throat. "Okay, boy, let's go."

Followed by the trotting Appaloosa and roiling smoke, Cole ran for the open doors. Reynolds jogged ahead of him with the mare. Outside, they gulped fresh air and uncovered the horses' eyes, releasing the animals toward a nearby pasture. Cole turned around, looking for Matt.

The smoke thickened. The crackling grew louder. His little brother didn't appear.

"Matt!" Despite his flagging energy, Cole started back in.

Reynolds, a strapping man as big as Cole himself, grabbed him from behind. "You can't go back in there, Boss," he shouted over the fire's snapping. "The smoke'd get you for sure."

"I have to get him out of there!" Cole fought to free himself. Before his injury, he would've gotten free.

Reynolds held tight. Cole's body ached. Swirling gray smoke filled the barn's entrance.

"Matt!" he yelled into the billowing darkness. "Matt!"

His eyes stung from smoke and tears. He couldn't lose his brother, the only person he loved and who loved him. How could he go on without him, go on knowing he'd been unable to protect Matt after all? Not even here on the ranch.

Guilt burned inside him as hotly as the fire. Years ago, he'd lost his mother, unable to save her from his father's beatings or the later toil she'd endured for her boys. Now he might lose Matt, too. Tonight, no train robbers had targeted his little brother.

Cole gasped, seized at the memory his mind had kept from him. Beside the train, he'd heard the bandits talking. They hadn't been after the express shipment. They'd wanted the expressman, Matt, dead.

Smoke poured from the broad entrance. Cole jerked out of Reynolds's grasp and raced for the barn. ''Ma-att!''

The rush of air and the crackling of flames grew louder.

Before Cole could enter, a ghostly apparition emerged from the churning charcoal clouds. A bare-chested, soot-covered man trotted in front of a horse wearing a shirt over its eyes. Matt led Dancer by the sleeves tied under the horse's neck. Cole expelled his breath in a rush and stepped back. Tears slipped over his lashes.

Matt's chest heaved with coughs and the effort of gulping clean air. Reynolds ran up and took the horse.

Cole led Matt away from the barn. When his little brother's coughing fits lessened, he shook him roughly. ''Damn it, Matt! I ought to punch some sense into that head of yours. You scared the life out of me. Don't you ever do that again!''

Matt's broad smile broke through several more coughs. ''Gladly. Just stop rattling the brains I've got.''

Cole was shaking. His body trembled with fear and relief. He pulled Matt to him, hugged him tight.

"Whoa! I guess I did scare you," Matt said. "I can't remember the last time you hugged me."

Cole squeezed him once more, then shoved him away. "Yeah, well, don't expect it to happen again anytime soon. What the hell happened in there?"

"Dancer was living up to his name. He backed himself into the corner, sidestepping and making noise. He didn't want to let me close. He's not used to me yet. I finally threw my shirt over his head, and here I am." Matt held his arms out to his sides. "And damn glad about it."

"You took a big chance."

"I couldn't leave Dancer in there. You gave him to me."

Cole felt tears threatening again, blinked hard. "Someday, Matt, that soft heart of yours is going to get you killed."

"Nah, you're always around to get me out of trouble." He peered up at the flames shooting into the sky. "I'm sorry about your barn, Cole. It sure was a beauty."

"Yeah, it was." Cole watched the men working in vain to douse the fire. Glowing embers rose, floated on the slight breeze and fell back to earth. Others drifted toward his home.

Cole's heart stopped. "The house!"

He raced toward the men, Matt and Reynolds following. "Lucas! Forget the barn!" he yelled to the short but powerful foreman. "Water down the house!"

All the men turned toward the culmination of

Cole's boyhood dreams. Embers landed on the wooden shingles.

"Come on, boys. Get those full buckets to the house," Lucas shouted. "Clancy, get that ladder from around back. Then climb up and take the buckets. Toss the water onto the roof."

The men ran to their positions and passed buckets back and forth. Cole took over at the pump, one hand being enough for the job.

A tiny blaze broke out on a corner of the roof, but Clancy, the youngest ranch hand, quickly doused it. The men kept the house wetted down and an eye on the outbuildings. Clancy sloshed another bucketful of water across the roof when a great creaking sound echoed over the yard.

The massive beams in the barn's ceiling groaned, shifting with the loss of support beneath it. The men turned in unison. Cole stopped pumping. A knot formed in his gut.

The roof collapsed with a thunderous roar. The walls around it fell inward like a house of cards. Black clouds billowed upward, dots of orange swirling within.

How had this happened? His barn was destroyed the same day it was finished. In town, someone had spread the rumor that his finances were in trouble. And on the train ride to Williams, a bunch of outlaws had targeted Matt for death.

Cole didn't believe in coincidences.

Jennie stood at the empty lunch counter. Although several people had looked in the window, she'd waved them off. The restaurant was closed for the night. Miss Thompson had already retired, and Jennie would help Rae turn out the lunchroom lamps. But her thoughts kept going to George Lampton. Since his appearance several days ago, she had been considering her options. To leave Williams or to stay and risk James Easton's finding her.

George would soon arrive in the East. Had her identity dawned on him? Would he contact her parents? Would James hear the news and come after her? An incentive of twenty thousand dollars awaited James once he had a ring on her finger. A future of power, position and more money would follow. He would not give it up easily, if ever.

"Jennie," Rae said, breaking into her thoughts, "you're brooding about something again. Why won't you tell me what it is?"

Sadly she peered down at the younger woman. "I'm thinking about leaving, Rae."

"But why?" Her friend's expression was stricken. "No. You can't go."

"I think I have to. A gentleman was here the other night. A passenger on his way back to Boston."

"He recognized you?"

"Not exactly, but he knew he'd seen me somewhere before. I know his family."

"Maybe he won't remember." Hope shone in her eyes.

"I can't risk it, Rae. Even if he doesn't remember on the train, my name could come up in conversation and then he would remember. I want to ask Miss Thompson for a transfer to another Harvey House."

"Jennie, even if she gave you the transfer, everyone here would know where you'd gone. If Easton or anyone else came looking, they'd learn your whereabouts very quickly."

"Then I should just leave. Board the train and find another town, another job." She hoped to avoid working in a saloon. Maybe she could clerk in a bank. Though she'd never seen a female clerk, they probably existed. Her father had taught her how to keep accounts. Or maybe a town doctor needed an assistant.

"You can't keep running, Jennie."

Running. She didn't like that word, the way it related to the choices she'd made. Should she have tried harder to convince her father of James's vicious nature?

She'd shown him her bruised wrist, but he accused her of lying, blaming the bruise on one of the "ruffians" who came into the dispensary. Jennie had never lied to her father, and his distrust hurt worse than anything. They'd been so close when she was a girl. He had allowed her "headstrong" ways back then, had treated her like a son, taught her to ride astride and given her an education more suited for a boy. That had all changed when she began maturing from a lanky girl to a developing woman.

"I don't want to run, Rae, but I don't know how to fight James." She thought about Cole, a man who never ran from a fight. He faced his fears, no matter the consequences. If he were in town, Jennie knew she would feel safer. But seven miles away over rough road seemed as far as Boston right now.

"You'll figure out a way. Remember the cowboy whose instep you stomped on?"

"Yes, but—"

"And Matt told me you actually stuck one of your needles into Cole's backside to make him behave. Was he telling me a fib?"

Jennie shrugged. "Well, no, but those situations were entirely different."

"Once you decide to stand up to James, you'll do fine. Besides, you have the rest of the Harvey House to back you up."

She smiled uncertainly but said, "You're right. I need to stop worrying about something that hasn't even happened yet. Might never happen."

Just the same, Jennie wished Cole were a whole lot closer.

Not far from the Williams livery, a man leaned against the wall of a night-shadowed doorway. The smell of horses and straw hovered in the air. One animal whinnied. Another kicked his hoof against a stall. The man unbuttoned his wool frock coat and ran his fingers over the chain of his shiny gold pocket watch.

He smiled. Everything was working out perfectly. The fire had been a complete success, although he wouldn't have complained if the house and outbuildings had also burned to the ground. But, one thing at a time.

The man had to admit even the botched train job had turned out rather well. Every day that Cole Bryant had to live as less than himself, see a cripple in the mirror, was a day for celebration. The Wells Fargo detective who had ruined the lives of three people deserved every minute of his suffering.

"You here somewhere, Mr. Big Man?" came Slim Carter's voice from a few steps away. His rank body odor preceded him.

"I'm here. Won't you join me?"

Carter slipped into the doorway. "It's done."

"It certainly is. Excellent work. I heard it blazed like the fires of hell. I'm deeply sorry I missed it."

"It was mighty pretty, the sky all lit up like it were day," the outlaw said. "But we didn't stick around too long."

"Of course not. That would have been risky. Are you sure no one saw you?"

"No one. The man who set the fire moves quiet as an Injun. Didn't even raise a stir out of the animals."

"Excellent. I did wonder why you waited, though."

"The building wasn't finished. We thought it only fittin' the barn be all done before we burned it."

He laughed deeply, and it felt good. "I like the way you think, Carter. Yes, indeed. Again, I wish I could have been there myself."

Carter shifted from one foot to the other. "Glad you're so happy. Now give me my money. The men and me got things to do."

"Of course. Here you are." He removed a stack of bills from his coat pocket. "It's all there."

Carter weighed the stack in his hand. "I'm sure it is. 'Cause if it weren't, you know you'd be hearing from me again. And you wouldn't like it."

"I have no doubt." As Slim moseyed away, the man said, "Just a minute, Carter."

The outlaw twisted around. "What?"

"Are you interested in another job?"

"I told you we got things to do."

"We can discuss the timetable. And the price."

Carter stepped closer. "How much?"

"I'm prepared to pay you one thousand dollars more. And if you limit your little group to three, that will leave a bigger share for each of you."

"Now I like the way you think, Big Man." Carter tipped his hat back on his head. "So what's the target this time?"

"You mean, *who* is the target?"

"Okay, who then?"

"A woman."

Carter scratched his scruffy beard. "What are we supposed to do with a woman?"

"Whatever you and your men like," he said, smiling with anticipation. "There's just one condition. She comes back somewhat alive."

Jennie sat on her narrow bed, her legs folded beneath her. The lamp on the bureau lit the two Indian rugs decorating the walls. Rae sat on her own bed massaging her sore feet.

"We've been here almost a month, Jennie. Do you think our feet will ever get used to this?"

"I doubt it. I have calluses on top of calluses. My mother would cringe if she knew. When I was a girl, I used to run barefoot through the house and gardens. My mother was appalled by my behavior, but my father said, 'Abigail, let the girl have her fun.'" Jennie smiled at the memory.

Rae laughed, the sound musical and long overdue. Since Matt's departure, her manner lacked its normal cheerfulness. "Jennie, do you miss your family very much?" Rae's hands paused in their kneading.

"I think of them often." Jennie worried about her mother. Abigail Andrews had suffered health problems ever since Jennie's difficult birth. Was her mother doing all right, or had Jennie's flight put her in bed? "Yes, I miss them. I like it here, though. The

West is so open compared to the city. There's a certain freedom to it.''

"Will you write your folks again? It's been a few weeks.''

"I don't know. There's so little I can say when I want to say so much. I want to tell them everything that's happened, about Cole and Matt, the Harvey House, even Miss Thompson.'' Jennie leaned back against the wall. "Sometimes I feel sorry for her, you know.''

"Miss Thompson?'' At Jennie's nod, Rae added, "She doesn't have very many friends.''

"I didn't know she had any. I've only seen her work or disappear into her room.''

"I was being kind,'' Rae said. "I don't think she has any, either. She's not very friendly to anyone, especially men.''

"She was good to Evan the other night.''

"Yes, but he's still a boy.''

"She must be lonely at times.'' Jennie remembered the consuming loneliness she'd felt when sitting on the train as it chugged away from Boston.

"I think she's chosen to be alone. Maybe she's been a Harvey Girl for so long that she's tired of seeing all these faces every day and prefers to avoid everyone in her off time.''

Jennie pulled her knees to her chest, stretching her white cotton nightdress over them. "I can relate to that. If any train passenger from last week came through this week, I wouldn't know it was the same person.'' Unless it was George Lampton. She still worried that he had identified her, but so far nothing had come of it.

Rae stretched her legs out in front of her and raised

one dark blond eyebrow. "What about that rich young Englishman who took a fancy to you the moment he walked in the door?"

Jennie turned up her nose. "He looked like a dandy, all self-important and…"

"And what?"

"Just *and*. He didn't interest me in the least."

"Because he's not Cole Bryant," Rae said matter-of-factly.

Jennie narrowed her eyes. "Rae Hansen, what are you trying to say?"

"I'm saying that whether you admit it to yourself or not, you're smitten with Cole."

"That is not true. Cole is only a friend. Barely even that. We can scarcely speak to each other without arguing."

"Mmm-hmm. Well, I think he likes you, too."

"Why on earth would you say that?"

Rae chuckled softly. "Because I saw you together outside the Harvey House before he left. I saw the way he looked at you. And touched you."

Heat crept into Jennie's cheeks at the memory of his gentle touch. "You shouldn't have seen that. And he shouldn't have done it. He's engaged."

"I think he forgot that fact just then."

"I think that your experience of falling in love at first sight hardly makes you an expert on men."

"I know enough. With three older brothers, I learned quite a bit. Otto, the oldest, has been married for two years now. I saw how he looked at the girl who became his wife. He still looks at her that way."

"Oh." Rae had her there. Growing up more like a tomboy than a young lady, Jennie had never paid much attention to the unspoken signals and special looks that passed between men and women.

"Maybe Matt will bring Cole to the spring dance tomorrow night," Rae said. "Then you can see exactly how he looks at you."

"It doesn't matter how he looks at me. He's still engaged."

"But not married yet. Besides, a marriage between him and Katherine Dawson would be a mistake."

"Now you sound like Matt."

"Well, he's right. I served Katherine at my station a week ago, and she is not the woman for Cole. You are."

Jennie had also seen her in the lunchroom, but she'd had no time to introduce herself or observe the pale young woman for more than a few seconds at a time. But in those few moments, their gazes had met. Katherine had smiled at her, obviously aware Jennie was the woman who helped Cole.

"You and the other girls can hardly wait for that dance." Dancing partners for the Harvey Girls would be in ample supply.

"I bet you'd be excited if Cole was coming."

"Rae, I am not in love with Cole, but I do care about him and worry about him." Especially when so many terrible things kept happening to him.

Word of the fire that burned his new barn reached town a few days after the blaze. Apparently, it was deliberately set. Jennie wrapped her arms around her knees and hugged them tight. Who could want to hurt Cole? Damage his property?

She shivered, afraid for him, afraid the danger would only grow worse.

Chapter Thirteen

He was winning and, God, it felt good.

Two miles from town, with Matt close on his tail, Cole stayed low over Storm's neck, urged his Appaloosa faster. His low-crowned hat shaded his eyes from the late afternoon sun.

Rhythmic hoofbeats pounded the earth. Storm's sides heaved, his breath sawing in and out. His white coat, dappled with what looked like fat black raindrops on his hindquarters, glistened with sweat.

Cole breathed deeply, relished the scents of horse, leather and pine. Racing over the reddish terrain, a cool wind searing his face, he felt whole again.

He risked a look over his shoulder, careful not to upset his balance. A dust cloud separated him from Matt. Dancer, a quarter horse, couldn't stay with the endurance-bred Appaloosa. Cole felt like shouting when he crossed the invisible finish line on the outskirts of town. Four weeks ago, he didn't think he'd ever feel this alive again.

Matt pulled up beside him as he slowed Storm to a walk. "No fair, big brother," he said, breathing hard. "Storm is stronger over the long haul."

"Then I challenge you to a short distance race. You name the day and the course." Cole leaned forward, reins in hand, and patted Storm affectionately on the neck. "We'll be there."

"It's a race, then," Matt answered. "And Dancer will cross *that* finish line first."

"I don't think so," Cole said, unable to keep the corners of his mouth from turning upward. Lately, he'd occasionally found himself wanting to outright smile, and he wasn't sure what had come over him.

The livery loomed up ahead. Cole glanced over at Matt and Dancer, reined in at the rail and dismounted. His brother followed suit and untied the saddlebags.

"Matt, you go on and get us a room. I'll take care of the horses. Then I'm going to see the sheriff." Cole wanted to know if anything had come of the list he'd sent to Sheriff Conklin, names of men who might be holding a grudge.

After the fire, Cole had surveyed the charred timbers and ash, and found a set of tracks that led into the pines. There, he came upon more evidence. At least four men had hidden behind the broad trunks. Further in, the hoofprints of six horses left their mark, the same number of horses used in the train holdup. And that bothered him.

Reynolds, a good tracker, and another ranch hand followed the trail, hoping to get a look at the outlaws. But the sign vanished in the rocky, hard-packed country dropping toward the desert.

"You think Sheriff Conklin will actually have some answers for you?" Matt asked.

"Probably not, but it's worth a try." Cole wanted to know the identity of his enemy, wanted to confront him before anything else could happen. Before a second attempt might be made on Matt's life.

"Good luck." Matt handed Cole his reins and took the saddlebags. "After I get the room, I have a little shopping to do at the dry goods store, then I owe you a beer."

"You buying something for Rae?"

"Not exactly." Matt looked sheepish. "A new tie for me."

"Going to look good for your sweetheart?" Cole teased, knowing he planned to look good tonight, too, despite one missing hand. It was time to move ahead with his life, let Katherine get used to his injury and make himself forget Jennie. Thoughts of the outspoken redhead had interfered with his sleep too often.

"I'll be lookin' my best," Matt said. "And dancing every dance with Rae, unless she agrees to step outside for a little sparking." He winked.

Cole thought about doing some of the same with Katherine, but he had a hard time picturing it. For some reason, kissing her didn't appeal to him as much as it once had.

"See you later." Matt sauntered away.

Cole took a step after him, the horses turning their heads with the movement. "Matt, be careful, will you?"

His brother turned back. "You worry too much, Cole. What could happen on the street in broad daylight?"

"I'd just feel better if you kept an eye out."

"Okay, big brother. I promise. You take care, too." Whistling, he strolled away, a little skip to his walk.

As Cole turned back to the horses, a ten-year-old boy he knew well came running out of the livery stable. Dirty blond hair straggled over hazel eyes. Freckles dotted most of his face. "Hey, Joey," Cole called out.

A smile split the boy's face as he approached. "Mr. Cole!" He slowed his steps as he neared the horses.

"Joey, this here's Dancer. You already know Storm. They've worked real hard today. Can you give them some of your special care?"

"Yes, sir." The boy ran an approving eye over Dancer. "He sure is a beauty. You always got good horses, Mr. Cole. I'll rub 'em down real good."

"That's a boy." He handed him the reins, expecting to see him lead the horses away. But Joey's feet didn't move. His head did, though; it turned this way and that, examining the end of Cole's sleeve.

"How's your arm, Mr. Cole? Is it all healed up?"

"It's doing good," he answered, not sure how he should feel about the boy's scrutiny and frank questions. Remembering Katherine's visit, her averted looks, Cole decided he approved of Joey's candid curiosity.

"Glad to hear it," Joey said. "I sure wish I coulda been there. Seen the explosion. It woulda been so excitin'."

"I think you were better off here, Joey."

"Ah, that's what my pa says. But nothin' really interesting ever happens round here." He kicked the dirt with the toe of his dusty boot. "I wish I coulda seen you get sewed up by that redheaded Harvey Girl. Do you think she'd tell me about it?"

"I wouldn't be surprised," Cole answered, knowing Jennie's love of medicine. "You'll have to ask her."

"Oh, boy!" Joey bounced on the balls of his feet.

"I've seen her from a distance. She sure is pretty." His face flushed pink.

"So you've got your eye on Jennie, have you?"

His blush deepened. "I've got my eye on lots of things."

"Well, you've got good taste. She is pretty. And good at doctoring."

"Are you taking her to the big dance tonight? We been real busy today 'cause of it."

"No, I'm taking another girl."

"Oh," Joey said, disappointment in the single word. "The reverend's daughter."

"You know an awful lot for a boy working at the edge of town," Cole said, impressed.

He shrugged and patted Dancer's nose. "I got ears. I also notice things."

"Like what?" What else did a boy notice besides a pretty redhead?

Joey gave him a sideways glance. "Like I saw the rev's daughter and Mr. Wilkins from the bank out walkin' together. More than once."

Cole tensed. His fiancée had been out walking with the pimply faced bank clerk? He tried to keep his voice as carefree as before, but it was a struggle. "You do see a lot. If your eyes light on Jennie, maybe you should invite her to dance with you. Have you got a pair of dancing shoes?"

"Heck, no! I ain't no twinkle toes." His face screwed up like a pug dog's. "'Sides, I don't wanna touch no girls."

He relaxed slightly, looked forward to the day he would have a son like Joey. But then he remembered what Joey had witnessed.

Cole ground his heel into the dirt. Was the family

he wanted so badly slipping out of reach? Had Katherine replaced him, gone back on her agreement? What would she say if he confronted her with Joey's information?

Cole intended to find out.

Jennie and Rae finished their duties as quickly as possible, then dashed up to their room and helped each other dress. Local townspeople, Harvey employees, railroad men and cowboys from the surrounding ranches would be stomping their feet tonight.

Jennie dressed in a bright green taffeta skirt and matching shirtwaist, its collar made of delicate white lace. The bodice, sewn with tiny pleats, hugged her curves, the corset beneath showing her small waist to advantage. Leg-o'-mutton sleeves projected beyond her shoulders.

Rae gave Jennie an encouraging nod. "If Cole comes tonight, he won't be able to take his eyes off you."

"I am not trying to gain his or any other man's interest, Rae. I'm just tired of wearing black and white all the time." To be honest, though, Jennie did find herself hoping to see Cole. She wanted to dance with him, show him he was as acceptable and desirable a partner as any man. But would he want to dance with her?

"I'm sick of our uniforms, too." Rae spun around, her yellow gingham dress flaring below the wide white sash circling her slender waist. "What do you think?"

"You look like a clear summer day. Matt will notice no one but you."

A bright smile lit Rae's face, and her eyes sparkled. "I can't wait to see him."

Jennie envied Rae's excitement, wished she were meeting someone special at the Opera House, too.

Several knocks resounded on their door. Muffled voices said, "Jennie. Rae. We're all ready. Come on."

Jennie opened the door to the other four Harvey Girls dressed in a variety of bright colors. "We're coming." She and Rae grabbed their coats. "Let's go."

Descending the stairs, the girls chattered and laughed. As they filed out of the building, Jennie, at the end of the line, noticed Olive Thompson standing alone in the hall. "Miss Thompson, are you coming to the dance?"

She stiffened. "Don't be foolish."

"But it will be fun. It'll be a nice change. Why don't you come with us?"

"I have no interest in going where there will be men and liquor," Olive said harshly. She made "liquor" sound like the devil himself.

Jennie wondered why. She remembered the two drunken cowboys who had accosted her and Rae in Kansas. Had Olive suffered a similar experience? "I was given to understand only punch would be served at the dance."

"Nevertheless," Olive said, sniffing disdainfully, "the men could have gone to a saloon first. You girls be careful." She turned on her heel and disappeared up the stairs.

Jennie considered her sudden departure and the concern Miss Thompson had shown. The older woman confused her, but she decided to think about her another day. Tonight was for having fun.

Buttoning her coat, she ran out into the brisk night air and caught up with Rae and the other girls. Brilliant stars studded the sky, and glowing lamps lit the Opera House veranda.

Thirty minutes later, after twirling to square dance numbers and bouncing to a polka, Jennie was breathless and declined another invitation so she could rest a moment. She'd already lost count of her partners.

Matt had arrived alone, greeted Jennie long enough to say Cole would be coming with Katherine Dawson, then swept Rae into his arms and whisked her around the dance floor. He hadn't let go of her since.

When the next dance started, a young cowboy pulled Jennie onto the floor. She smiled at him and his slicked-back blond hair. He appeared freshly shaved, although Jennie didn't think he needed to shave on a regular basis yet.

Onstage, a fiddler and caller accompanied men playing accordion, harmonica, spoons and other so-called musical instruments. Despite needing to pay attention to the dance steps she was learning, Jennie kept one eye on the door. She looked forward to seeing Cole in good health again. Happy.

But when he still didn't arrive, her spirits sagged. Where was he?

Cole turned up Second Street toward the parsonage at the First Methodist Episcopal Church. After supper at the Cabinet Saloon, Matt had helped him with his cuffs and tied his string tie, but it had taken longer than Cole planned, so the dance was already in full swing.

He could hear the square dance music high-steppin' right out the Opera House door and through the streets. Cole's excitement grew. Katherine would be waiting for him, and, in exactly two weeks, they would be saying their vows.

Tonight, not even the lack of news he'd received from the sheriff could curtail his spirits. Most of the men on his list still languished in prison. Others were far from Arizona, some even building new and respectable lives for themselves.

At the corner of Second and Sherman Streets, the church's tall white spire rose into the clear night sky. The scent of new grass drifted on the air. Cole headed for the pristine white parsonage. Warm, welcoming light glowed from the windows.

He stepped onto the cleanly swept front porch and rapped at the door. Footsteps shuffled inside, and the door opened to reveal Reverend Dawson. "Good evening, Cole."

"Reverend. It's good to see you. Is Katherine ready for the dance?"

The man's spare face wore an uncertain expression. Behind his spectacles, his eyes appeared larger than usual. "I think so. Just a moment." He called into the small house. "Katherine, Cole is here to escort you to the dance."

"Coming," she answered, her voice toneless.

The reverend attempted a smile. "You're looking well."

Some of Cole's excitement waned. "I've been working and healing."

The man nodded, glanced away and continued nodding.

Joey's story about the skinny bank teller came back

to Cole, even though he'd decided during supper that Joey must've wrongly interpreted what he saw. Now Cole began to wonder.

Katherine, carrying her wool coat, came around the corner from the parlor to stand beside her father. "Good evening, Cole." Her gaze skipped right over him and out the door. "It's a beautiful night for a dance, isn't it? I was so afraid it might rain. Or even snow. You never know up here, do you?"

"No, you never do," he said slowly. She'd never chattered on about the weather before. He eyed her closely, the straight sleeves of her unadorned navy-blue dress, the matching ribbon tied in her tightly up-swept hair, and the stiff smile pushing up her cheeks. "Are you ready?"

"Yes. Let me just put my coat on."

"I'll help you." As he extended his hand, she shivered. Was she cold from the open door? Or did her reaction have to do with him?

"Please, don't trouble yourself, Cole. Father can help me."

The reverend bit his lip, then shrugged and helped his daughter. "Have a good time tonight, my dear."

She kissed him on the cheek. "I won't be long." Katherine slipped past Cole, preceding him off the porch. "Shall we go? We're already late."

"I'm sorry about that," he said, following. "It took me longer to get ready than I expected."

"That's all right. I didn't mean to complain." Still without looking at him, she stepped into the street and kept going. She moved like a rabbit running from a hungry coyote.

"You seem to be in a hurry, Katherine. Are you

meeting someone at the dance?'' Cole kept his voice low and even.

Her step faltered as she shot him a surprised look, a guilty look. ''Wh-what do you mean?''

The steak Cole ate for supper felt like lead shot in his stomach. ''I heard you and young Wilkins from the bank have been out together.''

Her mouth dropped open. ''I...no, I mean, yes. I've seen him on several occasions, but we are friends.'' She started forward again, not quite so fast. ''Since I keep the accounts for the church, he has been helping me understand bookkeeping better. That's all.''

''I see.'' Her explanation was a good one, but Cole felt only marginally more at ease. ''How are our wedding plans progressing?''

This time, along the dimly lit road, she stumbled outright. Catching herself and avoiding Cole's aid even though his good arm was closest to her, she haltingly said, ''They are moving along well.''

''Take my arm, Katherine.''

''Oh, no, that's not necessary.'' Her pace increased again. ''We'll be there soon.''

''Take my arm, Katherine.'' He heard the challenge in his voice. ''There's nothing wrong with this one.''

Her breath rasped in and out, and she briefly closed her eyes, as if in pain. Finally she inched her hand through the space between Cole's good arm and his body.

He forced himself to remain outwardly calm, but inside, his emotions seethed, twisting and poking like barbed wire. Little had changed since he last saw Katherine. As he mounted the Opera House stairs, he felt his future sliding away.

Cole sucked in a deep, fortifying breath. He

couldn't give up yet. Wouldn't. He would offer Katherine one more chance to prove herself.

Jennie smiled at the young cowboy she still danced with, but her gaze again strayed to the doorway. This time, she saw him. Cole Bryant entered the Opera House with his fiancée.

Jennie missed a step at the sight of him. His commanding presence filled the large room, although the muscles of his face looked etched in stone. Wearing a black frock coat over black pants, a black silk waistcoat, and a high-collared white shirt, he appeared as presentable as any gentleman in Boston. A bow of black ribbon was tied at his throat. His hair, neatly combed, reached below his collar. Jennie's heart raced, and she yanked her gaze away from him, afraid of giving away her thoughts.

As the music ended, her young partner whirled her around one final time. She lost hold of his perspiring hand, gave a small gasp and landed in the arms of an older gentleman.

"Oh! I'm sorry," she said, regaining her balance with his help.

"I'm not," he said. "I've been wanting to meet you, Miss Andrews." He let her go, swept a lock of silvering hair off his forehead, pushed his spectacles back up the bridge of his nose and bowed. "Earnest Goodman, M.D., at your service."

"Oh! How do you do." Jennie straightened her skirt, flattered that he recognized her. "I wondered if I'd ever meet you. You're away a great deal, aren't you?"

"Too often, I'm afraid. It was fortunate you were

on that train when Cole needed you. Your work is to be commended."

His compliments warmed Jennie with pleasure. "Thank you. I must confess I didn't feel very sure of myself out there."

"You did very well. I'd like to know more about your medical experience. Cole tells me you are neither a doctor nor a nurse." The music began again, a waltz slowing everyone's steps and relaxing the mood of the crowd. "Shall we?" he invited.

She smiled and moved into his arms. Looking over his shoulder, her gaze fell on Cole once again. This time, though, she paid closer attention to the young woman beside him. Katherine wore a pinched smile and an unbecoming blue dress. Her arm was tucked in Cole's, but just barely.

As they moved past the people lining the wall, Katherine kept a wide distance between herself and Cole. Jennie frowned. Was the woman still squeamish about his injury? Couldn't she see that her manner was hurting him?

"Miss Andrews?" The doctor tilted his head in front of her. "It appears you are still keeping an eye on your patient."

Warmth rose into her cheeks. "I suppose I am. Since he elected to come tonight, I had hoped he would enjoy himself."

In time to the music, the doctor turned her around, his own gaze following the ill-at-ease couple. "That doesn't appear to be the case, though, does it? Cole has come a long way since the explosion, but I'm afraid the outside has healed more quickly than the inside."

"His fiancée isn't helping much." Jennie continued to watch Cole. "It must be so hard for such a self-reliant and responsible man to adapt to losing part of a limb." Her heart went out to him. She wished Katherine could show him more compassion, accept him and help him to accept himself.

She saw Cole release Katherine, then step in front of her. He held out both arms, inviting her to move into them. Jennie read his lips. "May I have this dance?"

She held her breath, waiting for the woman's response. Dr. Goodman stopped moving and watched, as well. The waltz music continued, but the room seemed to grow quiet, expectant.

Katherine looked around wildly, a hunted expression in her eyes. "I...I, oh, Cole. I can't," she said. "I'm sorry."

Jennie released her breath in a painful rush. The woman was heartless. Thank goodness, Cole didn't love her, or he would have been even more devastated.

As though testing her, giving her one last chance, he moved a step closer to her. Katherine shuddered and skittered backward into the young bank clerk Jennie had seen behind the teller cage. He put his hand on Katherine's shoulder.

Cole's already hard gaze turned to cold iron. "You can't what, Katherine?"

"I can't...dance with you." Her voice quivered, and she stared at the floor. "And I can't...marry you."

Cole's body went rigid. Jennie wanted to slap the girl for hurting him, but at the same time, she felt a tremendous relief. He was better off. Cole and Katherine would never have been happy together. Although, knowing his stubborn streak, he probably wasn't ready to accept that yet.

He slowly turned his back on Katherine, and his gaze raked the audience watching so intently. That gaze stopped on Jennie. Though his eyes were dark with fury, she saw through his anger to the humiliation and despair inside. When he abruptly turned and strode out the door, she ached for him.

And then she went after him.

Chapter Fourteen

Cole stalked past the wrought-iron gas lamps dropping pools of light along the veranda. His boots thundered down the stairs.

He needed to get out, away from the woman who made him feel less than a man. For weeks he'd fought his low periods and won. Tonight he'd lost the battle. Katherine showed him exactly what he was, a cripple no decent woman would want for a husband. He'd respected her, but she'd spurned him in front of the entire town, humiliating him.

She actually preferred Wilkins, the homely, gawky bank clerk. When the young man put his hand so tellingly on her shoulder, Cole had wanted to punch him, but even one-handed, he knew the fight wouldn't have been a fair one.

Still wanting to hit something, he kicked one of the round stones lining the path to the Opera House. It rolled end over end across the dirt and into a patch of bushes. Twigs cracked. Cole kept going, no destination in mind.

Muted sounds of the simple yet lively orchestra seemed to follow him. He also heard a pair of fast-moving footsteps and the rustle of a woman's skirt. Not the stiff cotton of Katherine's dress, but the tell-tale crackle of expensive taffeta. Cole knew who wore that skirt.

As he'd entered the Opera House, he immediately picked out Jennie, who was dancing with a young cowboy and then with Doc Goodman. She wore a green taffeta dress the exact color of her eyes. The bodice hugged her waist and breasts, her figure drawing the attention of even the oldest men present. Cole had forced himself to look away, concentrate on Katherine and his withering future.

Now, before reaching the street, he faced Jennie, intending to send her right back to the party.

She stopped in front of him, wearing no coat, her chest heaving with her rapid breaths. Cole swallowed against his suddenly dry mouth and realized he'd been a fool. He was no better than any of those ogling men inside. He wanted Jennie, the woman who haunted his sleeping and waking dreams.

He yanked his gaze up to her hair, thinking that would cool his mounting temperature. He was wrong. Several curls had escaped the loose knot on her head, tempting him to brush them away from her flushed face. He imagined those soft curls tangling around his fingers, and he gladly would have let them hold him prisoner. The alluring scent of roses surrounded her. But then he saw the sorrow filling her eyes, and it felt like a slap to his face.

Cole didn't want her pity. "Go back to the dance, Jennie. I don't want you here."

When she braced her hands on her hips, Cole knew he was in for trouble. Trouble he didn't want or need.

She leaned toward him. "I'll go back after we've had our dance. Not a moment before."

His jaw dropped, and then he snorted his disbelief. "You want to dance with *me?*"

"Don't you know how to dance?"

"Of course I do. But—"

"Well then?" She held out her arms as the strains of a waltz floated past them.

"You're doing this because you feel sorry for me."

She continued holding out her arms. "I feel very badly for you. Katherine Dawson did a terrible thing to you tonight. I'd like to kick her skinny derriere."

Cole actually felt a chuckle bubbling up his throat. It surprised him, and he forced it back down, listening instead to the remainder of Jennie's tirade on his behalf.

"For an avowed Christian woman, she showed you no compassion at all. In fact, I think her behavior shocked quite a few people back there." She paused for breath. "Now, will you please dance with me, Cole? My arms are getting tired."

He walked into them, took her right hand with his left while she settled her other hand on his shoulder. It was probably best he had no right hand to put on her back, because he would have been sorely tempted to pull her way too close to his heated body.

She smiled up at him. "Was that so hard?"

The woman had no idea what hard was. He remembered all the nights he'd lain in bed trying to get her out of his mind, and failing miserably at it. "You can be very persuasive."

The music's rhythm directed their matched steps, and Cole felt himself relaxing.

She tilted her head back. "It's nice out here under

the stars, away from the crowded dance floor. It was hot in there."

"You're not too cold without your coat?"

She looked down at herself and laughed softly. "I completely forgot about it. But it is a little chilly." She moved closer to him, pressing her breasts against his chest. Her soft curls feathered over his chin.

Cole almost groaned. Didn't she know what she was doing to him? He thought about Katherine's fear of him. "You're not afraid to get too close to me?"

"Have I ever been afraid of you?"

"Only when I start asking questions about your past."

"I wasn't afraid of *you,* only your questions."

"I see." Holding his breath, he raised his injured arm and placed it as far around her as possible. When she didn't flinch, he slowly released his breath. "Are you going to tell me now what you're running from?"

"I think you have enough to worry about. I don't want to bother you with my problems."

"They already bother me. Put my mind at ease, Jennie."

"Now who's being persuasive?"

"Come on, what happened back in Boston to send you cross country?"

She leaned her head against his chest and shoulder, looking away from him.

"You can trust me, Jennie."

"I know that." She turned her face back to him. "I've known it for a long time. But there were so many reasons not to tell you, the most important being to protect you."

"Protect me from what?" Even though Cole knew he could take care of himself, he liked that she cared so much about him. Few people in his life had ever cared enough to want to protect him from anything.

"From James Easton III," she said.

"That's a grand-sounding name. Who is he?"

"The man I'm supposed to marry."

"Ah," Cole said, not sure how he felt about a man who had a claim on Jennie. But what had happened to send her running from him? "Tell me the rest of the story."

She leaned harder on him. "My father knew I intended only to marry for love, but he very badly wanted a proper, well-connected son-in-law who could take over for him at the bank he owns and runs. My sisters' husbands have no interest or inclination. James, however, is related to a respected Boston family and worked in a bank in New York, where he was raised. So my father arranged a marriage between us."

"Against your will." Cole remembered figuring she was running from something to do with her marital status, but where did the danger come in? "You left because you didn't love the man, but—"

She stiffened in his hold and glared up at him. "I know you don't approve of love in a marriage, but—"

"Jennie, you didn't let me finish. Why are you afraid of him?"

"Oh." Her muscles relaxed a bit, but she didn't put her head back down against his chest. Cole missed that closeness already. He noticed the tempo of the music had quickened, but he had no idea when it changed. Rather than follow it, he stopped moving and just held her to him. She didn't try to move away. "James is a vicious man," she said.

"How do you know?"

She glared at him again. "Don't you trust my judgment?"

"I'm a detective, Jennie. Or was. I look at the evidence and then I make my own judgment. Why do you think he's vicious?"

"After my father told me about the marriage contract, I started asking some questions around town. Everyone in society had nothing but praise for him, but at the dispensary where I worked, one of the men Dr. Nicholson was treating heard us talking about James. The man said he'd seen the 'dandy' at one of the local pubs that the rough-and-tumble types frequent." She paused.

"Is that all?"

"No." Her body trembled, and he rubbed her back. "Shortly after James left the pub, the man went outside for some air. He found James wielding his riding crop, beating the boy who'd been minding his horse. The boy had fallen asleep."

Cole went rigid, thought of Joey at the stable. If any man tried the same on Joey, Cole knew he'd go after that man. He peered down at Jennie, saw something in her eyes that worried him—fear.

She looked away.

He put his fingers beneath her chin and brought her gaze back to his. "And?"

"And what? Isn't that enough?" she cried.

"You're holding something back. What is it? Did he do something to you?" Cole's heart started to pound. Had James Easton forced himself on Jennie? He dropped his hand from her chin and circled her waist with his good arm. He wanted to hold her, protect her and, God help him, kiss her.

"He threatened me. I tried to convince him a marriage between us would be all wrong, but he didn't agree, especially since he would receive twenty thousand dollars from my father on completion of the ceremony."

Cole whistled softly, relieved that the man hadn't forced himself on Jennie. "That's no small sum."

"It's a fraction of what he could eventually have, and he knows it. When I saw his determination, all I could think about was getting away from him, from Boston. Somehow, he read my thoughts."

"Your eyes do tend to give you away. What happened next?"

She leaned into him, as though needing his support. "James grabbed my wrist, twisted it until I cried out with the pain. Then he said, 'Don't even think about defying me. If you run, I'll hunt you down. And you won't like the consequences.'"

"Bastard," Cole swore, wanting to hunt the man down himself. "If he comes here, you send for me." Cole wished he could take Jennie back to the ranch with him. She'd be safer there. He didn't like thinking about the seven miles that would separate them once he went back. Too much could happen in the time it would take for him to get to her. "I think you should talk to Sheriff Conklin."

"I'm frightened, but I really doubt James will find me here. It's been two months since I left."

"I think he's probably eliminated a lot of possibilities and his search is narrowing. I know how to find people, Jennie. People who stick out in a crowd make searching fairly easy. You qualify as one of those people."

She groaned, glanced away. "You may be right.

Two weeks ago, I served a man at the Harvey House. He knew I looked familiar to him, but he couldn't place me and I wouldn't give him my name. He was from Boston, and his family knows my family.''

"Damn. Most likely, he's remembered your identity by now."

She shivered. Cole wanted to give her his warmth, reassure her. She'd been strong for a long time, and he admired her for it. He thanked the stars she'd been on the train with him.

"Come back to the ranch with me, Jennie. I can protect you there. When Easton comes, we'll be ready for him."

She straightened away from him. "No. I've decided I'm not running anymore. My mind is made up. This is where he'll come, and I'm going to take my chances at the Harvey House."

Cole blew out a frustrated breath. "But I can't help you if you're here and I'm on the ranch."

"I'm not asking for your help."

"But I want to help. I owe you my life."

She stepped out of his hold. "I told you before we were square."

Cole rolled his eyes. "Convincing a couple of roughneck cowboys to leave you alone does not equate to the value of my life."

"And I didn't treat you beside that train just because you'd helped Rae and me earlier. Stop considering everything a debt."

He understood her reasoning, but despite losing his hand and tonight his fiancée, he valued his life, more than he'd thought possible a few weeks ago. He still had his home, the ranch and his little brother.

When he didn't answer, she went on. "Besides,

you have your own problems to worry about. I heard about your barn being deliberately burned, and I remember how Mr. Gray at the mercantile didn't want to extend you any more credit. Then there's the attack on the train car Matt was in. Shouldn't you be more concerned about yourself and your brother?''

"I am concerned," he answered slowly, deciding to confide in her the way she'd just done with him. "I finally remembered something about the holdup."

"You did?" Her eyes widened. "What?"

"Those men weren't after the money in the express car. They meant to kill Matt."

She gasped and reached out to him, placed her hand on his arm. "But why?"

"That I don't know yet. The sheriff checked out some names for me, men who might hold grudges against me for putting them in prison, but nothing's come of it."

She moved closer. "I'm sorry, Cole. This must be so frustrating for you. And frightening. Do you think Matt is still in danger?"

"It's possible."

"You see, you have to stop worrying about me. I'll be fine here. There are always lots of people around me. Nothing can happen. And I'll even inform the sheriff of my situation if it'll make you feel better."

"It will." But not nearly enough. Cole didn't like leaving Jennie's problem in someone else's hands.

"And I'll keep my eyes and ears open around here for you," she said. "I often hear things at my lunch counter. The patrons talk amongst themselves, forgetting I'm standing there pouring their coffee."

He took a step closer, put his hand on her back, felt the rich fabric of her bodice and didn't want to let her go. "Jennie, don't put yourself in danger on my account." Just the thought of her risking her safety frightened him.

He heard her breath quicken as she peered up at him. "I won't be in danger." She swallowed visibly as he moved even closer, tightened his hold on her once again. "I'll be...pouring coffee."

"You still shouldn't take any chances."

She stared up at him, her eyes luminous. "Cole, I don't want anything to happen to you."

"Nor I to you," he said softly, feeling the moist warmth of her breath on his chin.

She licked her lips. They glimmered under the starlight, and Cole's muscles tightened. Though he wanted Jennie, he told himself his desire had nothing to do with love, and never could. He cared for her, yes, had been attracted to her from the very beginning, but tonight, he needed her to help him feel whole again. He needed to know that not every woman would shudder in disgust when he got close, when he wanted to kiss a woman.

Slowly he lowered his mouth over hers, brushed her parting lips with his tongue. As she opened to him, he tasted the sweetness of her mouth, lost himself in the welcoming warmth of her answering kiss. And in this moment, he wanted more of her, so much more.

On the Opera House veranda, a man stood outside the circle of light cast by a gas lamp. Out of habit, he tapped his shiny pocket watch with his finger. "Well, well," he whispered to himself, his gaze never leaving the couple now kissing where the street met the Opera House pathway. Behind them, the lights of a saloon silhouetted their melded bodies.

The man pulled out a cigar, bit off the end and struck a match. He sucked the flame onto the cigar. When the end glowed orange, he waved out the match. "How fitting," he mused. "Bryant's savior comes to his aid once again. And now she's coming to mine, too."

Inside, the man had relished Cole's humiliation at Katherine Dawson's hands; however, their breakup had effectively destroyed his most anticipated plan of revenge against Cole.

Now, however, things were looking up. He smiled at the couple oblivious of his observation. He could go forward with his plan after all. Carter and his men would have their fun with Jennie Andrews instead of the reverend's daughter.

The man contained his laughter, patted his broad belly and flicked a length of ash off the end of his cigar.

"Miss Andrews, you're going to be leaving us for a little while," he whispered. Once she'd been used and returned, Bryant would never forget what had happened to her because of him, and he would suffer for the rest of his life.

"You killed my boy and took my wife's sanity, Bryant. Now you'll pay."

Jennie's senses felt like they were awakening after a long sleep. She leaned into Cole, into his kiss, felt his heart pounding against her own. His tongue feathered across her lips and in her mouth.

The scents of soap and pine and the outdoors—all of them his scents—wafted around her. She forgot the cold of the night air, felt only a spreading warmth throughout her body.

She slid her hands from the muscular wall of his chest to his broad shoulders and around his neck, where she linked her fingers together. His soft hair brushed her hands.

His kiss deepened, and he held her as if he would never let her go. Jennie didn't want him to let her go. Under this starlit sky, she wanted to stay with him forever, safe and secure, comforted and cared for.

She opened to him, let his tongue dance with her own, slowly and tantalizingly at first, then faster and faster until their quick breaths seemed as loud as the dance music coming from the Opera House.

Cole jerked his head away from her.

Dazed, Jennie stared up at him, unable to read his expression. "What's wrong?"

When he tried to set her away from him, she linked her fingers more tightly. She didn't want to say good-bye to these few moments of wonder.

"Let go, Jennie."

"Why?"

"Because this kiss is finished. I thank you for it, but it's finished." His voice held only a trace of the warmth she'd felt in his embrace.

Slowly she released him and stepped back. The cold dropped over her like snowfall, reaching deep inside, chilling her. "You don't have to thank me for a kiss."

"Yes, I do. I kissed you for a reason, proved something to myself."

Jennie tensed, knowing she wouldn't like what was coming. "What reason?"

"After Katherine's rejection, I needed to know that not every woman would push me away."

She understood, but it didn't erase the hurt and disappointment his own form of rejection was causing. Only a minute ago, Jennie had felt so much a part of him, as if they were one person, but it meant nothing now. He had not felt the same, had used her. Feeling silly, she squared her shoulders. "I suppose, in my own way, I was using you, too."

His eyes narrowed. "How's that?"

"I was feeling scared because of James, and, for a little while, you made me forget him and feel safe." She looked up at the stars, wished she could rise up to them and leave all her worries and disappointments behind. "I was also feeling lonely. Rae has Matt now. I think it won't be long before they decide to marry, and once Rae becomes a wife, she can no longer be a Harvey Girl."

He pushed his hand into his pants pocket. "She'll make Matt a good wife."

"They have love on their side, even though you don't approve of that sentiment."

"I approve of it for them, just not for myself."

"Or for the woman you marry."

"With this—" he nodded toward his injured arm "—I may never find a woman willing to marry me, give me children."

A woman who loved him would happily do both, Jennie thought, but he didn't want to hear that, so she kept silent and felt a heartrending sorrow for Cole and what he was giving up. Even if he did marry and have children, the man in whose eyes she'd seen such a depth of love for his brother would one day regret not finding a love of his own.

Chapter Fifteen

James Easton III propped one square-toed leather shoe on the East Bluff Tavern's wood bar rail. A smoky haze hovered in the room crowded with evening patrons of Boston's lower classes. James stood alone at one end of the bar, the other customers leaving him a wide berth. Every so often, when he caught one of them eyeing him speculatively, he stared the man down until he turned away.

James drank from his second mug of dark beer. He liked this tavern, felt himself far above its clientele. And here, nobody asked your business or checked into your past. Jennifer's father, the almighty Edmund Andrews, had begun double-checking his references.

"He'll regret it," James said into his beer. "No matter what he finds out, he and I have a signed contract, and his daughter and money will be mine. Nobody tells me what I can and then can't have." His hand tightened on the mug. "I'll find the tramp, and she'll rue the day she ever defied me."

Tonight James hoped his detective, Thomas Fuller, would not bring him any more excuses. If he did, it would be fortunate for Fuller they'd had to meet in a public place. James missed feeling the power of sitting behind his uncle's massive desk, but on a Sunday night, Richard Easton stayed in.

As James drank a hearty swallow, the thick wood door opened. With the surge of fresh, salty air, the dense, tobacco-scented haze swirled in upon itself.

Thomas Fuller entered, looked around for a moment and crossed to James's side. The detective wore his usual overcoat. It hung open, revealing a rumpled brown woolen sack suit. James sneered; the detective had no class.

He set his mug down on the scarred bar. "Well? Do I have to wait all night to hear your report?"

Fuller eyed the other patrons, cleared his throat. "I've found her."

James straightened instantly. "Say that again."

"I've found her, Mr. Easton."

James felt a smile inch across his face. "Do go on, Mr. Fuller."

"I followed up on my theory about those letters posted from all over the country." He took a handkerchief from inside his coat and wiped it across his damp brow. "I thought to myself, Where does a woman have access to railroad people who can mail her letters? I didn't think *she* was the one traveling. That would cost money. And how was she supporting herself? There's been no activity with her bank account, and a woman of her breeding would avoid indecent work. Then it dawned on me."

"Fuller, this is all quite fascinating, but what dawned on you?" James started thumping his fist on the edge of the bar. "Where the hell is she?"

"Meals by Fred Harvey."

"What are you talking about, man?"

"Fred Harvey. The civilizer of the West. His company provides meals for Santa Fe Railway passengers. And he employs attractive young women to serve those meals. They often stay and marry the local men, thereby 'civilizing' the West. Jennifer Andrews is a Harvey Girl."

"And where is she supposed to be doing this, Fuller?" James asked skeptically.

"In the town of Williams, Arizona Territory."

James laughed. "You must be mistaken. Jennifer Andrews working as a waitress in the Wild West? I don't believe it. That area isn't even a state, for God's sake. The story her parents concocted about shopping for her trousseau in Europe is more believable."

Fuller removed a small notebook from his overcoat pocket and flipped it open. "One Jennie Andrews, redhead, was hired in Chicago on Tuesday, March eighteenth." He looked up briefly. "That's three days after your engagement announcement appeared in the newspaper."

"I know when it was. Get on with it."

Fuller cleared his throat again, annoying James. "On the nineteenth, she arrived in Topeka, Kansas, for one month's training. She then left for her first assignment, Williams, Arizona Territory. This has all been confirmed by the Harvey Company offices in Chicago and Topeka. I have not telegraphed Williams for fear Miss Andrews might be alerted."

James grudgingly gave his approval. "Good thinking. I can hardly believe it, but I suppose I must. The woman is too outrageous." James pursed his lips. "The Harvey Company volunteered her current whereabouts to you?"

"I explained that her parents were concerned since

they had failed to hear from her since she finished her training, and that there had been a death in the family.''

''You've lived up to your reputation, Fuller. I'm pleased.'' James lifted his mug to him.

''There's more, sir. I've had a visual confirmation.''

''Already?''

''It was pure luck. Just today, a family friend contacted Mr. Andrews. My informant said Miss Andrews served the man his dinner meal. However, he hadn't been able to place her until last night, when his mother mentioned the engagement.''

''Your source of information has been very helpful.'' James swallowed a mouthful of beer. ''Who is it?''

''One of the Andrews's staff. Her husband has a gambling habit, so she's always short of money.''

''Ah.'' James thought about his upcoming trip. ''Arizona is a good four days from here. Damn Jennifer for going so far. And to such uncivilized country. She can't possibly like it. Who knows? Maybe she'll be glad to see me, thank me for coming to get her.'' James laughed, enjoying the harsh, cold sound. ''I'll catch the westbound train tomorrow morning.''

''Mr. Easton,'' Fuller said hesitantly, ''I think there's something else you should know.''

''What?''

''Over the past few weeks, I spotted someone watching my comings and goings. He may be working for Mr. Andrews.''

James's gaze darted around the tavern. ''Did anyone follow you here?''

''No, no. I was very careful.'' Fuller looked back

over his shoulder. "But it's possible he has someone watching you, too."

"Damn it!" James wanted to fling his mug across the tavern, barely managed to refrain. "Andrews thinks he's going to break the marriage agreement. Well, he's wrong. No matter what Edmund Andrews discovers about me, once Jennifer and I are wed, he will bite his tongue for the sake of his and his family's reputation."

James began to smile, eager now to see Jennifer's expression when he confronted her.

Cole sat hunched over the open ledger on his desk. The afternoon sun shone on the large, earth-toned Indian rug that covered much of the hardwood floor. Books lined the shelves around him. He propped his elbow on the large accounts book in front of him and leaned his forehead against his hand. He couldn't concentrate any better today than he had during the four days since the dance. Lack of sleep didn't help.

He couldn't stop thinking about the danger to his brother, Jennie's reason for running and the kiss he'd shared with her. Cole rubbed his gritty eyes. The image of Jennie in his embrace, ardently responding to his kiss, haunted him daily when all he wanted to do was put her out of his mind.

He'd needed to feel wanted by a woman, but Jennie had given him much more than he expected, the kiss going on longer than he'd intended. He'd finally pushed her away because, with her hands linked around his neck and her body pressed against his, he'd felt more needy than ever, and he didn't like that feeling.

Not only that, Jennie deserved to keep her reputation intact for the man who would love her and want her love in return, not a man who thought only of the moment, of Jennie's warm, wet, inviting mouth opening to him under a starry sky.

Cole repositioned himself in the creaky wood swivel chair. Just thinking of those moments with her had his blood stirring.

Approaching footsteps drummed along the hall. Matt stopped inside the study doorway. Damp black hair fell over a face set in lines of absolute decision. He looked as though he'd been getting as little sleep as his big brother.

"Cole, I'm going to town Saturday morning."

"Are we low on supplies?" Cole teased with a straight face.

Matt scowled. "I'm not interested in supplies, Cole. I want to get engaged."

"Does Rae know about this?"

"She will. I'm gonna propose."

"Do you think she'll say yes?"

Matt looked at him as if he were loco. "She'd better 'cause I won't take no for an answer."

Cole decided he'd baited his little brother long enough. "Congratulations, Matt." He stood and clapped him on the shoulder. "You've made a fine choice." Then, he smiled.

Matt stared at him. "Cole, have you been at the whiskey?"

He laughed. "I have not."

Blue-gray eyes opened as big around as the double barrels of a shotgun. "You're laughing. I can't believe it. Something must be wrong."

"Can't a man laugh once in a while?"

"Most men, yes. You, I don't know. I can't remember the last time I saw you smile let alone laugh. And the way you stomped out of that dance, I didn't think you'd ever be happy again.''

Cole shrugged.

Matt's brows rose in understanding. ''Ah.'' He started nodding. ''This has something to do with Jennie, doesn't it? She followed you out of the Opera House and didn't come back for an awful long time. What were you and she up to outside?''

Cole stopped smiling. ''Drop it, Matt.''

''I'm right, aren't I? Ha! I knew it.'' He stomped his booted foot on the floor. ''From the very beginning I knew you fancied her. Didn't I tell you so that morning after she pulled Rae away from us at the depot?''

''There is nothing between Jennie and me,'' Cole said staunchly. ''You're jumping to conclusions.''

Matt chuckled. ''I knew that mousy Miss Dawson wasn't right for you. You never would've smiled around her.''

''I haven't smiled around Jennie, either.''

''Maybe not, but I think she's given you something to smile about.'' Matt hit his palm with his fist. ''This is great. You and Jennie and me and Rae.''

Cole rolled his eyes. ''Matt, you're—''

''Jennie will make a fantastic mother. Your kids will be smart and tough. Strong-minded. No weak Dawson blood running through them. And all the girls will be real lookers.'' Matt laughed. ''You'll have trouble with the local boys, though. No doubt about that.''

Cole too easily pictured the scene Matt painted, saw his beautiful daughters, as headstrong as their mother.

He shook his head hard to clear the image. What remained were thoughts he'd not considered before. If he and Katherine had married, would their children have been less than he hoped for? Might they have taken after her? He didn't particularly like that possibility. Cole wanted his children strong and independent, spirited and courageous.

Like Jennie.

But he knew she'd never be the mother of his children. She wanted to marry for love, had given up everything because of it. From him, she would not find the love she searched for, needed.

"Stop dreaming, Matt. Jennie and I want completely different things from a marriage. We will never be a couple." As he spoke, a hollow, unidentifiable ache opened inside Cole. He ignored the peculiar feeling.

Edmund Andrews rushed into his Beacon Hill mansion. A cold, blustery wind followed him through the massive doorway. He banged the door shut and tossed his travel case onto the marble floor.

"Abigail!" he shouted.

His wife appeared under the wide, arched entrance to the parlor. She held a blue-veined hand to her throat. "My goodness, Edmund, what is it? Why, every servant in the house must have heard you."

"Abigail, listen to me." He took hold of her slight shoulders. "I must leave within the hour or I'll miss the next train heading west. Get someone to pack my bag with clean clothes immediately. I don't know how long I'll be gone."

"What's happened?" Her anxious gaze peered up

at him. "Why the urgency now? We know where Jennifer is."

"James Easton left Boston over two and a half days ago for the Arizona Territory. My man's been trying to reach me ever since. I should never have stayed away so long." Edmund dropped his hands from his wife.

"You've only been gone a few days, Edmund."

He'd left the day after George Lampton paid a call on him at the bank, informing him of Jennifer's whereabouts. Knowing she was well and safe, and that James Easton was in Boston and being watched, Edmund had attended an important business meeting in New York. While there, he discovered the frightening truth about James Easton III.

"Now Easton's got a head start. Jennifer could be in grave danger." He looked toward the library. "I must take my pistol. I have to protect my daughter from that heinous man."

"Your pistol! Heinous man!" The color drained from Abigail's already pale face. "What are you talking about? James is an Easton, a fine young man."

"I was wrong, Abigail. Terribly wrong." His eyes burned with guilt and remorse. "Jennifer tried to tell me the truth, but I refused to listen, even accused her of lying. I'll regret that to my dying day."

"I need to sit down," Abigail said. After he helped her into a nearby Louis Quinze chair, she fanned her face with her hand. "I don't understand. Why would he hurt our Jennifer?"

"Because she refused to marry him."

"But does that make him so dangerous you feel you must dash off like this?"

He knelt before his wife, took her cool, delicate

hands in his. "Abigail, I have a terrible confession to make. I wanted a successor so badly that I was blinded by James's charm and family connections. In New York, I learned the truth. James extorted his glowing job recommendation from the bank manager."

"Oh, dear me." Her hands started to shake, and he held them tighter.

"It gets much worse. James murdered a man there."

She let out a tiny, horrified scream. "No!"

"The whole incident was hushed up, but it happened. And for the sole reason that the man defied James."

Her flesh went colder. "Wh-what can we do? Oh, Edwin, Jennifer is so far away."

"I will handle it. You mustn't worry about anything or you'll end up back in your bed with the doctor in attendance." Jennifer's abrupt departure had sent Abigail into a decline, but soon after, a reassuring letter had arrived from their daughter.

She lifted her chin a notch, her New England backbone returning. Color flowed back into her paper-thin cheeks. "I want to help, too. I have to do something."

"You cannot come with me."

"I know that. But I can send a wire to Jennifer, warn her of Easton's impending arrival."

"Excellent idea." He kissed the backs of her hands. "Now I must hurry."

Edmund hoisted himself up and went into the adjoining library. As he opened the felt-lined case containing his pistol, a thought struck him and he turned back to his wife.

"Abigail, don't tell her I'm coming. I don't want

Easton warned in case he learns of the wire. All I will have is the element of surprise.''

"Perhaps we should telegraph the constable there,'' she said. "They do have one, don't they?''

"I don't know. In any case he would be called a sheriff.'' Edmund considered her suggestion. "No, don't contact him. We'll let Jennifer decide what action needs to be taken. It's time I trusted her judgment.''

"All right, Edmund. Whatever you think is best.'' She pushed herself out of the chair. "I'll have Simon pack your bag. Cook can prepare a basket of food for you.''

As she glided out of the parlor on her tiny feet, Edmund checked over his gun and placed a box of bullets in his coat pocket. Then he leaned both hands hard on the desk.

"This is all my fault,'' he whispered, his heart drowning in guilt.

"Whew!'' Jennie exhaled loudly while wiping the back of her wrist across her brow. She watched the last train passenger rush out the lunchroom and into the night. "Another train here and gone.''

Rae wiped her own brow. "How do you suppose Miss Thompson has stood it for so long?''

"Maybe she has nothing else,'' Jennie said, curious about the older woman and able to relate to having no place to go. "It's not a bad life. Just a busy one, with long hours afoot. I've already heard the new girl in the dining room complaining.''

"She'll get used to it.'' Rae smiled. "But I think you're being wasted here. You should work in a doctor's office. I bet Dr. Goodman would be glad to have you."

Jennie wouldn't have minded that at all, would have happily volunteered to help him, but she needed a paying job, and in her experience, the people who needed the most doctoring could rarely pay much of anything.

"I don't think Dr. Goodman could afford to hire me. And where would I live? Here, I have my room, board, salary, and the rest of the staff to keep me company. But enough about my future. I think you are destined for marriage."

Rae rubbed at a spot on the counter. "I'm not sure yet."

"Oh, I think you are. I expect the new girl will soon be working with me here." And another would arrive fresh from training to take Rae's bed. "I'll miss you."

"Don't talk like that. Matt hasn't proposed yet."

"He will," Jennie said, no doubt in her mind. She had no idea what Cole's future held now, but Matt and Rae would grow old together.

Rae's big blue eyes took on a yearning quality. "If he does, I'd like to live on the land rather than in a town."

"A ranch isn't so different from a farm."

"But I don't know if Matt wants to stay with ranching. The C Bar M is Cole's dream and domain. I know he wants Matt there, but I'm afraid Matt feels the need to make his own mark. What if he goes back to guarding Wells Fargo express shipments? It's such a dangerous job. I'll worry about him all the time."

Jennie put her arm around her friend's shoulders.

"Tell him how you feel, and everything will work out. You'll see."

"I suppose you're right."

"Of course, I am, especially when two people love each other as much as you do." Jennie cast her a sideways glance. "I saw you and Matt looking at each other when you were saying goodbye after the dance."

After Cole's kiss, Jennie had returned to the Opera House alone. For her, the fun and joy had gone out of the evening. She didn't want to dance, but too many men needed partners, so she'd given them her hostess smile and kept her feet moving until the last song. All the while, she tried to forget Cole's devastating kiss and more devastating withdrawal.

"You and Matt didn't look like you wanted to part," Jennie added.

Rae smiled shyly. "You shouldn't have been watching us."

"Fair is fair. If I remember correctly, you implied something to me about a man looking at a woman the way he shouldn't."

She glanced away, then back, her fair face glowing. "Oh, Jennie, I can't describe what it was like when Matt looked at me so hard. I thought my legs were going to give way. Have you ever felt like that?"

Jennie hesitated, remembered one night. "Just once." Under the moonlight with Cole Bryant. "I was quite dazed."

"Isn't it wonderful? I'm going to dream about Matt tonight."

Jennie wished she had someone to dream about, but she couldn't even fantasize about Cole. He didn't want her. She gazed from the empty lunchroom to the dining room, where several local folks were finishing their Friday evening meal.

She spotted a frequent customer who had something to do with the Northern Arizona Savings Bank. Tonight he sat alone. Usually he dined with a rather frail looking woman. He dressed well and often twirled his shiny gold watch.

Jennie turned back to Rae. "Dreams are all well and good, but they won't get our stations clean."

Her friend groaned. "How true."

Jennie wiped her area, then went to check on the coffee.

Rae came up behind her. "Jennie, there's a customer seated at your station. Do you want me to take care of him?"

"No, thanks anyway." As she returned from the shiny brass coffee urns, she paid little attention to the man. His tailored suit was rumpled, as if he'd come off the train and decided to stay. She shrugged. Another face to serve and forget.

She headed toward the island in the center of the counter area and picked out a silver table setting, as well as one of the white Irish linens with the name of Fred Harvey woven into the cloth. Without looking up, she placed it all in front of the man.

"Good evening, Jennifer dear."

Jennie froze. Her stomach clenched. That voice. The same voice that called out to her in her nightmares. She barely breathed. A chill worse than a Boston gale blasted through her. Jennie forced her feet to back away. When the solid edge of the island pressed into her back, she finally looked up. Dared to confirm what she already knew. James Easton had found her.

Chapter Sixteen

Jennie, heart thudding, faced the man sitting at her station. A sinister half smile creased his sharp features. His small, dark eyes swallowed the light that shone upon them, just as in her nightmare. She shuddered violently.

Easton laughed, his amusement harsh. "I knew you would be glad to see me." He laughed again and leaned forward. "I told you I'd hunt you down. We *will* be married, Jennifer."

No longer suffering from surprise, and unwilling to let him see his effect on her, Jennie buried her fear. She squared her shoulders, gathered her wits and stood tall. "How did you find me?"

"I hired a private detective. He came up with the Harvey Girl idea and tracked you here. Then George Lampton confirmed it for us."

"I see," she said, actually feeling a sense of relief. The waiting and wondering were over now.

Rae appeared beside her, worry denting her forehead. "Jennie, is everything okay?"

"Jennie?" he said. "Is that what you're called out

in this empty wasteland? Honestly, Jennifer, couldn't you have found a more civilized place to hide?''

"I'm all right, Rae," she answered. "This is James Easton III."

The girl's eyes widened. She took one look at him and scurried away.

James laughed heartily. "I see that my reputation precedes me. I'm so pleased, my darling. Will this young woman be attending you during our wedding ceremony?"

Jennie's temper flared. She stepped forward, closer to him, and braced her hands on her hips. "There will be no wedding, James."

"Of course, there will be. Your parents are so looking forward to it. Not as much as I, but very nearly. Have you been in touch with them?"

Jennie said nothing.

"I thought not," he said.

She cursed her eyes, remembered Cole telling her how expressive they were. Oh, how she wished he were with her now.

"Allow me to tell you how society has shunned them," James continued. "You've brought disgrace upon the Andrews name."

"I don't believe you," Jennie said, but inside she felt as though he'd plunged a knife into her heart. She really had no idea what had happened to her family after her sudden departure.

"I assure you it's quite true. You caused quite a scandal. Your poor mother has been terribly ill. Such a delicate woman."

The knife twisted. Each word he uttered thrust it painfully deeper. Had her mother really become ill? Jennie shook her head in denial. Couldn't afford to let his words, true or false, affect her. "I will *never* marry you."

His smile shaped itself into a sneer. He placed his hands on the counter. "We have a contract."

"You and my father have a contract. Marry him."

"Don't mock me, Jennifer. I am not a pleasant fellow when I'm angered. The contract was duly signed and notarized."

"I didn't sign it, James. I am a grown woman, free to choose my own life and my own husband. I do *not* choose you."

Easton's hand swooped across the counter like a hawk going in for the kill. Jennie shrieked when his fingers ensnared her wrist. He jerked her toward him. Her lower body came up hard against the counter. She tried to pull away, but he squeezed tighter. Pain shot up her arm.

"Free her!" boomed a loud German voice.

The head chef, tall and powerful, appeared beside her. In his hand, a butcher knife glinted in the glow of the gaslights.

Jennie wanted to cry with joy and relief, but Easton hadn't released her yet.

"Did you not hear me, mister? I say free her!"

Jennie heard the sound of feet shuffling in from all directions and watched as Harvey Girls, busboys and kitchen staff, all dressed in black and white, surrounded her and Easton. They possessed various and sundry kitchen implements held threateningly high.

"This woman will be my wife," Easton shouted. "It has all been arranged. I came from Boston for her."

"You free her now or I will practice my carving," Chef proclaimed, slowly slicing the air with his knife.

Easton abruptly released her.

Jennie fell back, but Chef's brawny arm caught her. A thin, bony arm came around her next. It belonged to Miss Olive Thompson, who held a heavy saucepan at the ready. Tears of gratitude stung Jennie's eyes.

Miss Thompson spoke without taking her eyes off Easton. "Jennie, are you planning to marry this man?"

"No! Never!"

"Very well, then," she said. "The matter is settled. No one threatens one of *my* girls. Mister, get yourself on outta here. Now."

Easton scowled blackly, but after observing the army around him, he wisely chose to take her advice. He stood and retreated backward toward the door. Jennie watched as the people around him opened to form a narrow passageway. His nightmarish eyes fixed on her. "I will see you soon, Jennifer. Make no mistake about that."

James slammed the Harvey House door behind him. "She'll be sorry," he snarled, seething at being thwarted by a bunch of waitresses and kitchen lackeys. He stepped from the light of the building into the brooding darkness beyond. "Jennifer will pay for that. She can't stay under their protection forever."

Several steps later, he smiled as he remembered her look of genuine shock when he greeted her. He thought her parents might contact her before his arrival. Fortunately they hadn't, because he'd gambled and won when he lied about what Boston society thought of her parents. The big payoff had come when he mentioned her mother's poor health. Jennifer's lovely coloring had drained right out of her face.

Then his smile vanished. His betrothed was worried, but she'd refused him just the same.

He strode across the tracks, his gaze glued to the uneven, unpaved ground that waited to trip a man. He hated this place, the dirt, the small buildings, the board-covered sidewalks and the people. After his arrival over an hour ago, he'd registered at the Grand Canyon Hotel, but "hotel" hardly described the place. The building was half mercantile, for God's sake. Varied smells of food, tobacco, and other things he couldn't identify wound their way up into his gaudily decorated room.

James scowled. After four miserable days on a train, he wanted decent lodgings. Jennifer would also pay for the discomfort and inconvenience he'd endured on her account.

"Sir! Hold up there!"

James turned at the sound of a man's voice behind him. An older gentleman with a protruding belly hurried after him, his labored breathing noisy. What could the man want with him?

"Allow me to welcome you to our little town of Williams, Arizona Territory."

James squinted through suspicious eyes. "Welcome me? Who are you, the mayor?"

The man smiled broadly. "Perhaps one day. Let me introduce myself. The name is Benjamin Porter. I own a number of profitable businesses here in town, including the bank, if you care to open an account."

"I won't be here that long." James started walking again.

"Sir," Porter called out, "I am currently working on a project that may be of some interest to you."

"What are you talking about?" James threw back over his shoulder. "You know nothing about me."

Porter hurried forward. "On the contrary. I saw enough at the Harvey House to know that you and I could work very well together. I was finishing my meal in the dining room when you met with your...intended. You could benefit from a partnership with me. We share a mutual interest."

James stopped, his curiosity aroused. "What could *we* possibly have in common?"

"Why, Miss Andrews, of course," Porter said lightly.

James leaned menacingly closer to him, smelled coffee on his breath. "What interest is she of yours?"

"I had certain, uh, plans for her, but I am now rethinking them." He sighed and shrugged. "Sir, I am a very good judge of character, and in you, I recognize myself." The man reached inside his jacket and ran his fingers over the watch chain attached to his waistcoat. "You understand a man's driving need for revenge."

"Go on," James said, his interest piqued.

"I wish to make a particular man suffer. He and Miss Andrews have become quite close. In fact, I saw them kissing most passionately last Saturday night."

James saw red. "Jennifer was kissing another man?"

"I'm afraid so."

He considered returning to the Harvey House, but as the banker kept talking, the red haze receded.

"I would like to help you marry Miss Andrews. By accepting my help, you will be pleasantly surprised to find her a willing bride in our own local church."

James stroked a sharp fingernail across his whiskered chin. Jennifer would come to him willingly? The deal sounded too good to be true, but he couldn't discount it. He saw now that he needed assistance, preferably from someone who wouldn't arouse suspicion.

He put out his hand. "I am James Easton III, lately of Boston. What do you propose, Mr. Porter?"

Utterly drained, legs shaking, Jennie propped herself up against the counter. Though her saviors hadn't asked, she'd told them her story and was glad to do so. No more secrets.

"Jennie," Olive Thompson said, "you go on upstairs now. Forget about that horrible man and get some rest."

Jennie could hardly believe her ears. Miss Thompson was being so nice, then she remembered that her supervisor had been one of her mightiest protectors.

"That's very kind of you, Miss Thompson, but I'm fine." Her wonderful co-workers had returned to their jobs, and she wanted to do hers. "I want to finish cleaning up my station."

Miss Thompson realigned the knife and spoon where James had been sitting. "Jennie, I know I haven't always been easy on you, but I have to admit you're a hard worker, even though you come from money. I've never had much of anything, so sometimes my resentment gets the better of me. I'm sorry." She looked toward the door. "I see now why you became a Harvey Girl."

Jennie didn't know what to say.

"Well, anyway—" Miss Thompson straightened, putting the starch back into her spine "—I admire your desire to finish up for the night, but do as I say." Before Jennie could think to object, the woman gave her one of her most severe looks and pointed a bony finger toward the ceiling. "Go."

"Yes, Miss Thompson." Jennie crossed the lunch-room and slowly mounted the stairs. The boards creaked beneath her dragging feet. The entire encounter with James had left her emotionally exhausted.

At the door to her room, she stopped and placed her forehead against the cool white surface. What was she going to do? James would not give up. He'd get to her somehow.

"I wish Cole were here," she whispered to the door. "He'd know what to do." She closed her eyes. No. If he knew, he'd insist on helping her. She'd saved his life, and he wanted to pay the debt he felt he owed her. Jennie didn't want to put him at risk when he had his own problems to contend with.

She pushed herself away from the wood panel, groaned with the effort. After unlocking the door, all she wanted to think about was a full night's sleep in which she could forget everything, escape from the past, present and future for a few hours. She prayed the nightmare would remain at bay: it had already arrived once tonight.

Jennie started across the threshold when Evan, the busboy, called out to her. He trotted down the hall, waving a flimsy, folded paper in his hand. As he approached, Jennie saw him chewing on his lower lip.

"Miss Jennie, I did a terrible thing. I got so busy yesterday I completely forgot to give this to you."

"What is it?"

"A telegram. The telegraph operator asked me to

give it to you. I'm sorry I forgot. I hope it's nothing important.''

Jennie stared at the paper in his hand, didn't touch it. Could it be from her parents? They would know where she was now. Was it terrible news? Had her mother taken a turn for the worse?

"Don't you want it, Miss Jennie?"

"Yes, of course." The paper rustled as she took it in her trembling hand. "Thank you, Evan."

"Can you forgive me?"

"Uh, yes, sure," she answered distractedly, staring at the telegram. "Good night."

She closed the door, went to her bed and sank down on it. Clumsily she unfolded the sheet of paper, then read:

JENNIFER ANDREWS
HARVEY HOUSE
WILLIAMS, ARIZONA TERRITORY
EASTON HAS GONE AFTER YOU STOP WE ARE SO
WORRIED STOP CONTRACT DESTROYED STOP ALL
FAMILY MEMBERS WELL STOP BE CAREFUL STOP
LOVE MOTHER AND FATHER

Jennie ran her finger over the words and burst into tears. Clutching the telegram to her heart, she buried her face in her pillow and cried until sleep overcame her.

The next afternoon, Jennie stood in the lunchroom doorway and stared out at the dismal and darkening gray overcast. Since morning, the spring skies had threatened rain.

She'd worked as usual, grateful for the distraction.

The staff had treated her with compassion and offered to do things for her. She appreciated their caring and kindness, but she was not helpless, nor would she let James Easton rule her life. She just had to be vigilant.

Miss Thompson had given her permission to visit the telegraph office in order to reply to her parents' telegram. Since none of the locals had ventured out for a bite on such a blustery afternoon, now was the time to go.

"Are you ready, Miss Jennie?" Evan had offered to accompany her to the depot.

"Yes. Let's go." For the short trip, she didn't bother with her coat.

Evan held the door for her, still contrite over forgetting her telegram. "Are you sending a wire all the way to Boston?"

"Yes. To my mother and father." It had taken Jennie hours to formulate her reply, something that wouldn't frighten her parents and put her mother's health in jeopardy. She'd finally come up with *Easton has arrived. I am fine. Safer here than anywhere. Don't worry. Love Jennifer.* "I want them to know I'm all right." James had not shown himself again, but he hadn't left town yet, either.

Jennie shivered, not sure whether it was due to her thoughts or the wind gusting along the walkway. Dust, dried pine needles and bits of paper swirled between the Harvey House and depot. A sign marked Ticket Office hanging outside the building swayed and squeaked. Jennie put a hand to her loosely knotted hair. Her apron and skirt whipped against her legs.

"Are you sure you don't want to stay here, Miss Jennie? I could take it myself. I promise I won't forget between here and there."

She smiled at him. "I know you wouldn't, but I'd like to go as long as you are willing to escort me."

He nodded as another gust of wind pushed them along. Jennie lifted a hand and squinted to protect her eyes from the flying debris. Not fifteen yards away, a young man dressed in cowboy garb and a sheepskin coat ambled alongside the tracks in the opposite direction. He kept his head down, but just the same, he struck a familiar chord in Jennie.

"Evan, do you know who that is?" She gestured toward the cowboy. Had she danced with him at the Opera House?

"Nope. Haven't seen him before. Nice coat, though. If I had me one like that, I'd be real warm next winter."

She stared at the coat, then at the man's face. Her eyes widened with sudden recognition. She gasped, would've stopped moving altogether if the wind hadn't been behind her.

It was *him*. The train robber whose face she'd seen from the coach window. He looked exactly as she remembered. The faded red kerchief was tied around his neck, and every so often he hunched his shoulders, burrowing deeper into his coat. But now, instead of holding a rifle, his hand weighted the crown of his wide-brimmed hat. A holstered pistol hung below the hem of his coat.

This was one of the men who'd tried to kill Matt, who was responsible for hurting Cole. Why was he here? As if he felt her gaze, the man turned his head and stared right at her. Jennie missed a step.

Evan caught her arm. "Miss Jennie, is something wrong?"

She let him divert her attention, was thankful for

his presence. The man had not seen her on the train, but if she continued staring at him, he would become suspicious. "I'm fine, Evan. Thank you for asking. But let's walk faster."

Before entering the telegraph office, Jennie risked one more look at the outlaw. He'd disappeared.

Her mind churned as she went into the office. She could barely concentrate on the clerk's questions or the reply she wrote out for her parents. Had the robber come back to finish what he'd started? Kill Matt? And maybe Cole, too?

"Oh, God." Jennie ran out of the office with Evan on her heels. She would never forgive herself if she let anything happen to Cole or the brother he loved so dearly. Somehow, she had to warn them, protect them.

She burst into the lunchroom to find Rae at her station, folding linens. "Jennie, what is it?" Her gaze darted toward the door. "Is Easton coming back?"

"No, no," Jennie said breathlessly, reaching for her friend's hands. "It's worse, Rae. I just saw one of the train robbers. I think he may be here to hurt Cole. Or Matt."

Rae's hands gripped Jennie's. Her voice was barely a whisper. "You recognized him?"

"Yes. I remember him all too well." She tried to think clearly. What should she do? "Evan, run quick and get the sheriff."

"But, Miss Jen—"

"Please. If you don't hurry, it'll be too late. I don't know where the man was going. Only his general direction."

Evan's shoulders slumped. "I'm sorry, Miss Jennie. Sheriff Conklin and his deputy took the morning train to Flagstaff. They were escorting two prisoners there. I heard 'em say they'll be back tomorrow.''

"Oh, no! Is there another deputy?''

"No, ma'am.''

Rae's hands tightened on Jennie's. "What are we going to do?''

"Let me think.'' She stared up at the ceiling, then dropped her gaze back to Rae's frightened face. "Cole and Matt need to be warned. Cole told me how to get to the ranch. I'll get a horse from the livery and ride out there. It's not raining yet, but the sooner I leave, the better.''

"You can't.'' Rae's voice rose. "You'll lose your job.''

"I don't care.'' Jennie no longer cared about anything but keeping Cole and his brother safe. "I am sorry to leave you with so much work.''

"Don't worry about that. I'll manage.'' Rae released her hands.

"But what about that Easton fella?'' Evan asked. "He might see you.''

"I'll be careful. I'll go out the back and sneak around the depot. The livery is across the tracks from there. Rae, if you loan me your dark cloak with the hood, I can hide my face and hair. No one will know it's me.''

"Of course you can wear it, but why do *you* have to go? We can send someone else to Cole.''

Jennie stared at her friend as realization struck. "Rae, I love him. If I let someone else go, and something happens to him, or to Matt, I...'' She couldn't finish, had to take several deep breaths to regain her composure. "I have to do this myself. Protect him.''

Rae sniffed and wiped a tear from her eye. "I understand. Take my cloak and promise me you'll be careful.''

"I promise, and I'll be back as soon as I can." Safely, she hoped.

Chapter Seventeen

Jennie rushed upstairs, her heart beating frantically. She tossed her white apron onto the bed, but didn't change the black shirtwaist and skirt. The darker her clothing, the less conspicuous. If James Easton was keeping watch on her, she wanted to blend into her surroundings as much as possible.

Wearing Rae's hooded cloak, Jennie let herself out the back door. The wind still gusted. With bare hands she clutched the wool fabric around her face. She flew along the back of the Harvey House and behind the depot building. At the end, she peered around the corner. Seeing no one, she angled her way across the tracks.

Jennie burst through the broad, open doors of the livery stable, her breath coming in shallow pants. She held a hand to her heart, trying to slow its pounding. She'd made it this far, but seven miles still remained.

"Hello? Is anybody here?"

A boy's blond head and freckled face popped up from inside a stall. "I'm here. You lookin' for me?"

"I don't know. Are you the...man I need to see about getting a horse?"

When he came closer, his jaw dropped for some reason Jennie couldn't fathom. "Yes, ma'am, I mean, Miss Andrews. That's me. Joey. My pa is up to the house right now." Blood rushed into his face. Jennie wondered how he knew her name, but she didn't take the time to ask.

"Joey, I need a fast horse that will carry me to the Bryant ranch."

"I know Mr. Cole." Joey smiled. "He's a friend of mine. You saved him."

"That's right, and once again I'm worried about Cole. His safety. It's imperative I leave quickly."

He screwed up his face. "In-pair-a what?"

"I need to leave fast," Jennie translated, growing more worried and impatient by the minute.

"You a good rider?"

"Yes. My father taught me well. Please give me a good horse."

"Yes, ma'am. I'll saddle one up for ya in no time."

Joey ran to the stall and soon led a saddled sorrel through the big livery doors. "This here's Maggie. She's gentle and fast. Has a smooth gait, too, and don't spook easy. She won't give you no trouble."

"Thank you, Joey." Jennie patted Maggie's neck, then mounted, tucking her skirts beneath her and pulling the cloak around her. Outside the livery, she urged the horse into a gallop and headed south. Worry and love spurred her forward.

Dressed in his dark brown cutaway sack suit, a white shirt, and ribbon tie, Matt stood just inside the Grand Canyon Hotel and stared across the tracks at the Harvey House. He fingered the gold wedding band in his coat pocket and smiled, anticipation making his heart skip faster. He was going to propose marriage to the woman he loved.

"Sunshine," he said, not realizing he'd spoken aloud.

"I think we shall be seeing rain and a dark night before we see sunshine," said a man's Eastern-accented voice.

Matt glanced behind him to see a stranger dressed all fancy-like looking out at the bleak sky. His narrow face was set in tight lines. What was a man like this doing in Williams?

"You new in town?" Matt asked.

"I arrived recently, yes," he answered, his pointed chin held at a haughty angle.

"Will you be staying awhile?"

"Not long. Will you excuse me?" He sauntered into the mercantile.

Matt frowned after the retreating figure. Something about the man rubbed him wrong, but he pushed the feeling aside in favor of beating the storm to see his future bride. From the size of the gunmetal gray clouds charging down from the north, he needed to get a move on.

Matt started walking. He'd intended to be here much earlier, but a bunch of Cole's cows had gotten themselves mired in a mud hole of spring runoff. Pulling them out took most of the morning. Cole, expecting another kind of trouble, insisted Cordoba and Reynolds ride with Matt, fully armed. A cottontail rabbit sitting in the road and several mule deer scampering into the pines were the only surprises they met. Matt hoped his brother was wrong about the threat against them, but he knew better than to ignore Cole's instincts.

He stepped onto the boardwalk in front of the Harvey House. He hadn't expected to fall in love for a lot of years yet, but day and night, Rae filled his thoughts. Eager to see her before the dinner train pulled in, he'd given Cordoba his horse to take care of while he shopped for a ring and donned his suit.

Now, entering the lunchroom, Matt found Rae absorbed in polishing a silver tray behind the counter. Slowly approaching her, savoring the sight of her big blue eyes, he noticed worry etched in her usually cheerful features.

"Hello, Sunshine," he said softly.

She looked up and dropped her polishing cloth. "Matt!" A huge smile broke across her face, and he thought he recognized relief in it. Her gaze moved over him. "You're all right."

"Of course, why wouldn't I be?"

Her smile disappeared. "Because of the train robber."

"Whoa," he said, raising his hand. "What are you talking about?"

"Didn't you see Jennie? Didn't she tell you?" Worry crept back into her face just as a clap of thunder shook the building.

"Rae, start over. Isn't Jennie here?"

"No. Not an hour ago she saw one of the train robbers right outside. She went to warn you and Cole. Are you sure you didn't see her?"

Reaching across the counter, Matt took Rae's cold hands in his. "Jennie rode to the ranch?" When Rae nodded, he asked, "When did she go?"

"Forty-five minutes ago. Maybe a little longer."

"I was already in town then." He released her hands and strode to the window. Rain began pelting the dry earth. The storm would get worse before it got better. "Does she know how to ride?"

"Yes. She's a good rider."

"Then she should be okay. The storm is coming out of the north, so it won't hit the ranch for a little while yet. If Jennie's not there already, she will be soon. She'll be fine." He hoped he was right.

Rae came around the counter to stand beside him at the window. "Can you go after her, Matt?"

A bolt of lightning split the darkening sky.

"I'm sorry, Rae. Not in this." He took her hands again, squeezed them. "I will run over to the livery, though. Make sure she got a good start."

"There's something else." Biting her lip, she glanced outside. "A different kind of danger. Oh, Matt, the man Jennie ran away from came here last night. He insists she marry him." Rae told him the story, then cocked her head to one side. "You don't look very surprised."

"Cole figured she was running from something. You know he's been trying to puzzle it out ever since we all met."

"He knows the whole story now. Jennie told him the night of the dance. Oh, Matt, I'm so frightened for her. What if Easton saw her leave here? He might've gone after her."

"Is he a snooty-looking fellow, small eyes, big accent?"

She stared at him. "How did you know?"

"I just saw him over at the hotel. If he saw Jennie, he didn't go after her."

Rae put a hand to her heart. "Oh, thank goodness."

"Now tell me more about this train robber she saw."

"When she recognized him, she was afraid he must be here to hurt you or Cole. She wanted to tell the sheriff, but he and his deputy are in Flagstaff until tomorrow."

"Well, I wouldn't worry too much. The man will hole up till the storm is over."

"Are you sure?"

Matt wasn't sure about anything, except that Jennie had been right to question the outlaw's motive for being in Williams. "Just in case, I'll tell the hands who came in with me. Do you know what the robber looks like?"

"Evan, the busboy, was with Jennie when she saw him. He mostly noticed a sheepskin coat and red scarf. Said the fellow was young."

"Good enough. Now I'd better get on over to the livery and ask about Jennie." But he didn't go, not yet. Matt rummaged through his coat pocket. "Rae, I need to ask you a question first."

"What? Do you need something?"

"Yes, very much." He lifted her hand and placed the shiny gold ring in her palm. "I need *you*. Will you marry me?"

She gasped, her blue eyes shining bright in the storm's dim light. "Oh, Matt. Oh, yes. I love you so much." One tear and then another slid down her cheek.

He kissed her full on the lips, tasted the happiness of her tears and cherished them. Reluctantly he set her away from him. "I'll be back soon. I love you, too, Sunshine."

Dressed in a dark slicker and wearing one glove, Cole peered at the makeshift shelter through the light rain spitting out of the clouds. His horses were a hardy bunch, but he wished they had the protection of a barn.

Since the fire, his men had cleared away the charred timbers. Now, blackened ground was all that remained of the destruction someone had inflicted on him.

"Lucas, you and the men get on inside," he said, checking the latch. "This sky's going to open up any minute. There's nothing more to be done out here." Thunder growled in the distance. Cole looked forward to an evening of quiet reading in front of his fireplace.

"Gotcha, Cole," Lucas said. "Come on, boys."

The men filed into the bunkhouse, and Cole started toward the main house. The unexpected sound of approaching hoofbeats stopped him, had him fumbling left-handed for the gun holstered under his slicker. He swore at his ineptitude.

Cole forgot his frustration when he recognized Jennie atop the horse. Her black skirt clung wetly to her legs. The hood of her cloak hung down her back, and a good quarter of her hair had escaped its pins. "Jennie! What the—"

"Cole, I had to come," she said quickly.

The fear he heard in her voice unnerved him. His gut tightened like a vise. "Is it Matt? Is he hurt? Did somebody get to him?"

"What?" Creases appeared between her brows. "Isn't he here?"

"He went to town with two of my men." Cole took hold of the rawhide bridle.

"I never saw them," she said.

He refused to jump to conclusions, fought to think clearly. If Matt, Reynolds and Cordoba had been ambushed, their horses would've come home, and Jennie would have seen their bodies in the road. He sucked in a complete breath, the first since Jennie's arrival. So, if nothing had happened to Matt, what the hell was she doing here?

Gingerly and stiffly, she dismounted. Cole held the horse still, wishing he had a right hand to help Jennie down. When she turned toward him, he noticed her flushed cheeks. Rainwater dripped off her face and hair. She looked more beautiful than ever, alluring, desirable. And cold. She was shivering.

The rain started down in earnest.

"Jennie, you need to get inside. Go on into the house. I'll get one of my men to take care of the horse."

"No, I have to tell you something." She winced with the step she took toward him.

"It can wait. This horse cannot. We'll talk in the house where it's warm and dry."

"But—"

"No buts. Go on." He saw the frustration on her face. Ignoring it, he led the horse toward the bunkhouse.

Cole glanced back once. Despite Jennie's bedraggled appearance, or perhaps because of it, his body was already humming. So much for the quiet evening he'd planned. It was going to be a long night.

Jennie trudged toward a handsome, well-kept, two-story white clapboard house, but she was too cold, wet, tired and relieved to admire it now. The energy that had sustained her during the ride ebbed, flowing out like the tide. She was too tired even to mind Cole's refusal to listen to her. He was safe now, and

Matt was in town with two other men to watch over him. He would certainly go to Rae, who would tell him everything.

Jennie mounted the short staircase, exhaustion making her feet feel like anchors. A painted white bench on the wide porch beckoned to her. Just as she began to lower herself onto it, a gloved hand gripped her arm, pulling her back up.

"Not out here," Cole said. "You'll freeze. Come inside."

She let him pull her along, let herself rely on him and his strength. This was the man she loved.

He let go of her arm to open the door, then pushed her inside the front entry. After kicking the door shut, he removed his slicker, hung it on a hook and did the same with her cloak. When his gaze took in her saturated clothing, he cleared his throat roughly.

"You're soaked through." He pulled his glove off with his teeth, dropped it onto the bench and took her hand. "My God, your hand is near frozen. Why didn't you wear gloves?"

Jennie shrugged as he drew her into a cozy and masculine parlor decorated with earthen colors. She struggled to keep her teeth from chattering. "I didn't think about it."

"You didn't think to wear your coat when you came after me outside the Opera House, either."

She peered up at him. "I had you to keep me warm then."

His gaze locked with hers. "So you did."

Jennie felt a warmth start deep inside her. Her shivering began to abate, and her reason for coming here surged back to mind. "Cole, this afternoon I saw one of the train robbers."

His eyes went cold. He didn't move.

"Did you hear me? I recognized one of the train robbers. He was in Williams."

Cole strode to the beautifully worked stone fireplace, threw on another log and viciously stoked the fire until it roared. "Stand over here. I'll go get you something dry to put on. Then you're going to tell me everything."

Jennie shuffled closer to the fire. Its glorious heat stole through her, but it didn't remove the chill Cole's reaction had put into her.

He returned quickly, holding out a black flannel shirt and lightweight woven blanket. "Wrap the blanket around your waist like a skirt."

She took them. "Thank you. Where can I change?"

"Here." He turned his back.

"What are you doing?"

"Waiting. Get your wet clothes off so I can take them."

She heard the harsh impatience in his voice, but it didn't frighten her. "I'm not going to undress with you in the room."

He glanced back at her, his gaze hard. "You took your petticoat off in front of me."

"That was entirely different. A medical emergency. Besides, I thought you were unconscious at the time."

"If you come down with pneumonia and I have to strip your clothes off, will that count as a medical emergency?"

A heat even hotter than the fire suffused Jennie's body. Her fatigue retreated. The thought of Cole removing her clothes became a vivid picture, disturbing and exciting. She fought it, lifting her chin. "Go away."

"Fine. Call me when you're decent."

He disappeared down a hallway, but Jennie heard him grumbling all the way. Something about females and trouble and the house probably burning down.

She quickly removed her sodden garments—shirt-waist, skirt and petticoat—and dropped them onto the stone hearth. Jennie debated about leaving on her underclothes for the sake of modesty, but they were wet through, and good sense prevailed. She removed her corset, camisole and drawers, adding them to the pile. Her mother would have been scandalized, but Mother wasn't soaked to the skin in the Arizona Territory.

Jennie buttoned Cole's soft shirt and inhaled the clean scent of soap and man that still pervaded it. She liked its smell and feel. Her hands traced the long line of fabric. The shirttail dropped well below her hips. She smiled and rolled up the overly long sleeves. The blanket came next. It reached around her waist two times before she tucked it in place.

"Are you finished yet?" Cole shouted from another room.

"Yes!" Jennie eyed the sopping heap of clothing on the hearth.

He arrived seconds later and lit the lamp beside an overstuffed leather chair. "Sit down." He pointed to the matching sofa. "And start talking."

"What about my clothes?"

"I'll hang them up later. Now tell me exactly what's going on."

Jennie dropped onto the sofa. "I came to warn you about the train robber. I saw him outside the Harvey

House, walking east along the tracks. I don't know where he went, but I recognized him.''

"How can you be sure?"

"During the robbery, I saw him sitting on a horse and holding a rifle. He wore a sheepskin coat and a red scarf. Before the attack on the express car, the scarf fell down. I saw his face very clearly."

"And you didn't tell anyone?" His voice held a sharp edge, and he raked his hand through his hair. "Didn't you think the sheriff might have been able to use that information?"

"I don't like your tone, Cole Bryant."

"I don't care. Why didn't you tell anyone, Jennie? It might've made a difference to my barn."

"I'm sorry," she said, hearing her voice rising, "but I completely forgot until I saw him again. I had other things on my mind, like saving your life, working for a living and wondering if James Easton would find me."

Cole paced the floor and stopped beside the fireplace. Flames crackled in the grate. "Okay, I'm sorry, too. I just want to get this guy. And whoever is paying him."

"Apology accepted." She clasped her hands in her lap. "You still have no idea who that might be?"

"No, but it has to be someone from my detective days. Nothing else makes sense." He thumped his fist on the mantel. "I hate not knowing who to watch out for. And if that person will go after my brother again."

"Rae will tell Matt about the train robber. He'll know to be careful."

"He already knows. I haven't let him forget it."

"When you do find the robber, will you...kill him?"

Cole stared into the fire. "I've never killed because I wanted to. Although, in this case, I'm sorely tempted. That outlaw may have been acting on orders, but he was one of the men who took my hand, would've killed my brother if I hadn't interfered." He turned around. "But if I can take him alive, I will. And he'll get to the sheriff for a proper trial."

"Of course." She gave him a small, knowing smile.

"What are you smiling at?"

"You're a lawman with high ideals. You wouldn't kill for the sake of vengeance."

"Don't be so sure. If the man had gotten into my sights that first week after my injury, I *would've* shot him. No questions asked."

She shrugged, still smiling. "Maybe."

"If you want to believe in me, that's fine, but don't expect it to go anywhere, because I won't let it."

Jennie kept smiling. Finally she said, "Can something be done about my clothing now?"

He sighed. "Yeah." To her astonishment, he went straight to the pile and crouched down. "I put some coffee on in the kitchen. I'll spread these over the line I've got rigged up in there for days like this." He gathered the wet clothing with his good arm and dropped the other one on top to brace it all.

"Wait." Jennie hopped off the sofa and placed a restraining hand on his shoulder.

Cole twisted his head and stared up at her. "What?"

She glanced at her unmentionables directly under his injured arm. "I'll help you."

He scowled at her. "I may be a cripple," he said flatly, standing up and towering over her, "but I'm capable of spreading clothes on a line."

"No, you don't understand. I know you can do anything you want. I was just...well, embarrassed. No man has ever touched my, uh, clothes."

His gaze went to the drawers under his arm. "Oh, I see. I guess I'm still a little touchy about...you know."

"You're entitled, but not with me." Jennie smiled, wanted him to know she would never see him as less than the man she met beside the train.

Cole smiled back.

Jennie's eyes widened with shock. "Cole, you're smiling!"

He shrugged. "What of it?"

"I've never seen you smile. I wasn't sure it was possible."

"Anything's possible, Jennie."

"I guess so," she said, hardly able to believe her eyes. Even before his arm was injured, she hadn't seen him smile. Jennie decided it was probably a good thing, because she might have fallen in love with him right then and there if he had. "Why, you even have dimples."

His smile disappeared. "I think that's enough on that subject."

"I'm sorry. You took me by surprise is all. I won't mention it again. But I wouldn't mind seeing it again." And again and again. She longed to touch his mouth with her fingertips.

He stared down at her and, though he stepped back, Cole didn't turn away. His gaze traveled slowly over her. "My shirt's a little big on you, isn't it?"

His intent gaze banished all thought of smiles. "It's fine." With each rise and fall of her chest, the soft flannel of his shirt brushed her suddenly sensitive breasts.

Unsure of herself, Jennie turned away. She stared into the fire's crackling flames, tried to think of something other than the sensations Cole's gaze occasioned in her body. Sensations she'd never known before, but wanted to explore.

Chapter Eighteen

After spreading Jennie's wet clothes on the line in the kitchen, where the cast-iron stove kept the room warm, Cole returned to the parlor. He carried a small wooden cutting board with two cups of steaming coffee on it.

At the room's threshold, with his mind no longer distracted by her mention of the train robber, he nearly stumbled at the sight of Jennie sitting forward on the sofa, peering into the fire while fanning her hair over her shoulders to dry. The red curls weighted his shirt against her breasts. Her nipples pushed against the soft flannel. Cole's already knotted stomach felt as if it were being braided into a set of rawhide reins. A whole night with Jennie stretched endlessly in front of him. How was he going to keep his distance, when all he wanted to do was close it?

"Oh, I didn't hear you come in." She lowered her hands to her lap.

He approached, holding out the makeshift tray to her. "The coffee's hot."

"Thank you." She lifted a cup, cradled it in both hands. "It smells good."

His gaze once again focused on her curls. "I've never seen your hair down before. It's…nice." Tempting. He wanted to touch it, let those curls twine around his fingers.

Realizing where his thoughts were headed, Cole twisted away. His own cup almost slid off the board, which he quickly set on the table next to his favorite chair. He dropped onto the leather and stared at the woven rug beneath Jennie's feet. Bare feet. He lifted his gaze to her ankles, then higher.

She put her coffee aside, brought her feet up and tucked them beneath her. "Are my clothes all right?" She avoided his eyes.

"They'll be dry come morning."

"But I didn't plan to stay the night." She looked everywhere except at him. "I can't stay the night."

Cole glanced out the window, saw the rain pummeling the land in the last light of day. "You don't have a choice."

She bit her lower lip. "We won't be alone in the house, will we?"

"'Fraid so. Are you worried about the propriety of it?"

She finally faced him, and for once, Cole wasn't sure what he saw in her eyes, unless it was her own uncertainty. "My parents would be, but I'm not. This isn't Boston. Society isn't looking over my shoulder."

"It's worse here. Williams is a small town. Everyone will talk. I'll sleep in the bunkhouse," he offered, though he didn't relish the thought of bedding down with his men. And he downright wouldn't remove his shirt in front of them.

"No, no," she said quickly. "I'd rather you stay here."

"That's good, 'cause I'd rather stay here, too." He smiled again.

Jennie dropped her feet from the sofa to the floor. After her exhausting ride, she was starving. She also wanted to keep busy rather than sit with Cole so temptingly close. "Are you hungry, Cole?"

He didn't answer, seemed to be looking at her without seeing her. Either that or he was seeing too much. Jennie licked her lips, remembered the intensity of his gaze outside the Opera House. She also remembered the smell of his masculine, outdoor scent, the sensuous taste of his lips and mouth, and the feel of his tongue dancing with hers.

She watched him now, so tall and broad in his chair, his chest rapidly rising and falling. Long black hair shone in the light of the lamp beside him. Jennie wanted him to hold her again, wanted to feel his strength around her, the beat of his heart against hers. And she wanted to show him her love.

An unfamiliar excitement built inside her. Perhaps it was the impropriety of their situation, or perhaps it came from courting danger. How would Cole react if she tried to kiss him? He'd pushed her away once. Did she dare risk his rejection again?

Undecided, Jennie pushed her thoughts aside. "Cole?" She leaned forward. "Cole!"

His gaze focused. "What? What is it?"

"I'm famished. I asked if you're hungry?"

His stomach chose that moment to rumble. "I guess you have your answer." He smiled.

The sight of that smile brought Jennie's suggestive thoughts rushing back. "May I help in the kitchen?"

"Do you know how to cook?"

"No. But I'm very good at serving."

This time he laughed. Jennie reveled in the deep, wonderful sound, couldn't get enough of it. She wanted more. Of it, of his smile, and of him.

He stood, put out his hand. She didn't hesitate to take it, and he pulled her to her feet. The texture of his work-roughened hand around hers made her sigh inwardly with pleasure. But he let go too soon, and she retained only a fleeting impression of the warmth of his palm.

She followed him past an intriguing book-lined study. Entering the kitchen, Jennie saw her clothes and unmentionables strung across one end. The heat of embarrassment crept into her face, but Cole didn't seem to notice, or even look at her clothes in the light of the lamps.

"How does a quick beef stew sound to you?" he asked, dropping freshly washed carrots and potatoes onto a cutting board big enough for two people to use. Next, he brought out a slab of red beef an inch thick and put a clean iron skillet on the stove.

"It sounds delicious. What can I do to help?"

"Are you as good with a knife as you are with a needle?" He handed her a large kitchen knife.

"Almost."

"Good enough." He took up another knife. "I can cut raw meat without a problem, but carrots and potatoes tend to roll around on me."

Jennie smiled and arranged a carrot on the board. "I suppose they would, wouldn't they? How impertinent of them!"

He smiled back. "Chop them up small so they'll cook faster."

"Coming right up." Several times, Jennie glanced over at Cole, who diligently cubed the beef. He stood beside her, so close she could touch him. But she didn't. Jennie liked working alongside him, didn't want to risk breaking their companionable atmosphere.

"Cole," she asked, her knife poised over the last carrot, "what kinds of books do you have in your library?"

"Mostly practical stuff. Police work, politics, ranching, agriculture. My mother worked hard to instill in Matt and me the importance of an education and book learning. While I worked for Wells Fargo, there was plenty of time to read between destinations."

"I miss reading. My father has a wonderful library at home, but here, the Harvey House has nothing. Besides, there's little time for reading." She started peeling the potatoes.

"You're welcome to borrow whatever you like. I have some books on world history and even a few of Shakespeare's classics." His knife paused as he peered down at her. "'Holy, fair, and wise is she; The heaven such grace did lend her, That she might admired be.'"

Jennie opened her mouth in surprise. "That was beautiful," she whispered. "I had no idea you were so well-read."

Abruptly he returned to cutting the meat. "It was only a couple of lines from a play. They don't mean anything. That's all I remember anyhow."

Jennie didn't believe him.

He scooped a dollop of lard and dropped it in the heated skillet. While it was melting, he floured the beef. Using his knife, Cole lifted a line of meat pieces and tossed them into the pan where they sizzled and spat.

"Your mother is to be admired," Jennie said. "She's right that an education is important, but I also think firsthand experience is extremely valuable. I learned more from working in the dispensary with Dr. Nicholson than I ever did from his medical textbooks. More about medicine and about people."

"I'm grateful for that." He stirred the meat with a wooden spoon. "Did you by chance get that horse from the livery?"

"Are you changing the subject?"

"Not exactly. You made me think about a young friend of mine who works with horses."

"A precocious boy named Joey?"

"You met him, huh?" At her nod, Cole added, "Joey likes you, you know. He's seen you around and knows you fixed up my arm."

Feeling strangely flattered, she finished cutting up the potatoes and laid down the knife. "I guess that explains why he blushed and how he knew my name. I didn't take the time to ask him."

"He's a good kid." Cole picked up the pile of carrots, added them to the skillet, then did the same with the potatoes. "Smart, too. He wants to know all the gory details of my injury. I told him you'd probably be happy to tell him everything."

Jennie laughed. "You know I would. Do you think he'd like to be a doctor someday?"

"I think I won't venture a guess, but he's got the

brains, curiosity and stomach for it.'' He stirred the mixture on the stove.

''I'm amazed he was able to put my name with my face. I don't recall ever seeing him.''

''Joey sees a lot of what goes on in town. He also understands folks better than most.'' Cole tipped his head. ''You know, when we go into Williams tomorrow, I think I'll have a talk with him. If that train robber was walking around town to meet up with whoever's behind my troubles, Joey might've seen or heard something.''

Jennie watched Cole add water and spices to the pan. He continued to surprise her with his talents. ''You're very adept in the kitchen. I'm impressed. My father would be at a total loss.''

''It's what you're used to. Has he ever had to cook for himself or anyone else?''

''No. Never.'' She laughed, trying to imagine her father stirring a pan of bubbling, fragrant stew. ''I doubt he's ever been in our kitchen.''

Cole squinted at her. ''You sound like you're missing him. At the dance, you were still angry with him. Has something changed?''

She wiped her hands on a linen towel. ''The man who thought he recognized me finally remembered my name. I assume he told my parents, because they sent me a telegram. They understand now why I ran and are worried about me.''

''Worried about your being out West?''

''No.'' She twisted the dish towel. ''They're worried that James Easton might…cause me trouble. He's here now.''

Cole dropped the spoon onto the pan and stepped back. ''When? When did he arrive, Jennie?''

"Last night."

Through a clenched jaw, he said, "I told you to send for me if he came."

"It all happened so fast, and there was no need," she said, though she liked the protected feeling Cole gave her. "Everyone I work with came to my aid."

"What exactly happened, Jennie?"

She told him how Easton grabbed her and about Chef, Miss Thompson and everyone else helping her. "I haven't seen James since last night, but he's still in town."

"And probably planning something." Cole's gaze bored into her. "You took a huge risk riding out here today. What if he'd seen you?"

Hearing her own fears voiced, her shrug wasn't as nonchalant as she wished. "I was very careful."

He shook his head. "You worry me, Jennie Andrews. Will you ever be able to stay out of trouble?"

Since finishing supper almost two hours ago, Cole had stared at the words in a thick, leather-bound volume. Jennie sat on the sofa across from him, reading her own selection from his bookshelves. Thunder rumbled outside while a log shifted in the fireplace with a shower of sparks. Periodically Cole turned pages, but none of the words penetrated beyond his eyes.

One troublesome redhead was distracting him. Despite her wet ride and change of clothes, the fragrant scent of roses still clung to her. Cole inhaled deeply, and felt a hunger that had nothing to do with his stomach.

He cleared his throat and turned a page, struggling to think safer thoughts. Jennie had ridden all the way out here, disregarding her own safety to warn him of danger. He'd never known a woman like her. How was he going to get through this night without touching her the way he wanted to? All over.

"Is something wrong, Cole?" She covered her mouth against a yawn.

When her expressive green eyes invited him closer, Cole cleared his throat again. "No, nothing's wrong, but I do have something on my mind." More than he could say.

"What is it?"

"Jennie, did you get permission from Miss Thompson to leave the Harvey House?"

She avoided his gaze.

"Jennie?" he said, her name drawn out.

"There wasn't enough time. I had to leave right away."

"You didn't ask, because your supervisor would have said no. And rightly so."

She shrugged. "We'll never know for sure, will we?"

"Jennie, you've risked your job on my account. You shouldn't have done that."

She stiffened, and her tempting mouth became a thin line. "Your life and Matt's are more important than any job."

How did she manage to exasperate him at the same time that she charmed and tempted him? "I'm just worried about what will happen to you, Jennie."

Her body slowly relaxed back into the sofa. "Oh, well, you don't have to worry. Even if I lose my job, I won't be penniless. Now that my parents are on my side again, I can return to Boston. I have money there."

Cole stared at her. Return to Boston? He felt his heart execute an odd little twist. "You want to leave?"

"I didn't say that, but it's an option." Her mouth opened to another yawn.

"I suppose you'll stay for Matt and Rae's wedding, won't you?" he asked.

"What wedding?"

"Matt went into town to propose. I doubt they'll wait too long for the big day. Rae wouldn't refuse him, would she?" At the brilliant smile spreading across Jennie's face, setting it aglow, Cole swallowed hard.

"Refuse Matt?" She laughed. "Not a chance. Rae loves him with all her heart."

"Good, 'cause I'm not sure how Matt would react if she didn't."

"I know they'll be very happy. Has Matt said where he wants them to live?"

"Not to me, but they're more than welcome to stay here. I built this house for a big family, although I'd hoped it would be mine."

Her smile dimmed, and she looked away. "Someday it will be, Cole." Lightning flashed, brightening the room for an instant. "You'll find what you're looking for."

"I hope so," he said, not sure what he wanted anymore. Unless it was Jennie Andrews in his bed tonight, which was the last thing that could, or should, happen.

Chapter Nineteen

As Jennie stared out the window from her seat, she thought about returning to her life in Boston, to a life without Cole. The notion brought a desolate feeling to her heart.

The clock struck nine, and she peered over at Cole, whose long legs were stretched out over the woven rug, his boots crossed at the ankles. Her gaze followed the line of his body up to his face. She wanted to touch his shadowed jaw, tell him how much she loved him. But he wouldn't want to hear those words, so she said nothing. Only dreamed of how much she wanted to be with him, close to him, intimate with him.

"You've had a long day," he said. "You ought to get to bed."

She nodded. "I think you're right."

"I'll show you up." He stood, but didn't reach for her hand the way he had earlier.

Jennie missed his touch, wondered what had changed. She followed him out of the room. Though exhausted and sore from her ride, she didn't want to say good-night to him. Tonight might be her last chance to be alone with him.

At the bottom of the stairs leading to the darkened second floor, he stopped. "Wait. I'll get the lamp from the parlor." He returned within seconds, the glow lighting his handsome face.

At the top of the stairs, he stopped at the first open door, placed the lamp on a table just inside and motioned with his hand. "This is my room, in case you need me for anything."

He stood so close as she peered inside that Jennie felt his warm breath on her cheeks. Her pulse skipped a beat at the sight of the neatly made bed big enough for two people. She turned slightly and faced him. He gazed back, and the seconds stretched into timelessness.

Jennie breathed shallowly. With hope. With apprehension. She desperately wanted to show him her love, even if it was the only night she would ever have with him. She reached up and touched his jaw, felt the roughness of a day's growth of beard. Then she stepped closer, placed her other hand over his heart.

"Jennie," he said gruffly, "I'm only a man."

"That's all I want you to be." A man who wanted her, all of her. She raised onto her tiptoes and pressed a kiss to his rigid throat. "Cole, I want to stay with you tonight." Forever.

He groaned, then gathered her hard against him, against his warmth and strength. His mouth covered hers, his tongue tangling with hers. The world spun around her. All Jennie saw was Cole. All she heard was the rapid mingling of their breaths.

When they finally parted, his fingers traveled down

the buttons of the shirt she wore, unfastening them. A shiver of excitement shook her body, and she unbuttoned the shirt he wore, trailed her fingertips over the curling black hairs on his chest.

He moaned. "Jennie, I don't want to stop, but are you sure about this?"

"Very sure," she whispered, slipping the black flannel shirt from her shoulders. It puddled around the hem of her makeshift skirt.

He sighed. "You are so beautiful. I wish I could sweep you up in my arms and carry you to my bed. I'm tempted to try."

His sentiment touched her. "I don't mind walking, as long as you come with me."

He took her hand, brought it to his lips and kissed it so lightly it felt as though an autumn leaf were floating across it. "Do you mind if I make a stop along the way?" he asked.

"That depends on where."

"The bootjack." He smiled. "Unless you want a man who sleeps with his boots on?"

She smiled back. "Cole Bryant, tonight, I want nothing but you."

He yanked off his shirt and tore out of his boots and socks. Jennie stood beside the bed as he approached her. His fingers released the first two buttons of his faded brown Levi's, then paused above a distinct bulge. Her mouth went dry.

"I want you, Jennie Andrews." His lips came down over hers while his hand moved to the thin blanket encircling her hips. She felt his fingers release the last vestige of her modesty. Then he pulled her naked body against him.

"Oh, Cole," she breathed into his hot mouth. Her senses overflowed.

He kissed her more thoroughly, and she would have willingly drowned in that kiss. He broke away to help her onto the high bed. When she lay back, his gaze traveled over every inch of her, but she felt no shyness, only a curiosity about him and what would happen between them. In the yellow glow of the oil lamp, Jennie wanted to see him as he was seeing her.

He seemed to read her mind, because his fingers returned to unfasten the buttons below his waist. Cole slipped his pants off and stood beside the bed. Jennie let out a wondrous breath. His body was glorious, lean and powerful and aroused. She held out her arms to him.

The bed creaked under his weight. He lowered his head beside hers, and his lips nuzzled the hollow beneath her jaw. Contentment and a growing pleasure swelled within her. He nipped at a spot she'd never known was so sensitive. "Wh-what are you doing?"

His lips came up to her temple, his breath warm and sweet against her face. "What does it feel like I'm doing?"

"I—I'm not sure."

Cole kissed the corner of one eye. "Do you like it?"

"Oh, yes." Another sigh escaped her lips. "But I don't think I'm supposed to."

He laughed deeply, the sound resonating through her. "I think you'll like what I do next, too."

His hand moved to her breast, and his fingers circled the hardening nipple, massaged it until she arched upward and whimpered with the sensations he summoned from her.

Her body quivered beneath his touch. She'd never felt so alive. He smiled at her, and her breath caught at the raw hunger in his darkening eyes. With his weight to one side, he leaned down, opening his mouth over her breast.

His tongue roved over her nipple, sucked at her until Jennie gasped with pleasure and dug her fingers into the muscles of his back. She felt his body shaking, and a moment later, on their sides, he lifted her leg over his and pulled her so close she felt his arousal pressing intimately against her.

Her body tightened, reacting to his, then she opened herself to him, wanting him inside her. Tonight, they belonged to each other.

Cole woke up with Jennie burrowed against his chest. He smiled at the long, red curl dangling over her lashes. He brushed it back behind her ear, then leaned over and lightly kissed her soft cheek. She didn't stir. Her breathing remained even and untroubled.

As he watched her, his smile faded. He had never felt *more* troubled. Cole closed his eyes against the sight of her trusting form and the cheery midmorning sunlight streaming into the bedroom. All signs of the storm had been swept away while they slept. Now a storm raged inside of him.

Over the past five weeks, this passionate woman had done so much for him, and last night, she'd willingly welcomed him into her body. No woman had ever made him feel so good, not even before his injury. She'd said nothing about loving him, but he'd seen it in her eyes, and he'd taken advantage of it when he should have shown her to the guest room and walked away.

Cole rolled onto his back, sat up and swung his legs over the edge of the bed that creaked beneath him. He raked his hand through his hair. She shouldn't have stayed with him. Jennie deserved the kind of man she wanted, a man who could love her. Now she would never have that.

When the sheets rustled behind him, he glanced around.

"Good morning, Cole," she said, a secret, satisfied smile on her beautiful face. She stretched languorously, the sheet and wool blanket slipping down to reveal one creamy breast tipped in rose.

Cole stifled a moan. He wanted her again.

He jumped up, grabbed his pants and yanked them on as best he could. To keep him in line, he fastened several of the buttons. When he turned back to her, she'd pulled the blanket up to her neck and confusion furrowed her brow. "What's wrong?"

"Everything. Jennie, you've risked a great deal. Not only by coming here, but by sleeping with me. I never should've let it happen."

"It was my choice, too," she said, "and I don't regret a minute of it."

"You should," he said, aware that he didn't regret any of it either, only the consequences. "Jennie, I know you want to marry for love, marry a man who loves you, but it's not possible now. You see that, don't you?"

"What are you talking about?"

"You'll have to marry me," he said somberly. "I've rui—" He didn't finish, looked away. "It's the only thing we can do."

"You meant to say you've ruined me."

His gaze met hers straight on. "Yes."

"So out of guilt and obligation and honor, you're offering to marry me."

"Is that so terrible?" He shoved his hand into his pocket. "You do love me, Jennie."

Her eyes widened. "I never said that!"

"You don't have to. I can see it in your face. And last night, you never would have…slept with me if you didn't love me."

Her gaze darted away from him. "You're wrong. I did what I did in case James Easton somehow has his way with me. I didn't want him to be the first."

Her effort to disguise the truth amused him. "Jennie, I know you love me just as I know you're lying to me now. You can't hide your feelings from me."

Her chin rose. "All right, maybe I do love you."

"Maybe?"

She brought her heel down hard on the mattress. "Fine! I love you! But that doesn't change how you feel about me or the kind of marriage you want." She yanked at the sheet. "Cole, if you want to hear the truth, I'll tell it to you. You're afraid to love a woman. Afraid to let a woman's love into your life because you're also afraid of losing it."

He said nothing. Was Jennie right? Was it fear that kept his heart closed to love? To her?

"I realize," she went on, "that your feelings are due to your difficult childhood, your mother's broken heart. I can't imagine what you suffered as a boy. I wish I could help you, but I won't surrender my own convictions about marriage. I will *not* marry you, Cole."

He should have felt relief at her refusal, but instead,

he only felt empty inside, as if he were missing something he needed. Cole fought against the hollowness. What did it matter if Jennie never stayed at the ranch again? Never welcomed him into her body again? And never let him hold her again?

He forced himself to think logically. "Jennie, what if you and I made a child last night?"

Abruptly she brought a hand to her stomach. The fight seemed to go out of her. But a moment later, she squared her shoulders. "If there is a child, I'll be quite capable of raising it myself back in Boston. You'll have nothing to worry about."

Cole stomped over to the bureau, grabbed a fresh shirt from a drawer and slammed it shut. The woman had an answer for everything. "I think you could manage without me. But it wouldn't be right. I want *my* children raised on the C Bar M."

"You won't have that choice. Whatever happens is now my responsibility. I will leave Williams, Cole. And you'll have nothing to say about it."

He ground his teeth. Stubborn, headstrong woman. Then he frowned over an impending sense of loss he didn't understand, was afraid to look at too closely. He didn't really want to marry this troublesome redhead, did he?

The road, dotted with mud puddles and broken pine boughs, stretched before her. Birds chirped in the pines and squirrels chattered back and forth before scampering up the tree trunks. The sun warmed the day, making yesterday's cold seem like a distant dream. Jennie wished she could enjoy the day, but the lighthearted sounds mocked her misery.

Wearing her own clothing and Rae's cloak, she

rode Maggie beside Cole and his Appaloosa, but she wished she could gallop away from him and the two ranch hands who followed, men Cole said could be counted on in a fight. He expected trouble. He wore his gun over his left hip, and his gaze constantly swept the landscape. If trouble didn't find him, Jennie knew he would go in search of it. He wanted that train robber.

She worried about Cole even though she didn't want to, didn't want to think about him at all. He'd offered her marriage, but not for the right reasons, not the one reason that would have her instantly by his side in a church.

Jennie wondered how soon she could leave Williams, board the train that would take her away from the heartache she'd found out West. Soon Rae and Matt would marry, and she would be alone.

"Jennie, will you be all right if we go a little faster?" Cole asked.

"I think the faster the better." Then they could part company all the sooner, and she could give in to the tears she hated admitting wanted to fall.

"I just thought you might be sore after your long ride yesterday and the, uh—" he glanced back at his men, then lowered his voice "—you know, last night."

"I'm fine," she said, ignoring the pain from yesterday's ride; however, she couldn't ignore the memories his comment brought back. In his bed, he'd carried her to heaven and back. His fingers and mouth and body had heated her flesh until she thought she might die with pleasure and the longing for more. "How soon until we arrive?" She wanted to think of anything but the sensations he'd wrought in her.

"Another fifteen minutes if we kick the horses up into a lope."

"Why don't we gallop instead?"

One corner of his mouth turned up, and she spotted one of the dimples that had taken her so by surprise while they sat in his cozy parlor. "You in a hurry?"

"Yes. Rae will be worn out from the extra work my leaving caused her."

"Uh-huh," he said, as if he didn't entirely believe her. "That's a good reason, but I can't afford to tire the horses too much, especially if I have to go back out."

"Cole, why not just tell the sheriff what I saw and let him handle it?"

"We're going to tell the sheriff, but I'm not running away from my best chance at finding out who's behind the attempted murder of my brother," he said, his voice harsh.

Jennie squeezed Maggie's sides, signaling her into a lope. She didn't want to hear any more about Cole's hunt. Or the danger he'd be putting himself in.

Almost fifteen minutes later, just as Cole had said, they slowed their horses, bypassed the livery and stopped in front of the sheriff's office. The door was open, apparently to allow the spring day's warmth inside. A wagon clattered past and several of the townsfolk strode along the boardwalk.

The men dismounted and looped their reins around the hitching rail. Jennie moved more slowly, winced as she started to swing her leg over Maggie's back.

"I'll help you down." Cole stood below her, his hand reaching for her waist.

"I can manage, thank you," she said, her foot still

in the stirrup. With her back to him, she lowered herself to the ground. Her legs buckled.

He caught her against him, held her steady. Jennie felt herself wanting to run from him at the same time that she wanted him to hold her forever, whisper in her ear, "I love you, Jennie."

"You'll get your legs back in a minute," he said, shattering her daydream.

She shifted her weight from one foot to the other, testing her limbs. "I think they are already back. You can let go now, Cole."

But he didn't.

"Cole?"

"Uh, yeah." He stepped back.

"Thank you." Jennie turned, mourned the growing distance between them, but knew that unless he could love her, they had no future together.

He tied her horse to the rail. "After you tell the sheriff about that outlaw and what he looks like, I'll have Lucas walk you to the Harvey House. I'll return your horse to the livery when I go talk to Joey."

"I appreciate that. Please tell him I will come by later to pay him."

Cole leaned over her, pierced her with his gaze. "No, you won't. I'll pay him and you'll stay put at the Harvey House."

She braced her hands on her hips. "I rented the horse, so it's up to me to pay for her."

"Why do you have to be so contrary, Jennie? You rented the horse for my benefit, so I will take care of it."

"I am only trying to pay what I owe."

"Well, don't, because if you leave that Harvey

House, you'll be putting yourself in danger. And that's the last thing I want.''

"Why?" Jennie demanded, then held her breath, hoping against hope.

"Because you saved my life. Because I owe you.''

She exhaled her disappointment, berated herself for thinking he might say something else. "I'll do as I please," she said.

"Jennie, I'm sorry I can't give you what you want most, what you need, but I do care for you in my way. If you don't stay put, where I know you'll be safe and out of Easton's way, I'll worry about you when I should be concentrating on that train robber. After all the trouble you've gone to to help me, would you want me distracted when I most need to focus?"

Slowly Jennie shook her head. She didn't think she could bear it if something else happened to Cole, especially if she were responsible.

"Then promise me you'll stay at the Harvey House."

She took a step away. "Very well. I promise." After another step, she said, "Unless, of course, someone needs my help. Medical attention, perhaps."

He rolled his eyes. "Jennie, one of these days, you really will be the death of me."

Chapter Twenty

Cole led Jennie's horse along Bill Williams Avenue, scrutinizing the faces of the people he passed, some on horseback, some on wagons, others promenading on the boardwalk. Most averted their gazes, none of them matched the man Jennie described, the same man Cole remembered seeing before he heard the robbers talking.

At the livery, he yelled into the semidarkness of the stable. "Hey, Joey, you here somewhere?"

From inside a stall, a blond head popped up, the hair spiked and unruly. "Mr. Cole!" Joey leaned an old rake against slatted boards and skipped out. "You got Maggie there. I knew she'd get Miss Jennie to you okay."

"She did at that. Thanks for taking care of Jennie." Cole handed him the reins followed by several clinking coins. "Does that cover what's owed you?"

"Sure does." Joey dropped the money into the pocket of his baggy canvas pants, led the horse into a stall and quickly returned.

Cole reached out and mussed the boy's already

wild hair. "When are you going to get yourself a comb?"

The boy scuffed the toe of one boot in the dirt. "Ah, I got me one. Ma makes me use it every mornin', but my hair just don't take to it."

Cole laughed.

Joey stared up at him in disbelief.

"Something bothering you?" Cole asked, still smiling.

"I ain't never heard you laugh before. Or seen you smile."

Cole sighed. "I'm afraid it may be becoming a habit."

"And that's bad?"

"I don't know yet. I'll have to let you know." He leaned against a wood post.

"I think it's good." The boy looked out the big doors. "I bet Miss Jennie likes it, too. When she come here yesterday, I wanted to ask her 'bout your arm, but she were in a big hurry to see you."

"Yeah, she had something important to tell me. Maybe she'll talk to you another day." *If she stays in Williams long enough.* "Joey, I need to talk to you."

"About what?" One of the horses nickered, drawing Joey's attention for a moment.

"You're a smart boy, and you know a lot about what goes on in this town." Joey nodded as Cole spoke. "Have you noticed anyone acting kind of suspicious?"

"Like how?" Joey asked.

"People doing things they wouldn't normally do."

"Like you laughing?" he asked seriously.

Cole closed his mouth and ran his tongue over the

front of his teeth. "Yeah, like that, but more important." ·

Neat little creases appeared in Joey's forehead, and his light-colored brows knit together. "Well, last week when I was checkin' on the horses at night, I seen Mrs. Benson sneak up to the old shack over yonder." He gestured to the south. "Mr. Gray from the mercantile went up there, too. I got tired of waiting to see when they'd come out, so I went on home."

"That's real interesting, all right." Cole coughed to hide his amusement. "Anybody else doing odd things?"

He thought again. "The banker, Mr. Porter, went to the shack, too. But no lady met him. It was a man."

Ben Porter. The man who knew his account balance, who could have started the rumor about his finances. Cole straightened away from the post. "What did the man with Porter look like?"

"I couldn't see real good, but he was younger than Mr. Porter. And he acted kinda funny."

"Funny how?"

"He kept hunchin' into his sheepskin coat like he were freezin'."

Cole stiffened instantly. The leader of the train robbers had done the exact same thing. Between Jennie's information and Joey's, it had to be the same man. Could Porter be behind everything that had happened? Cole frowned. What had he ever done to Porter? "When was this, Joey?"

"Gosh. I don't know." He counted back on his fingers, touching each one, screwing up his face and starting over. Obviously mathematics was not Joey's strong suit. Then his eyes lit up. "I remember! It was just after we heard your barn burned."

A payoff for a job well done?

"And last night," Joey said, interrupting Cole's thoughts.

"Huh? What about last night?"

"I saw Mr. Porter last night, too."

"You sure it was him?" Cole asked, the back of his neck starting to itch. If Porter had met with the outlaw again, then something bad was bound to happen soon.

"Of course, I'm sure. He was twirlin' that gold watch like he always do. You know."

Cole had also noticed Porter often played with his pocket watch. If Joey didn't become a doctor, Cole decided he'd make a fine detective. "Was the other man there, too?"

"Not that I saw. But I had to get on home to bed. Ma doesn't like me checkin' on the horses too late." Joey shrugged. "Sorry."

"There's nothing to be sorry about. You've done good, Joey." Cole affectionately mussed his hair again, then reached into his pocket. "I've got to get going now. You keep your eyes open like always, okay?"

"Okay, Mr. Cole."

"If you see Mr. Porter do anything strange, or if you see the other man again, you come get me at the hotel or the Cabinet Saloon. If you can't find me, go for the sheriff. Got that?"

Joey nodded briskly.

"All right then." Cole pulled two coins from his pocket. "Here. These are for you. You've already been a big help to me." He dropped the coins into Joey's palm.

"Gee thanks, Mr. Cole! I'll sure keep watch for you."

Cole waved to the boy on his way out the broad doors, then he tried to think what to do next. He had no evidence to accuse Porter of attempted murder, not even a motive for it. And who would believe such an accusation? Benjamin Porter was the town's esteemed banker, guilty of nothing but foreclosing on luckless landowners.

Cole knew he needed more, something that would tie Porter to the train robbers. But what? Even if he watched Porter's every move, the man had already met with the outlaw. The back of Cole's neck itched worse. Was he too late?

Edmund Andrews relentlessly drummed his fingers on the armrest. The passenger coach rocked and swayed, carrying him toward Williams in the Arizona Territory. He'd been riding for days, praying for his daughter's safety, praying he wasn't too late to help her.

The train was hours behind schedule, making him more and more fidgety. It was supposed to have made its dinner stop at Williams, but they'd stopped at the Harvey House in Winslow, Arizona, instead. Edmund found it difficult to imagine his daughter in the black and white of a Harvey Girl uniform.

He pulled out his pocket watch, stared at it for the umpteenth time. He tried to calm himself, but instead, he glanced at the bag on the empty seat beside him. Inside lay his pistol. If he had to, Edmund knew he would use that pistol against James Easton III.

Exhaustion rounding her shoulders, Jennie watched Evan lock the door to the lunchroom for the night.

He disappeared inside the kitchen, where the noisy clatter of pots, pans and china being washed and dried preyed on Jennie's nerves and did nothing to take her mind off the pain hammering away at her heart.

She'd left Cole at the sheriff's office hours ago and let his foreman escort her to the Harvey House. Rae had greeted her with a hard hug; Miss Thompson had greeted her with a deep scowl and raked her over the coals.

"Look at the mud splattered on your uniform," she'd said. "You're a disgrace to the Harvey House tradition. You also scared the life out of me with your thoughtless stunt. How am I supposed to take care of my girls if they go traipsing around the country on horseback in the middle of a storm?"

Jennie didn't bother correcting her supervisor about the timing of the storm, but she did explain her reasons and apologized profusely for worrying her. Jennie hadn't lost her job, but she'd been given a stern warning and put on probation.

After cleaning herself up and changing into a spotless uniform, she'd scrubbed the counter and polished the silver with zeal. Her station had sparkled. Fred Harvey himself could've taken a white glove to it. Throughout the usual dinner rush, she had kept it just as clean, constantly swiping at the stray crumbs and drips of soup or milk or coffee.

Now little remained to occupy her. She couldn't even count on Miss Thompson to distract her; the woman had retired upstairs ten minutes ago. The girls from the dining room had also gone up, leaving the lamps in their section dark.

Jennie's thoughts strayed to the possibility that she

might be carrying Cole's baby. He wanted his children to grow up on the ranch, but Jennie's image of sharing a happy family life with him was only a dream.

She peered over at Rae. She'd congratulated her best friend on her engagement, but it had been difficult to muster the appropriate enthusiasm. Rae had asked her question after question about the C Bar M, her face shining with excitement. It shone even now, as if Rae held some wonderful secret in her heart. Jennie envied the love the girl shared with Matt.

"Are you finished, Jennie?" Rae extinguished a wall sconce.

"Yes." She placed her wiping cloth beneath the counter and came out to help with the rest of the lamps. When a man's face appeared at the window, Jennie absently called out, "We're closed until morning." The face disappeared.

Rae came up to her, eyes sparkling. "Oh, Jennie, I have to tell you."

As another pot clanked in the kitchen, Jennie took her friend's hands. "Why, you're trembling, Rae."

"I know. It's so exciting. Ever since you got back, I've been dying to tell you, but I couldn't risk anyone else hearing or guessing." She uttered a deep sigh. "I do wish you could've been with us, though."

"Rae, what is it? You're keeping me in terrible suspense."

More pots clanged as her friend began pulling a chain from inside the collar of her uniform. "Last night, Matt and I—"

The lunchroom door crashed open. Three men rushed in, one of them wearing a sheepskin coat and red scarf. Jennie's eyes widened in recognition. Before she could think to scream, a grimy hand covered her mouth. She watched in horror as another man clamped his hand over Rae's mouth and grabbed her around the waist.

A fourth man sauntered inside. "Good evening, Jennifer," James Easton III said with a gloating smile.

She swore at him, but the hand that smelled of dirt and spilled whiskey muffled her harsh words. Jennie fought against her captor, lifted her heel to smash his instep. But he moved at the last second and she slammed her foot against the hard floor, jarring her already aching body.

The man's gruff laugh made her struggle harder. She wanted to scream, bring the noisy kitchen staff running. "Little lady," the outlaw said, holding her tighter than any corset she'd ever worn, "we is going to have us some fun tonight."

Easton's smile turned feral, but it wasn't aimed at her. "That one's mine. You can have the blonde, if Miss Andrews here fails to do what she is told."

Jennie's heart stopped. Rae was in danger because of her.

"But I like 'em spicy," the man said. "I want this one."

The train robber stepped in. "Jack, you heard the man. We got us a plan, and we're gonna stick to it. The redhead belongs to him. Just bring her outside."

Jack grumbled but lifted her right off the floor and started toward the doorway. Jennie didn't know whether to feel relieved or not that James had prevailed, she only knew that Rae's virtue, and possibly her life, depended on what Jennie did.

Her stomach churned when Rae was roughly pulled

away. The girl's heels dragged across the wood planking until they dropped over the side of the walkway, leaving a trail in the dirt. Her captor picked her up, and Jennie heard her friend's fearful whimpers as she was taken west past the depot. The darkness swallowed her and, too soon, Jennie heard nothing more.

"Rae!" The sound of her shout was like a muffled sob. Jennie went slack in the outlaw's arms.

"I think you can safely release her," Easton said. "She won't do anything stupid now that we have her friend. Will you, Jennifer?"

"No," she said behind the hand, defeated.

Jack thrust her at Easton, who wrapped his arm around her waist and pulled her to his side. When she flinched, he said, "You might as well get used to my touch, Jennifer, because you'll be enjoying a lot of it." He laughed. "Now, unless you want some harm to come to your friend, you'll come with me. We have a little formality to take care of."

He steered her toward town, and Jennie moved woodenly alongside him. "Where are we going?" she asked, afraid she already knew what "formality" he spoke of.

"We're going to the altar, my dear," he said smoothly. They crossed the deserted main street. "I've gone to great expense and come a very long way to wed you. I refuse to wait another hour."

Olive Thompson tucked the last few strands of gray-streaked black hair beneath her white cotton nightcap. She checked over the few toiletry items laid out on her bureau. Everything was in its place, lined up for morning. Satisfied, she moved across the room, her long-sleeved, high-collared white nightgown swishing against her limbs. She extinguished the lamp and stood a moment, letting her eyes become accustomed to the dark. Habit propelled her toward the window, which overlooked the tracks.

Olive stared at the few lights still burning in town—in the saloons. She had never entered one in her life and did not care for anyone who did. The men drank and gambled away their savings in such places, just as her father had, forcing her to leave home and search for work as a young girl. Now she was old and getting older. She didn't have much to show for her labors, but she had her independence.

The whistle of the westbound Number 1, several hours overdue, shrilled in the distance. Olive glanced to the left to see the train chugging toward the station. Out of the corner of her eye, she caught sight of something white on black moving toward town.

She squinted into the darkness, pressed her nose against the cold glass just as two figures passed through the light of a gas lamp. She inhaled sharply. "Jennie!"

The Boston fellow held her to his side. Mincing steps replaced Jennie's usual purposeful strides. Something was wrong.

Olive squinted harder. Where were they going? As the train pulled in, the locomotive's billowing clouds of steam obscured her view. When it dissipated, Jennie was nowhere in sight.

"Oh, no!" Olive clutched the neckline of her gown. "I have to do something."

She pushed away from the windowsill and jerked out dresser drawers. Over her nightgown she threw on her black skirt and shirtwaist. After shoving her feet into low-top oxfords, she nearly tied the laces into knots. One thought revolved in her mind. She had to get Sheriff Conklin. He would know what to do, how to protect Jennie.

She tore open her door, left it gaping for the first time ever. Holding her skirt much higher than was proper, she sprinted for the staircase.

Ahead of them, a church spire rose into the sky. Jennie longed to escape James Easton's grasp, but with Rae in danger, she had to sacrifice her convictions. She would marry a man she could never love. A man who wanted to hurt her, use her for his own gain.

James yanked her onto the front porch of the parsonage. "Get up here."

Despite the late hour, the windows were still lit. James pounded on the door, then, finding it unlocked, shoved it open and pulled Jennie in behind him.

Katherine Dawson was coming toward them, her sewing clutched in her hand. "What is it? Is there an emergency?"

James pushed past her into the parlor, where the reverend calmly set his reading aside and hoisted himself out of an armchair. "Can I help you, sir?"

"Marry us," James ordered. "Tonight."

"Not another one," the reverend muttered. Then he said more loudly, "It's quite late. If you would come back tomorrow." He nudged his spectacles higher on his nose.

James drew a small silver gun from his pocket and pressed the muzzle against the reverend's cheek. The preacher swallowed visibly. "Get your coat on, Reverend. Now!"

"Yes. Yes." He backed away from the gun. With

a shaky hand, he plucked his black coat off the nearby sofa. "Y-you stay here, Katherine. I—I won't be long."

James waved the gun toward her. "She's coming with us. As a witness. I want this done right."

Katherine's face drained of color. She looked as if she might swoon. Jennie felt sorry for her and knew without a doubt that Katherine Dawson could never have been the kind of wife Cole needed.

Still clutching her mending, Katherine started to reach for the coat hanging on the wall. At the girl's movement, Jennie caught sight of a shiny silver needle sticking out of calico fabric. While James was occupied with the reverend, she knocked Katherine's sewing out of her hand, caught it, snagged the needle and let the rest drop to the floor. She pricked her thumb but didn't even flinch.

"Oh, I'm sorry," she said to Katherine. "Your mending." With her back to James, Jennie bent down, weaving the needle into her apron before attempting to pick up the fabric.

James hauled her upward. "What are you doing?"

Her stomach tightened. Had he seen what she did? Was the needle visible? She couldn't imagine why she had risked taking it. Using it was out of the question as long as those men held Rae hostage. "I was just getting Miss Dawson's sewing."

He stared at her, and she struggled to keep her eyes from giving her away. She'd told him the truth, part of it anyway.

He kicked the sewing aside and narrowed his gaze at her. "I don't trust you, Jennifer. Not since you ran from me. But you won't run again, because I'll be watching you." He smiled then. "For the rest of your life."

Chapter Twenty-One

Olive dashed out the Harvey House door. The train, taking on water and disembarking several passengers, blocked her path. Her breath came in quick pants as a well-dressed older gentleman surveyed her clothing and rushed over to her, no doubt hungry. Olive tried to step around him. Couldn't he see the restaurant was closed?

He matched her movement. "Madam, do you work in the Harvey House?"

"We're closed, sir." She decided to climb on the train, cross through the vestibule, and jump down on the other side.

"Please, I—"

"I don't have time to talk, sir. I must go."

He placed a hand on her arm. "Please," he begged, "my daughter works here, but a man is after her. I'm very worried. Help me."

Olive gave him her full attention. "A man? From Boston?"

"You know about him? About my Jennifer?"

"He's got her." She flailed her hand toward town. "He took her that way. I'm going for the sheriff."

He released her arm, shifted his bag from one hand to the other. "I'm going with you."

"Then follow me. And hurry." She led him in and out of the train. They raced into town, skidding to a halt in front of Sheriff Conklin's office. Light still shone from inside, and she thanked God for it.

The hinges protested loudly as Olive thrust open the door and stumbled inside. "Sheriff!" she cried.

He jumped up from behind his desk, the chair scraping backward across the wood floor. "Miss Thompson! What on earth!" His gaze locked on the top of her head. "Why are you wearing your night-cap?"

Olive reached up and touched it, then waved a hand in dismissal. "One of my girls has been kidnapped."

"Sheriff, I'm…Edmund…Andrews," the older man said between breaths. "My daughter, Jennifer, has been…taken against her will."

"You saw her taken?" the sheriff asked.

"No, but—"

"I saw it," Olive interrupted. "Jennie never would have gone with him willingly. And he was holding her so tight that she couldn't walk normal."

"Was it that Easton fella? The one who intended to marry her?"

"You know about that?" Mr. Andrews asked, finally catching his breath.

"I heard about him from several sources, including Jennie herself just this afternoon."

"It was him," Olive said, starting to shake. She'd never been so ruffled before. But then, no one had ever kidnapped one of her girls before. What would the man do to Jennie?

"Miss Thompson, come sit down." Sheriff Conklin tried to direct her into a chair, but she stood her ground.

"You must organize some men to find her," she said. "He brought her into town, but I lost sight of them."

"My deputy's still in Flagstaff, but Cole Bryant's in the Cabinet Saloon with his men. He'll help us. Come on." The sheriff grabbed two rifles from a gun rack, and Mr. Andrews removed a pistol from his bag. Their hurried steps rang out over the planked boards outside.

"Sheriff Conklin," Mr. Andrews said, rushing alongside, "where is the local church?"

"Over thataway." He pointed with one of the rifles. "But this is no time for churchgoing, Mr. Andrews."

They continued on, but when Olive and the sheriff turned right toward the saloon, Edmund turned left.

Cole paced back and forth across the rear area of the Cabinet Saloon. His brother and three of his men—Jones, Cordoba and Lucas—sat at a scarred round table in the corner, glasses of barely touched beer in front of them. Dense smoke hovered over the local men and area cowboys who stood drinking at the bar or playing cards at the tables.

The Sunday night crowd talked in subdued tones, possibly the result of his anxious presence. Cole didn't care, just wanted something to happen. He hated this waiting game. Reynolds was keeping watch on Benjamin Porter's house, but so far, the banker had done nothing suspicious.

The swinging double doors banged open. "Bryant!"

Cole halted midstride to see Sheriff Conklin bearing down on him. Every head in the place turned. Miss Thompson, of all people, marched in after him, wearing a white cotton nightcap with ruffles around the edge. Her face was pinched with worry.

Cole's gut clenched. "What's happened?"

"Miss Thompson here saw that fellow from Boston bring Jennie Andrews into town."

"Willingly?" Had Jennie changed her mind about Easton? No, Cole couldn't believe that. Wouldn't believe it.

"I don't think so," Miss Thompson said, wringing her hands. "He was holding her tight to his side."

"Did you see a gun?"

She shook her head. "They were already halfway into town when I spotted them. And then the train came. It blocked my view."

Desperate to know everything, Cole leaned closer to the woman, spoke faster. "Do you have any idea where they were going?"

"No, I'm sorry." She wrung her hands harder.

Sheriff Conklin cleared his throat. "The girl's father is in town, but we lost him between my office and here."

Cole straightened. "Lost him within a block?"

"One second he was asking for the local church, and the next he was gone." The sheriff shrugged.

"Church?" According to Jennie, James Easton wanted to marry her and would do whatever was necessary to achieve that end. Jennie would never marry him though, even at gunpoint. Would she?

Cole felt a sharp pain inside his heart. Before he could reflect on the cause, the saloon doors crashed open again.

"Mr. Cole! Mr. Cole!" Joey cried, charging up to him, gulping air.

"Joey! What is it?"

"I've been keepin' an eye out like you said." The boy had to take two more breaths. "I saw Miss Jennie's friend, the blond Harvey Girl, with three men. One of them were that man Mr. Porter met with."

Behind Cole, the legs of a chair screeched across the planked floor. It toppled over backward. Matt stood with feet splayed, gun at the ready.

Cole held up his hand. "Hold on, Matt. Let's hear what else Joey has to say." As his mind started sorting the puzzle pieces, he turned back to the boy. "Were they on horseback?"

"They sure was, Mr. Cole. That's how I found 'em. My horses smelled 'em, so I went to investigate like you would. I hid in the bushes real quiet-like and watched. The blond girl was real scared, cryin' into the scarf they had tied around her head. They took her away with 'em."

Cole glanced at Matt. The skin of his brother's face was stretched taut. He checked the chambers of his gun, snapped the barrel into place and looked up. Pewter eyes glittered. Cole had never seen his little brother so intense, ruthlessly so. But he understood exactly how he felt.

"I'm going after her, Cole."

"I know. And I'm going after Jennie." As he said it, the puzzle pieces rearranged themselves in his head, and suddenly Cole realized Jennie had no choice but to marry Easton. Somehow, the man had gotten into league with Porter and his outlaws. Rae was being used to insure Jennie's surrender. Cole kicked himself for not realizing the danger in which he'd put the two girls. Porter's previous targets had been people and things Cole cared about. Jennie and Rae fell into that category.

"Joey, what direction did the men ride?"

He bounced on his feet and pointed. "West, toward Bill Williams Mountain."

"Listen up, boys," Cole said. "Lucas, Jones, you get over to the livery with Matt right now. Saddle the horses. Cordoba, you fetch Reynolds from Porter's house and follow them. Reynolds can track with the best of 'em. He'll find Rae."

Matt strode halfway across the room before turning back to Cole. "Where do you plan to find Jennie?"

"At the church," Cole answered flatly, checking his own gun. As Matt and the others paraded out, Cole faced Sheriff Conklin. "Sheriff, you go with Matt. There's at least three of those outlaws and only one of Easton. I'll deal with him."

The sheriff glanced at Cole's injured arm. "Are you sure? Maybe I should come with you."

Cole stiffened. "I can manage."

"All right. He's all yours then." The sheriff strode out.

"Joey, you stay here with Miss Thompson." Cole started toward the door. At the threshold, he turned back and eyed the boy. "You did good, son."

Joey beamed him a smile.

Cole ran out, the doors swinging behind him. For the first time in his life, he prayed. Prayed that Jennie wasn't hurt. Or married. He wanted her for his own, wanted no other man to touch the woman he now knew he loved.

Cole ran faster, each step bringing more fear into his heart. He couldn't lose Jennie, not now. Not ever.

* * *

Candles flickered on the altar. Jennie stared into the flames, wishing this were one of her nightmares. She stood as stiff as the pulpit. In front of her, Reverend Dawson peered through his wire-rimmed spectacles. He blinked frequently, his gaze darting from his black leather-bound book to James's pointed face. Katherine, looking even more frightened, stood to Jennie's left. The church smelled faintly of tired flowers.

James Easton's manicured fingernails dug into Jennie's hand. She wished she could fight him or flee from him, do something to help herself, but she kept still.

"Read," James ordered.

The reverend jumped and opened his holy book. "'Dearly beloved, we are gathered…'"

Jennie stopped listening. In a matter of minutes she would be a married woman, but not married to the man she loved. She cherished the night spent in Cole's bed, his arm around her and his body against her own. His touch had set her every nerve ending on fire.

Jennie didn't regret her choice to stay with him. For a little while, she had actually felt loved by him, her body worshiped by Cole's eyes, lips and fingers. She might soon be married to James, but he would never possess her the way Cole had—body and soul.

"'Into this holy state these two persons…'" the reverend droned on.

Jennie tried to imagine her life beyond tonight, but no image formed. Perhaps because she would attempt to escape as soon as she knew Rae was safe.

The reverend looked up from his book. "Sir, I need to know your name if I am to continue with the ceremony."

"James Easton III." He held on to Jennie's arm. His other hand rested on the gun in his coat pocket.

"Very well. James Easton III, wilt thou have this woman to be thy wedded wife, to…"

Jennie started to shake as a cold hopelessness crept into her body. James's hand tightened on her, his nails clawing her tender skin through her sleeve. Even knowing she could do nothing to stop the ceremony, she looked around wildly. The rest of the small church appeared empty, the corners and back dark where no light reached. Her nightmare was coming to an end, reality overtaking it.

"I will," Easton answered.

"And the young lady's full name?" Reverend Dawson asked.

He'd directed his question to her, but Jennie couldn't answer. Her mouth felt as dry and gritty as sand. James answered for her. "Jennifer Andrews."

"Jennifer Andrews, wilt thou have this man to be thy wedded husband so long as ye both shall live?"

Her legs wobbled, as if she were a baby standing alone for the first time. James pinched her arm hard. "Answer him," he snarled.

She swallowed several times, didn't speak.

James whispered into her ear. "Remember your dear friend and the men who took her. If they don't hear from me, well, you don't want to know." He left the threat to her imagination.

She trembled all the harder, knew she had to go through with this. "I—"

"Don't answer, Jennifer," shouted a familiar and beloved voice.

Jennie whirled toward the wonderful sound. "Father," she whispered, as the front door shut behind him.

Edmund Andrews strode into the center aisle carrying a large pistol. "Let her go, Easton!" He raised the pistol higher and stopped. "I don't want to use this, but I will if I have to. I now know what kind of man you are."

James laughed. "Ah, how nice. Another witness to our vows, my dear. And a family member, no less. We are so pleased to see you, Edmund. If you'd arrived earlier, you could've given away the bride. Why don't you come closer and join us?"

Her father paused beside the fourth pew. James shifted behind Jennie, trapping her with one arm around her waist. The cold metal of his gun pressed against her cheek, destroying her elation. "Father, there's nothing you can do."

"No good can come of this, Easton. Release my daughter." His voice had lost some of its earlier strength.

James spoke sharply. "No one's going to stop me now." He pressed the gun deeper into her flesh.

She winced but forced her voice to remain calm. "Father, there's no reasoning with him."

"Listen to her, Andrews. She knows what she's saying."

Her father pursed his lips. Jennie didn't want to die, nor did she want her father hurt. She offered him what she hoped looked like a reassuring smile. He'd come all the way from Boston to rescue her. She wished she could rush into his arms, feel like a little girl again, protected and loved.

"It'll be all right, Father. Really."

James smirked. "Put your gun down, Andrews. Now. Before I get really annoyed."

Jennie watched him hesitate. "Please, Father. There's no choice. His partners—outlaws—are holding my best friend hostage. I have to go through with this."

Jennie watched her father's strength flow out of him. His shoulders slumped, and he set the pistol on the seat of the wooden pew beside him. Jennie was pleased yet surprised. She'd never seen her father knuckle under so quickly and completely to another man. The Edmund Andrews she knew would have disarmed himself but stiffened his shoulders even more. Was he exhausted from his trip, resigned to his failure, or only biding his time? Was he preparing to put himself in danger for her sake?

A chill traveled up Jennie's arms, as though confirming her thoughts. She fought her growing panic. How was she going to keep him from trying to be a hero?

Matt forced himself to stay behind Reynolds, letting the tracker cut for sign. Only the sound of hoofbeats in the softened ground, the occasional snort of a horse and a slight breeze rustling the pines broke the quiet. Matt held back a jittery Dancer. The horse seemed to sense his fear, worry and impatience.

Reynolds pulled up. The other riders stopped behind him. No one spoke.

Matt smelled the smoke of a nearby campfire. He tightened his grip on the reins and stared at a rise on the edge of the forest. Rae had to be on the other side.

Sheriff Conklin quietly dismounted. "Leave the

horses here,'' he whispered. ''We'll go in on foot and surprise 'em.''

They swung off their horses, led them into the trees and tied them securely. Then they crept toward the rise. Matt fingered the grip of his holstered revolver and swallowed hard. He'd never killed anyone, but if any of those men were hurting his Sunshine, he would pull the trigger.

When they neared the top, they spread out, dropped to their knees and crawled to the crest. Matt clamped his jaw tight and peered over.

She was there. His wife was there. And she was sitting apart from the men. Her face shimmered from the campfire's flames. Her hands and feet were tied, but her clothing was in order, and she didn't appear to be in any pain. No scarf covered her mouth.

Matt breathed more easily. He listened to the outlaws, whose voices were loud in the quiet. They didn't seem the least bit worried about visitors. Matt fixed his gaze on Rae, willing her to know he was with her.

She looked up.

He inhaled sharply, and his heart reached out to her. Could she really know he was there?

One of the outlaws poked a stick into the fire. Orange embers floated upward. ''So how long we gotta wait here, Slim?''

''Just the night,'' answered a man wearing a sheepskin coat. ''That Eastern dandy will be married and headin' back to the big city on the mornin' train.''

Not if Cole had anything to say about it, Matt thought.

Another man spoke, his voice deep and gruff.

"Hows about us havin' a little fun with this purty gal? I've never had a woman as fine as this one."

The one called Slim laughed. "Why not? We got us a whole night to pass."

The man with the stick said, "I thought we wasn't supposed to touch her. Ain't that what was said when we took her?"

"That was to get the redhead to do what she was told," Slim said. "The boss man just don't want the blonde dead. The dandy didn't care one way or the other."

Matt carefully drew his gun; his hand tightened around the grip.

The gruff-voiced man stood, put a hand to his crotch and started toward Rae. "This good ol' boy's aching for you, missy."

Rae scooted backward, pushing with her heels. "D-don't come n-near me."

"Ah, come on. You know you're gonna like it." He laughed.

Matt's nostrils flared, and he breathed as heavily as a bull readying for a charge. He rose from his belly to his knees, digging the toes of his boots into the dirt.

The man leaned down and grabbed Rae's chin, roughly tilting her face up.

Matt vaulted to his feet. The sheriff and other men followed his lead. He raced across the open ground. "Get your filthy hands off my wife!"

The three outlaws looked up in astonishment. Before they could jump to their feet, revolvers and rifles were aimed at their chests.

Matt dropped his gun, launched himself at the outlaw near Rae and knocked him flat. The man grunted.

Matt straddled him and let his fists fly. The man's head snapped from side to side. Each blow splintered the quiet.

"Matt! Please stop," Rae cried. "Matt!"

He heard her voice as if it were coming from afar.

"Please," she said. "I'm all right."

He sat back and looked down. The man sprawled beneath him barely moved, only moaned. His face was bloody, his nose broken and lips split. Matt hauled in a breath and lifted himself off. Then he crawled to Rae.

He stared into her understanding eyes. "I've never done that before, Rae. I was so mad. He touched you. Wanted to—"

"I know," she said, leaning toward him, trembling. "I understand. Thank you for coming after me."

"I love you so much, Sunshine. If any of those men had hurt you, I would've ki—"

"Shh. Don't say it." Her blue eyes looked overlarge in her face. Tears flowed in rivulets down her pale cheeks. "I love you, too, Matt."

"Don't cry, Rae. It's over now." He gently brushed the back of his hand across her tears, then reached for the ropes binding her wrists and feet. "I'm taking you to the hotel with me. No more Harvey House dormitory. You're my wife, and we're going to be together. Tonight and forever." The knots parted.

He helped her to her feet. She swayed toward him. "Hold me, Matt. Please. Just for a moment."

He clasped her to him, stroked her back and pressed his face to her soft hair.

Sheriff Conklin coughed several times. "Matt, we

need to get these men to town and check on Cole. You comin'?''

He lifted his head. ''Yeah.'' Rae stared up at him, worry in her eyes. ''Is Jennie all right? Is that how you found me?''

He rubbed her shoulder. ''No. Joey from the livery saw the men riding away with you. We know Easton took Jennie. Cole went after her.''

''Do you think he'll find her?'' Rae's voice shook again.

''Cole's very good at finding people. And Jennie's father is here, too.'' He squeezed her shoulder. ''Don't you worry. Cole won't let anything happen to Jennie.'' Matt peered back toward town and hoped Cole wasn't too late.

Chapter Twenty-Two

At the church, Cole stealthily mounted the steps. Outside the double doors, he put his ear to the crack. Inside, the reverend's strained voice spoke the words of a marriage ceremony.

Cole balled his hand into a fist, then slowly stretched out his fingers. He had to stay calm.

He lifted the thong off his Colt, wishing he could enter with gun drawn. But he had to use his one hand to get the door open first, which would give whoever stood inside a clear shot at him.

He listened again, heard a man's voice repeating the reverend's words. The ceremony was close to finishing, and Cole had to stop it. He soundlessly inched the door open and peered in. Candles illuminated the altar and people standing in front of it. He slipped into the shadows at the back, drew his gun just as silently.

An elderly gentleman, Jennie's father no doubt, leaned against the fourth pew. To the left, Katherine stood shaking, her hands clasped together. The reverend was swaying on his feet as he intoned another part of the vows Easton would repeat. Easton's gaze flicked between the reverend and Mr. Andrews, and he held a small-caliber gun to Jennie's head.

Cole longed to race to her rescue, feel her arms around him as she offered him her gratitude. He wanted to see her smile, feel the love that she had shown him in his bed. Instead, he forced himself to stay still, assess the situation and think. For example, why was Easton holding Jennie between himself and her father? Did Mr. Andrews have a gun?

Cole crept around the right side of the church, closer to Easton's back, where he could get a clear shot if necessary.

"'...to love and to cherish, till death us do part,'" Easton finished.

Cole raised his gun.

The reverend instructed Jennie to repeat after him.

"Don't do it, Jennie," Cole commanded.

She spun toward his voice, surprising her captor and inadvertently coming between Cole and his target. "Cole!"

"Move away from him, Jennie." He kept his voice even. Inside, his stomach knotted with fear.

"I can't. I have to marry him. Some other men have Rae, and they'll hurt her unless I do what James says."

"You had better listen to her," Easton said, a self-satisfied smile on his narrow face.

"No, you listen to me. If you want to see Boston again, you let her go."

Jennie worried her lower lip. "But, Cole, he—"

"Don't worry about Rae," he said. "Matt's gone after her along with the sheriff and some of the boys. Joey saw the direction they went. You don't have to do anything you don't want to do."

Easton's grip tightened on her. "She *is* going to marry me." He pressed the gun behind her ear. "She's mine or she's no one's." A wildness glittered in his eyes.

Sweat dripped down Cole's spine. He'd seen that look before in other men, cornered men. And unstable men. He started to lower his revolver.

"That's a good fellow, Bryant," Benjamin Porter's voice said from the shadows. "No, don't stop. Keep bringing that gun down. All the way to your side."

Though Cole did as the banker said, he gripped his gun handle even tighter. When Porter stepped into the flickering light, a double-barreled shotgun was aimed directly at Cole's chest.

"Porter. I should've known," he said calmly, though inside he seethed. He should've expected this, should've brought the sheriff with him after all.

"I thought you must've figured out something. I saw those men taking shifts outside my house. Were they yours?"

"My ranch hands."

Porter nodded. "When I saw one come running for the other, I decided it was time to attend a wedding. Reverend, you go right ahead with the ceremony."

Cole didn't take his eyes from Porter, but in his side vision he saw Jennie fooling with her skirt. Cole turned slightly, eyed her more closely. What was she up to now?

"What have you got against me, Porter?" he asked, stalling for time and wanting to get to the bottom of the attacks on the people he cared about. "Were you the one who burned my barn and attempted to kill my brother?"

When Porter smiled, Cole had his answer.

"I didn't do it personally, you understand," Porter said. "If I had, your brother would be dead, as planned. But I have to admit, your losing a hand was a plus I hadn't anticipated." His smile broadened as his gaze passed over the shortened length of Cole's arm.

Cole forced himself not to move, for Jennie's sake and his own. A hole in his chest wouldn't help either of them.

He watched her now. Easton had lowered his gun from her head, and she was still playing with the folds of her skirt. A sparkle emanated from one of those folds. A tiny, momentary twinkle of light reflected from something small and metal.

Cole nearly groaned aloud with realization. She had a needle. From personal experience, he had no doubt about her intentions, or what might happen if Easton caught her before she could surprise him. "Porter," he said, anxious to keep everyone distracted from her, "you haven't answered my question. What did I ever do to you?"

The man's smile disappeared. "You have to ask? You bastard, you killed my son."

"I don't recall shooting anyone named Porter."

"He was using his mother's maiden name. Hardin."

"Your son was Fred Hardin?" He remembered the young man who'd forced him to fight, put a bullet in his arm. Cole had brought Hardin into Prescott the last way he'd wanted, draped crosswise over a saddle.

A muscle twitched in Porter's cheek. "My *only* son!" His voice echoed inside the church. "When you killed him, my wife's sanity went with him."

"I'm sorry about your wife and her suffering, Porter. Yours, too. But that young man stole Wells Fargo gold and refused to give it up. It was my job to get it back. He fought. Shot me, in fact. I've got the scar to prove it.''

''He was only a boy.''

''He was a young man, Porter.'' Cole shifted his position so the wood pew hid his hand. ''Eighteen years old and riding with a gang of outlaws that robbed a train. I had to go after him.''

Porter's face twisted with hate. ''But you're the one who's still here.'' He raised his shotgun higher.

''If he'd given himself up like the others did, he'd still be here, too.''

''You're going to pay, Bryant. Nothing you say changes the fact that you took my son from me. I want you to suffer like my wife and I have suffered. Tonight, you're going to lose the woman you love to this Easterner. Then you'll die.''

Jennie laughed loudly, drawing everyone's attention. ''Mr. Porter, you're a fool if you think Cole Bryant loves me.''

Cole watched Porter's gun waver. He wouldn't refute Jennie's statement now. Later, when they were alone, he'd tell her the truth. ''Listen to her, Porter.''

The banker turned his gaze to her. ''It's true,'' she said.

Cole caught sight of Jennie's father reaching down toward a pew. When his hand cleared the side of it, he held a long-barreled pistol.

With one arm still around Jennie's waist, Easton waved his gun at the reverend. ''I don't care who this cowboy loves, Jennifer is marrying me. Now! So get on with it, Reverend.''

As the reverend glanced down at his holy book,

Jennie surreptitiously raised her hand toward Easton's grasp.

Cole waited, body tensed. The candles flickered on the altar. Katherine looked as if she would crumple at any moment.

Jennie, her hand poised over Easton's, appeared frightened but fierce. "I won't marry you, James." She stabbed the back of his hand.

"Yowww!" He shrieked and jumped back from her.

Jennie dove for the nearest end of the altar. Cole wanted to cheer.

Easton stared at the needle embedded in his hand, then yanked it out. He raised his gun as Jennie scrambled on her hands and knees to get away. "Jennifer, no one defies James Easton III."

"Easton!" Cole shouted.

Gun extended, Easton swung toward him. Hate contorted his features, and his trigger finger moved.

Cole fired and instantly dropped behind the pew for cover. The report exploded in the confines of the church. Two other shots blasted. A window above Cole's head shattered. Pieces of glass rained over him, landed on his hat. Then he watched Easton staring down at the blood spreading over his fancy waistcoat. His mouth dropped open and astonishment softened his sharp features. A moment later, his body collapsed, landing in a heap on the floor.

In a crouch, Cole shuffled several steps away from his last position. He stuck his head up and glanced around. Porter and Mr. Andrews were both out of sight. Jennie was thankfully staying down behind the altar. Katherine had slumped to the floor like a rag doll, but her eyes were open. The reverend stood stock-still, the hymnal open in his hands.

"Get down, Reverend," Cole yelled.

The man didn't respond.

Cole debated the idiocy of leaving his cover to get the reverend to safety. Then he heard a groan from where he'd last seen Porter.

"It's all right, sir." Mr. Andrews rose from the center aisle. "This man's shotgun is now in my possession."

Cole stood slowly and holstered his gun. He glanced at a motionless James Easton and sidestepped between the pews until he came to stand beside Porter's writhing body. Blood soaked the area around his gold watch and chain.

Cole stared down at the man who'd come so close to killing his little brother, who'd taken his hand and burned his barn, who'd nearly let the woman he loved be taken away from him. Porter didn't deserve his compassion, but just the same, Cole felt sorry for the father who had lost his son.

"Porter, I'm truly sorry this had to happen. I never wanted to kill your boy."

The banker's expression hardened. Anger replaced his pain. He tried to say something, but only a gurgle erupted from his throat. Then, nothing. Cole closed the man's sightless eyes and stepped back.

"Sir, I wish to thank you for protecting my daughter. I am Edmund Andrews of Boston, Massachusetts." He extended his right hand.

Self-consciously, Cole shook with his left hand. Jennie's father didn't flinch or look away, and Cole's estimation of the man rose higher. "Cole Bryant.

Your daughter did a pretty good job of helping herself. She's very good with a needle.''

"Yes, although her mother and I prefer she use it on needlepoint canvas rather than people.'' He smiled. "But Jennifer has always followed her own mind.''

Cole knew exactly what her father meant. He also knew that this strong, willful, stubborn woman needed looking after. Needed someone to keep her out of trouble. She'd probably send his life into disarray, but Cole realized that he needed someone to look after. His little brother was a grown man now, with a woman of his own. Matt didn't need Cole watching over him anymore. It was time to let go.

"In any case," Mr. Andrews continued, "I am indebted to you.''

Jennie approached them, her expression cool. No loving smile, or even a grateful one, greeted Cole. His heart suddenly weighed as much as a boulder.

"Father, there is no debt to be paid. Mr. Bryant and I are square. I saved his life, and he has now saved mine. Nothing more need be said.''

Cole knew there was a whole lot more to say, but not here. Not in front of her father, Katherine, the reverend and two dead bodies. "We'll discuss our so-called debts later, Jennie.''

"There's nothing to discuss," she said, chin angled high.

"There is, but now is not the time. Why don't you welcome your father properly? He came a long way to protect you, and managed to protect me in the process.''

When she turned to her father, a smile warmed her

face. "Oh, Father, I'm so glad to see you." She threw her arms around him, hugged him hard.

Cole found himself envying her father. He stepped away.

"Jennifer," her father said, "I made a dreadful mistake trying to force you to marry that man. I'm so sorry."

She was quiet for a moment. "I still don't understand why finding a successor was so important that you would barter me away."

He winced. "I had no right, but I was getting desperate. Your mother's health was becoming more precarious, and I wanted to spend as much time as possible with her."

"Is she all right now?" Worry edged Jennie's voice. "The telegram said the family was fine."

"She is fine, though worried about you. She'll be anxious to see you."

"I'd like to see her, too," she said. Cole heard the yearning in her voice and felt more and more distant. She would return to Boston, leave him behind.

"Jennifer, I said some terrible things, accused you of lying when you'd never lied to me before. Can you ever forgive me?"

She took his hands in hers. "I know what desperation feels like, Father. Yes, I do forgive you." She kissed him on the cheek.

Mr. Andrews kissed her back. "Thank you. And I promise I will make it up to you."

Cole turned away, trying to imagine his life without Jennie. He didn't like it. He offered his hand to Katherine and pulled her to her feet. She was so distraught she let him touch her.

He brought her to her father, who shook his head

repeatedly. "My church has been the site of violence and death."

"I'm sorry, Reverend," Cole said. "When the sheriff returns, he'll take care of the bodies. I'll escort you and Katherine back to the parsonage."

He nodded. "Thank you, Cole. You're a good man."

They started toward the double doors, Cole supporting Katherine.

Jennie stopped them. "Cole, how can I find out about Rae?"

"Go to the Cabinet Saloon. Miss Thompson should be there with Joey."

Her eyes widened. "Miss Thompson?"

Her father put his arm around her shoulders. "Miss Thompson saw Easton abduct you. When I descended from the train, she was running for the sheriff."

"Still wearing her ruffled nightcap," Cole added.

"Oh, my goodness," Jennie said.

"It was quite a sight." Cole steered Katherine toward the door. "I'll meet you at the saloon after I get the reverend and Katherine settled. Then we're going to talk."

When he saw Jennie again, Cole intended to tell her exactly how much he loved her, how much he needed her in his life.

Chapter Twenty-Three

Along the darkened boardwalk, Jennie walked arm in arm with her father. Her steps were light. She could hardly believe he was here with her, had come so far for her sake, and admitted he was wrong. Since they'd left the church, he'd apologized several more times. He wanted to take her home right away, make up for his mistakes.

Jennie saw no reason to stay in Williams. Rae and Matt would soon be married, starting a new life. And Cole would continue his search for a dutiful woman who didn't need or expect his love. Jennie inhaled slowly, sadly.

"Are you well, Jennifer?" her father asked, peering over at her. "You seem terribly preoccupied."

"I'm just thinking about all that has happened." She remembered the first moment Cole made his presence known inside the church. All her fears and worries had lifted. He'd come just when she needed him most. She knew she would always love him, but she couldn't stay with a man who could never love her in return.

"Tell me about the girl you're worried about."

"Her name is Rae Hansen." Jennie smiled. "We trained together in Kansas. She's from a large farming family in Iowa, and she's the warmest, most loving person I've ever known. She and Cole's brother are engaged." Just as they reached the corner near the Cabinet Saloon, approaching hoofbeats made her turn.

"Jennie!" Matt yelled. He rode at the head of a procession of riders. Rae sat behind him, her arms holding tightly to his waist. She peeked around his side, her blond hair and smile shining in the moonlight.

Jennie let go of her father's arm and clasped her hands together. Her throat tightened with relief and joy.

Matt reined his horse to a halt and gently lowered Rae to the ground. The other riders, one being the train robber Jennie had recognized, rode past with the sheriff.

She rushed up to Rae but stopped two steps away. Her gaze roved over the younger girl. "Oh, Rae, I'm so sorry. They didn't hurt you, did they?" She would never forgive herself if they did.

"No, no. I'm fine. Did Easton hurt you?"

"He tried to force me to marry him, but when Cole said Matt knew where to find you, I stabbed James with a sewing needle."

"You didn't!" Disbelief rounded her eyes.

"I most certainly did. Then Cole shot him." Jennie's voice lowered. "Easton's dead, Rae. I'll never have to worry about him again."

Rae opened her arms, and Jennie fell into them. Tears slid down her cheeks and dropped onto the man's wool coat Rae wore over her uniform. Jennie held onto her friend until the loud crash of the saloon doors pulled them apart.

Joey burst from the building followed by Olive Thompson. Jennie wiped her eyes with her apron and stared in awe at the half smile on the older woman's lips.

"That boy has been pacing the floor ever since the men left." She crossed her bony arms over her chest. "Well, I see that you girls are thankfully unharmed. I'm pleased that I didn't run to the sheriff in my nightcap for nothing."

"Thanks to you we are very well." Jennie kissed Olive's cool, thin cheek.

"We are both grateful." Rae kissed her next.

Miss Thompson waved them away, but in the light from the saloon windows, a blush of embarrassed pleasure stained her cheeks. "I take care of my girls."

"I helped too," Joey piped up. "Didn't I tell you which direction the bad guys went, Mr. Cole?"

Cole strode up to the group. "You sure did, Joey. And Matt got his girl as a result."

Joey stubbed the toe of his boot on the boardwalk. "Ah, shucks." He glanced down at the wood planks, then looked shyly up at Jennie.

She watched the boy who had helped her get to Cole's ranch and helped to save Rae. "You are a remarkable young man, Joey. You deserve a hug, too."

She bent down and pulled him into her arms. He stood as stiffly as Miss Thompson had and blushed even more deeply. Then he wrenched free, sprinted across the street and headed toward home.

The others laughed at his rapid flight.

"Will he be all right alone?" she asked Cole.

"He'll be fine. He knows his way around better than anyone." Cole turned to Rae.

"I'm glad to see you're all right."

"Thank you, Cole," she said. "And thank you for watching over Jennie."

He shrugged. "It was no trouble."

"Of course it was," Matt said, smiling as he hooked his arm around Rae's waist. "Jennie's always getting into trouble. Isn't that what you've been saying since we first met her?"

Cole glared at Matt, said nothing.

Jennie glared at Cole. "Is that true?"

He turned his narrowed eyes on her. "You know it is. I've made no secret of it. You need someone to look after you. Someone like—"

"Me," her father said. "And I fully intend to do a better job than I have. Now, Jennifer, will you make the proper introductions, please?"

Before her father's interruption, Jennie had intended to argue with Cole. She could take care of herself. She wanted to make that clear to her father, too, but not tonight. Not after he'd come all this way and even shot a man to protect her. "You've already met Miss Thompson, but this is Rae Hansen, my best friend. Rae, my father helped rescue me. Arrived just in time."

Rae put out her hand. "Then I'm very pleased to meet you, Mr. Andrews."

Matt leaned down toward Rae and whispered something in her ear.

She smiled shyly. "I'm sorry, Mr. Andrews. Jennie made a small mistake. My last name isn't Hansen anymore. It's Bryant. This is my husband, Matt."

Cole and Jennie said, "What?"

Matt beamed. "Congratulate me, big brother. I'm a married man. We got hitched last night after Rae got off work."

"Is it true, Rae?" Jennie asked. "Is that what you were trying to tell me earlier?"

She nodded excitedly. "We thought to keep it a secret because of my job and the trouble Cole was having." Fear quickly clouded Rae's eyes. "Cole, is it finished yet?"

"Yeah," Matt added, "what's happened with Porter tonight?"

"He's dead," Cole answered, removing his hat. "He was in on what happened to the girls. Arranged it like he arranged the train robbery and the barn burning. He was trying to hurt whatever or whomever I cared about because I killed his outlaw son."

"Well, thank God that's finished." Matt kissed his wife's cheek. "Rae, you're coming to live with me. For good. Cole, when you put in that lumber order for the new barn, you'd better order some extra 'cause I'm going to build Rae a house of her own."

"Our own," she said, eyes shining as she looked into her husband's face.

Jennie smiled for her friend's happiness, but an emptiness opened within her. Rae's new life had already started. It was time for Jennie to go. The Harvey Company would quickly replace her with another girl, and it would be as if she'd never been here at all.

"Matt," Cole said, fingering the brim of the hat, "you know I've wanted you to work the ranch with me."

"You've hardly let me forget it."

"Well, I understand now that you have your own life to live. One in which you may not want your older brother always looking after you." He pulled at the collar of his flannel shirt. "What I'm trying to say is, well, you're free to make your own choices. You don't have to stay if you don't want to."

Matt released his bride and pulled his brother into a rough embrace. Jennie sniffed as she watched Cole hesitate at first, then hug his brother back.

"Big brother, I've already made my choices. Rae, you and the C Bar M. I'm afraid you're stuck with me."

With an affectionate thump on Matt's back, Cole pushed him away. He said nothing, only nodded. Jennie saw the muscles of his throat working. She'd never felt more happy for someone and yet so dispirited at the same time. She loved him, but his offer of marriage had come only because it was the honorable thing to do.

Her father pulled his watch from his waistcoat. "What time is the morning train east?"

"Eight o'clock," Rae, Jennie and Miss Thompson said together.

"Then I think it's time we retired, Jennifer. We have a long trip ahead of us."

Silence fell over everyone. Jennie couldn't look at the faces of her friends, the friends she'd be leaving behind. Rae placed her hand on Jennie's arm. "Jennie, you can't leave. Please don't go."

"It's for the best." Tears pricked her eyes.

"But I thought you liked it here," Rae said.

"You're my best friend and I don't want you to leave."

"I have to go, Rae."

"Why?"

Jennie wanted to share her misery with the closest friend she'd ever had, but she wouldn't give in to the weakness. It would only make saying goodbye more difficult. "You'll always be my best friend, Rae. I'll miss you terribly, but you and Matt will have a wonderful life together." She swiped at her eyes.

Miss Thompson drew Rae back. "Jennie, there's an empty room available at the Harvey House. Mr. Andrews, if you would like to stay near your daughter, you'd be welcome."

"I appreciate that, Miss Thompson. You're very thoughtful." He held out his arm. "Jennifer?"

Cole stepped forward. "Jennie, I need to speak with you for a moment. Alone."

She took her father's arm, didn't want to talk to Cole. She knew where he stood, what he wanted. "My father's right, Cole. It's late and I have to pack my things."

"But there's something I need to say to you."

"I don't think so. Good night, Cole." She started walking away with her father.

"Jennie," Cole said, "we—"

"Good night, Mr. Bryant," Edmund Andrews cut in. "Perhaps you'll see us off at the station tomorrow."

A heavy silence followed them as Jennie and her father strode toward the Harvey House, but it was no heavier than the despair, hopelessness and yearning in Jennie's heart.

* * *

Cole sat in the overstuffed armchair of the Grand Canyon Hotel's reception area. Morning was slowly pushing the night away, and he hadn't slept at all. Matt and Rae were in a room upstairs, probably not sleeping much themselves. Cole envied their reasons.

He was still kicking himself for not forcing Jennie to listen to him, but he hadn't wanted a confrontation with her father. He respected Edmund Andrews, and he wanted the older man to respect him.

When Jennie had walked away last night, Cole had considered shouting out his feelings in front of everyone, but his mouth had gone desert dry at the thought. And he'd lost his chance.

This morning he would talk to her. No train was going to take her away from him.

Jennie stood inside her room, heard the shrill whistle of the approaching train. Her father had already taken her bag to the depot's platform. She took a last look around, felt a worse loneliness than when she left Boston. The room seemed empty without Rae in it.

In the dining room and lunchroom, both already half filled with passengers, the Harvey Girls bustled between tables. The occasional clank of a pot or pan came from the kitchen. Jennie didn't stop to say goodbye, couldn't bring herself to express everything she felt. It was easier just to go.

Outside, the morning air was brisk. She inhaled the scent of pine and knew it would forever remind her of Williams and Cole. She glanced around, longing to see Cole. But he didn't appear.

"Shall we board, Jennifer?" Her father motioned toward the door.

She hesitated, peered at the tracks that would take her to Boston. Take her away from Cole. Jennie bit her lip. Was she doing the right thing? Or was she running away again? Leaving before she'd even begun to fight for what she wanted? Cole and his love.

Jennie looked at her father, who was watching her with his head tipped to one side.

"What is it, Jennifer? Have you forgotten something?"

Cole awoke to the sound of familiar footsteps pounding down a staircase. He rubbed his itchy eyes, knocking his hat off in the process. Had he fallen asleep in the parlor?

"Cole," Matt said, "what are you doing there?"

He opened his eyes, saw the reception desk and remembered where he was. "I guess I fell asleep."

The skirt of Rae's uniform rustled as she hurried to join them. "We overslept. I know a married woman isn't supposed to work as a Harvey Girl, but with Jennie leaving I told Miss Thompson last night that I would help out. She'll be wondering where I am."

"I doubt that," Cole said, grabbing his hat, hoisting himself out of the chair and stretching. His brain felt fuzzy from lack of sleep. "I think she knows."

"I suppose she does, but I can't miss saying goodbye to Jennie." Rae started toward the door.

Cole jumped to attention. "What time is it?"

"Seven forty-five," Rae said. "We have fifteen minutes."

He slapped his hat on his head and beat her out the door. When he arrived at the depot, he saw Jennie near the front passenger coach conversing with her father. She wore the same forest green traveling suit he remembered from their first meeting. Perched on top of her auburn curls was the same hat, minus one long, dyed-green feather.

He smiled at the memory, their first disagreement. Cole looked forward to many more. He marched toward her, Matt and Rae further behind. Passengers began filing out of the Harvey House, blocking his view of her. The locomotive's bell clanged and the conductor yelled, "All abo-oard!"

He got to her before she could step any closer to the coach, put his hand on her arm. "Jennie."

She turned, her green eyes bright with pleasure. Either she was happy to see him or happy to be going. He didn't much like the second option. "Cole."

"We have to talk," he said.

"I agree."

"You do?" He dropped his hand from her.

"Yes. Come over here." She led him away from her father. "I love you, Cole, and I don't want to leave without giving you a chance to learn to love me. Running away isn't—"

"I already do."

Jennie held up her hand. "Please, don't interrupt. I haven't finished."

"Jennie, did you hear what I said?"

She rolled her eyes. "Would you listen to me, Cole?"

He placed two of his fingers over her lips. "No. You listen to me, Jennie Andrews. I love you. With my heart and my soul. All of me.'' He slowly withdrew his fingers.

She stared at him. ''You do?''

''I do. And I want to marry you. Not because it's the right thing to do, but because I need you in my life, need your love, and need to love you. Don't get on this train, Jennie.''

''You really do love me.'' A luminous smile spread across her face.

Feeling his heart expand, Cole took her hand in his. ''Will you marry me, Jennie?''

''Oh, yes,'' she breathed. ''Yes, yes, yes.''

He laughed, and he thought his smile must be as big as hers. Cole brought her hand to his lips and kissed it, then he led her back to her father, who stood with Matt and Rae. ''Mr. Andrews, I'm going to marry your daughter, and I'd like your permission. Do I have it?''

The area below the man's thinning hairline furrowed. ''Mr. Bryant, you must allow me to consult my daughter first. I failed to trust her good judgment once. I won't do it again. Jennifer, do you wish to marry this man?''

She nodded. ''I love Cole, Father, and we'd both like your blessing.''

''In that case, you have it. Congratulations, my dear.'' He hugged her hard, then faced Cole. ''I trust you'll love her and look after her? She can be quite troublesome at times.''

''Don't I know it.'' He winked at Jennie, who gave him a halfhearted scowl. ''I'll take good care of her, sir.''

''Very well.'' He shook Cole's hand as steam

hissed and the train began pulling out of the station. "Apparently, I will be staying for a wedding."

Matt slapped his brother on the back. "Congratulations, big brother. I knew you'd come around sooner or later."

Cole laughed. Rae kissed him on the cheek and hugged Jennie tightly.

When the caboose passed them, Jennie threw her arms around Cole's neck. "I love you so much."

He clasped her to him. "And I you. Don't ever leave me, Jennie Andrews."

"I won't. Not ever."

Cole kissed her in the most tender and cherished of all kisses. Everyone and everything else ceased to exist. When they finally separated, both dragging in air, cheers and loud banging noises made Cole turn. Together, he and Jennie looked back at the Harvey House.

"Oh, no," Jennie exclaimed, briefly burying her face in his chest.

The entire Harvey staff stood outside the eating house. Everyone held a large metal spoon in one hand and a pot or pan in the other and struck them together like cymbals in a parade. The racket would awaken all of Williams, and possibly some of the outlying ranches. Bill Jacobs, the Wells Fargo agent, stepped out of his depot office. After waving to Cole, he covered his ears with his hands.

Jennie put a finger across her lips, trying to shush the staff.

The noise only got louder.

She pulled Cole's head down and yelled into his ear. "Do you think Reverend Dawson is up yet?"

"If he wasn't before, he is now," Cole shouted back, gesturing toward the boisterous orchestra.

"Let's go see him," Jennie shouted. "Then I want you to take me home, to the C Bar M."

Cole smiled down at her, his heart full to bursting. "Yes, ma'am."

* * * * *

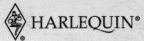

*Each month
you can find three
enchanting new stories from
the leader of inspirational romance—*

Love Inspired®

More than heartwarming tales of inspirational
romance, these original stories celebrate the
triumph over life's trials and tribulations
with an editorial integrity you can trust.

Featuring new releases each month by the
world's most respected authors, Love Inspired
is the name you count on most for value,
convenience and above all else, integrity.

Available at fine retailers near you.

Steeple
Hill™

Tyler Brides

It happened one weekend...

Quinn and Molly Spencer are delighted to accept three
bookings for their newly opened B&B, Breakfast Inn Bed,
located in America's favorite hometown, Tyler, Wisconsin.

But Gina Santori is anything but thrilled to discover her
best friend has tricked her into sharing a room with
the man who broke her heart eight years ago....

And Delia Mayhew can hardly believe that she's
gotten herself locked in the Breakfast Inn Bed
basement with the sexiest man in America.

Then there's Rebecca Salter. She's turned up at the
Inn in her wedding gown. Minus her groom.

*Come home to Tyler for three delightful novellas
by three of your favorite authors: Kristine Rolofson,
Heather MacAllister and Jacqueline Diamond.*

HARLEQUIN®
Makes any time special™

ANN
COLLINS

Ann is a world traveler with a love of foreign languages, photography, writing, needlecrafts and the outdoors. She taught English in Japan, snow skiing in Colorado, Italy and Switzerland, and sailing in Martinique and Mexico. Ann grew up watching Westerns on television and loves a good Old West adventure. She even took part in a three-day dust-eating cattle drive in California's eastern Sierra. Ann lives in San Diego, California, and is a doting aunt to her little nieces. You can contact her at P.O. Box 927894, San Diego, Ca 92192-7894.

HHBIO542